Books of Merit

INTO THAT DARKNESS

INTO THAT DARKNESS

Steven Price

a novel

THOMAS ALLEN PUBLISHERS

TORONTO

Library and Archives Canada Cataloguing in Publication

Price, Steven, 1976–
    Into that darkness / Steven Price.

ISBN 978-0-88762-737-8

I. Title.

PS8631.R524157   2011   C813'.6   C2010-907346-0

Editor: Patrick Crean
Cover design: Michel Vrana
Cover image: kallejipp/photocase.com

Published by Thomas Allen Publishers,
a division of Thomas Allen & Son Limited,
390 Steelcase Road East,
Markham, Ontario L3R 1G2 Canada

www.thomasallen.ca

ONTARIO ARTS COUNCIL
CONSEIL DES ARTS DE L'ONTARIO

Canada Council
for the Arts

The publisher gratefully acknowledges the support of
The Ontario Arts Council for its publishing program.

We acknowledge the support of the Canada Council for the Arts, which
last year invested $20.1 million in writing and publishing throughout Canada.

We acknowledge the Government of Ontario through the
Ontario Media Development Corporation's Ontario Book Initiative.

We acknowledge the financial support of the Government of Canada
through the Canada Book Fund (CBF) for our publishing activities.

15 14 13 12 11   1 2 3 4 5

Printed and bound in Canada
Text Printed on a 100% PCW recycled stock

for Esi

Who can tell what purpose is served by destinies
And whether to have lived on earth means little
Or much.

— CZESLAW MILOSZ

This book would not exist without the extraordinary grace of Lise Henderson. For advice, support, and encouragement, I am also grateful to John Baker, Jeff Mireau, and Anne McDermid; to my family, Bob & Peggy, Brian, Kevin Potato; to Patrick Crean, for his judicious eye; to Jack Hodgins, for his wisdom and friendship; and especially to Jacqueline Baker, who is, as ever, a light and a reason.

INTO THAT DARKNESS

The child was breathing quietly at the parlour cabinet, his teeth glinting small and sharp in the half-light.

It's alright, his grandfather said. Go ahead. Open it.

He looked up.

His grandfather's shaggy head, upraised and watching. A law-book clutched in one fist, a knuckle marking the page. When the old judge shoved back his chair and walked over and ran a hand along the child's neck his seamed palm felt ghostly and cool. What you're looking at there would be a million years old at least, he said to the child. The oceans were once full of them. He fumbled with the book in his fingers. Your father found it for me. Do you know where he found it? Under the trestle in Sooke. In the mountains.

In the mountains?

In those days all this was under the ocean. Even the mountains.

The child cradled the fragment of shale in his hands with great delicacy. Its surface was small and very black and tattooed upon it was a tiny black chambered shell spiralled like a goat's horn.

His grandfather took the fossil from his open palm and stooped looking down at it. I once thought it was very valuable, he said. I thought myself lucky to have found it. For it to have come down across so many millennia to end up here, in this room, in my hands. Can you imagine. It's a piece of a vanished world, Arthur, a world that will not come again. Wouldn't you think that's worth something?

The child nodded. Yes sir.

His grandfather cleared his throat as if from a long way off. Set the fossil down again on its shelf. He shut the cabinet fast and the glass door pinged as it shivered to. Well, he said. I guess I did too. I guess I keep it as a reminder. Of another kind of law. He clasped his hands in the small of his back and leaned in and peered at the fossil as if to read a secret writ upon it.

There have been many ends of the world, he said softly. This was one of them.

IN THE ROARING

I'll be buried here too.

You don't think about that when you're young. Or it isn't the same somehow. I was born in this city and I'll be buried in it. My parents are buried here, and my grandfather, who raised me. He was a big man, his skin was grey as old paper. He served as a judge for half his life. He considered it a kind of duty. He told me a question doesn't have to be something you ask. It's a way of looking at the world. I don't know. I guess I've tried to look at the world like that. It's strange to think he was younger than I am now when he died.

I go out to his grave sometimes to pick off the dead flowers, lay a fresh bouquet. I think the dead deserve more from us. That might just be my age talking. My eyes drift over the low iron fences, the crumbling monuments, the shady tree-lined paths to the sea. The sea like wimpled metal. The sea with its terrible coins of light. I don't like to look at it now, it hurts my eyes.

When I go to his grave I think mostly about my own life. What I didn't achieve. What I didn't hold on to. The work I might have painted, but didn't. Not about what's come apart down in that darkness, the wood planks, his second-best blue suit that looked so green in the coffin. His body. I don't know if that's selfish or just the way we're built. Maybe a bit of both.

Two years back I remember going out to his grave and finding the stone overturned, broken at its base. Someone had spray-painted something on the stone I couldn't read. It was in purple paint. I guess it was kids. You see them sitting on the streets begging for change, or running out to wash windshields at intersections. They have hard eyes, flinty eyes. Still I don't know what would make a kid do a thing like that. I don't understand it. I guess we must have been that way too once. But we never desecrated the dead. We never would have done that.

I looked a long time at that mess.

Callie always said I had a draftsman's eyes, not a painter's. I suppose she was right. I don't know that I ever saw anything truly. I tried. I guess you could say that was the real work. Seeing. Callie would have laughed at that. She didn't think truth was something you saw. She said change was the only constant in the world, and it was change she wanted to find in her sculptures. She saw with her hands, her fingers were her eyes. Callie had enormous hands. Her palms were always hot. She would put them on my naked back in bed and it would be like a furnace. I can still feel that heat. The pressure of her knuckles, like she was shaping me as I slept.

We were young together once. It's strange to think about now. I could have gone after her I guess. I could have left too. I don't know. She wanted so much to love, it was as if she loved. It was never enough for me. I wonder if it would be enough for me now.

His wife did not die in autumn and yet autumn was when he dreamed of her. He sat on the edge of his bed, an old man now and coughing in the darkness, white sheets tangled at his waist. His dead wife blurred and fading from the curtains. He sat and he coughed and he rose.

On the stairs his bare feet tracked moist half-prints over the oak which shrank at once and were sucked up invisible. He wore pale corduroy trousers soft as the skin of a peach and a collared white shirt and a heavy silver watch on his left wrist. The big waist of his trousers was cinched tight with a belt notched to the last notch but one. When he came down into the kitchen the low sun in the east was red and the easterly sky red also and at the table he stood drenched in that light as in another man's blood and it was this light he saw by.

The cupboards were bare. He filled an old kettle and set it to boil on the stove and he took his mug from its hook above the sink. Unscrewed the lid of a white ceramic jar. Spooned out coffee and left the lid off and the spoon standing in it and when the water was boiled he poured and stirred and drank his coffee. It was the second Tuesday in September, the end of his sixty-ninth year. His name was Arthur Lear.

Some days he would speak to no other living soul. Some days he would scrape at his memories like charcoal, rub his past between dry fingers. This house had been erected in the third decade of the last century and with its arched ceilings and narrow corridors and weird arterial plumbing some days the pipes in the walls would mutter and hiss eerily like a chorus of the dead, and those ghostly voices would be the only voices he'd hear.

Days and days.

The old man took his greatcoat down from its wooden pin and went out.

Locked the deadbolt deliberately, pocketed the key. Then standing in the street he turned back to double-check the door. The grey cedar shakes on the sides of his house were splitting. Yellow spears of grass sprouted under the low casement windows, the boot-pulped porch steps slumped crazily. He had been a painter for most of his life and he wondered when he had stopped noticing such details. In the bay window he could see the shapes of old canvases, props, brushes fanned out in unwired jars. But that was all of another life. That was another life.

He went on up the street, his big hands curled at his sides like grey spiders. At the first intersection a black dog loped across the street some soft thing in its jaws and the old man watched it go. The streets were quiet here. His black shoes were clean but unpolished, their hard heels clicked softly. The sidewalks looked bleached and windblasted. An early sunlight was etching the very edges of things.

When he reached the neighbourhood pub he peered into the glass doors and ran a hand through his hair. Waited for a break in the traffic, jogged across to the bank on the far side. The coins in his long pockets swung heavily. The streets were filling with figures scarved and pale and moving with purpose towards parked cars, bus stops, the city itself. The old man glanced at the faces he passed but no one met his eye.

Then he turned the corner and peered across the street at the tobacconist's. Through the windows he could not make out her shape. Her shop fronted a square of shops and boutiques below an old wooden theatre and on the far side stood a bench and fountain where he would often sit and read in the mornings. Just beyond these a big oak tree thrust forth rooted and powerful from the cobblestones like a great upwelling of earth. In a café window next to the tobacconist's he saw a black child's face pressed against the glass, his thick plastic eyeglasses distorted and watery in the light, and then the boy was craning his neck upwards. Two women in tailored coats had paused beside the old man and were pointing at the sky and then a rushing sound like fast water could be heard and the old man too raised his eyes.

He raised his eyes. A dark cloud of gulls burst over the storefronts down the street and poured past inland and he stood amazed. Seabirds many hundred strong. Flying fast and silent and sinister in their silence over the streetlights and trees and old buildings.

They passed from sight. The sky felt all at once larger, darker.

Then a second flock hurtled up and over the buildings as if following the first. The old man shivered and lowered his gaze. The black child in the café window was watching him and raised one light-skinned palm to the glass in what might have been a gesture of greeting or farewell.

The old man hurried across.

The boy watched the old man long and thin in his greatcoat striding along the far side of the street and thought: *I did not want to go anyway and even if I did want to go I would not go now.* Thought: *They will find out it was Tobey and then they will be sorry.* He had one sharp elbow pressed into the math textbook open before him and he was chewing small ribs into a pencil as he brooded when the old man stopped suddenly and lifted his drained grey face and all at once a darkness poured like dampness down the building behind him.

The boy shivered. There was a warpling in the upper windows along the street as if the very glass itself were bending and the boy blinked and adjusted his eyeglasses on his small nose. He rubbed one elbow on the café window though his mother did not like him to do this. Then he lifted up his eyes.

He lifted up his eyes and saw them. The seabirds. Rivering past in a thick black torrent.

And he could not help himself and whispered, very deliberately: Holy *shit*.

Then glanced quickly back at the counter. His mother had not heard. He pressed one palm to the cold window his fingers splayed as if to blot the shadowed street out but the rope of birds was already thinning, already the last stragglers like scraps of cloth were being blown past. When he lowered his eyes the old man was coming towards the square.

He flushed suddenly, as if he had been caught out. And thought again: *No I would not want to go even if they wanted me to even if I was allowed.* Thinking of the museum with its moth-eaten tusked mammoth, its creaking old explorer's ship, the dark streets of its mining town on the second floor. The smell of tar and the clatter of horses and the recorded cries of miners in their tunnels. Then thinking of his classmates in the school bus and the plastic seats with the stuffing frothing up out of the seams and his teacher in his stiff angry manner glaring back at them. Thinking of that and then not thinking of that.

The boy set his chewed pencil with a click sullenly down. Pulled the textbook into his lap and curled two hands over the top corners. The espresso machine roared, steamed off.

The door banged open in a gust of cold air and the old man stamped in. He scraped his shoes twice on the mat. The boy saw his own watery reflection swing into view in the door, his tight black hair cut short to the skull, his nose and lips small in his wide face. His mother often told him he had his grandfather's face but he was not so sure. He was ten years old and short for his age but his narrow shoulders and compact arms were strongly built and he was not finished growing.

The old man met the boy's eye and the boy looked away.

What can I get for you? his mother asked.

The old man stood six and a half feet if anything. His skin was grey, leeched, and in his old greatcoat he loomed over the boy's mother like some terrible figure from nightmare. His voice dry as old leaves.

Coffee, he said. Just a small coffee.

Then reached deep into his left pocket and withdrew a lean brown billfold. His knuckles were red with the cold. The boy could see very distinctly the old man's silver wristwatch and the hour hand where it pointed to twelve o'clock. The big brass clock on the wall read ten past nine.

The woman hauled a rack of steaming mugs from the dishwasher and set it clattering to cool. She looked at her son, thought of him that morning and of his quarrel with his sister. She could not recall why they had fought. His sister was sixteen. She supposed that was reason enough.

Then the door banged open, an old man ducked in. With his white hair and grey skin and pale clothing he might have been covered in dried clay, so grey and ghostly and strange was his pallor. He was very tall and made taller by his reserve. Only his eyes were dark.

Just a small coffee, he said gruffly.

And reached down, took his change, nodded to her. His fingers were callused and cold. When he was gone she stood a moment with one dark wrist pressed to her brow watching the space where he had been and then she grimaced and smoothed her skirt over her thighs. Her torso was ribbed and sexless like a dancer's and she was proud of her thinness after two children.

I'll be checking that, she called across to her son. Don't think I won't be.

The boy glanced at her then again down at his math book. He was sitting at the table beside the electric fire. It was a narrow coffee shop she owned but the windows were tall and blue in the early blue light. The red leather couch behind him gleamed.

I don't see you writing anything down, she said. You better have one heck of a memory.

He blew out his cheeks, picked up his chewed pencil. He picked it up very slowly.

It was then that the woman realized the old man had left his billfold standing open on the counter. Shit, she muttered. And glanced quickly at her son to be sure he had not heard. Mason, she called to him. I'll be right back honey.

He looked up.

Someone forgot their wallet. I won't be a minute.

I can watch the counter.

She snorted. You just tell anyone who comes in I'll be right back.

In the square outside she found the old man with his thorny hands clasped in the small of his back and the coffee held there by its lid and his greatcoat bunched up under the elbows. He was stooped, peering down at a window display where a mobile of a clown in a circus tent turned lifelessly. The leaves of the big oak tree rustled in the square behind them. In the street the traffic was slow and the stoplights swayed though there was no wind.

Someone in the crosswalk was shouting. The brake lights of a truck flared.

You forgot this, she said. Feeling the cold through her shirt-sleeves. Sir? She touched his sleeve softly and he turned, startled, peered down at her.

She held out the billfold. You left this on the counter.

He took it. His fingers touched hers.

And just then something, a tremor, shuddered up from under her feet. Something in her stomach pitched and rolled and the old man caught her elbow with his left hand.

Are you alright? He was holding her elbow and his grip was gentle.

I'm fine, she said. She was not certain that she was. She shook her head. He was looking at her, waiting, and suddenly she blushed. You didn't feel that? Just then?

What?

She stepped back and scraped the toe of one shoe over the cobblestones as if to get her bearings. The cars in the street poured past without slowing. She felt light-headed, strange.

God, she murmured. I haven't felt a tremor in years, not since I was a girl. Then peering up at the old man looming pale and spectral in that light she added, My dad and I used to feel them all the time. Earthquakes, I mean. He said they were good luck if they came in the morning.

She did not know why she had mentioned her father. Perhaps it was the old man's voice, low, crackling, like a tire driven slowly over crushed rock. She heard her father in it.

He was from Trinidad, she added. I guess they reminded him of home.

But the old man just cleared his throat and frowned and cleared his throat again.

Well, he said. And after a moment, as if he did not know what else to say, he said, Well. Thank you for the wallet.

And he nodded to her with one hand held to his heart, a gesture from another time, and he turned away.

When the old man entered the tobacconist's he did not at first see her and he called a greeting into the gloom. She was in her shirt-sleeves, sweeping out back. She pulled on a brown cardigan and walked slowly to the counter and propped her broom behind it. The old man's head was not clear and he shook it slowly thinking still of the fainting woman in the square outside. He set his coffee on the counter to cool. The tobacconist was peering up at him through her bifocals as if he were an inventory to be checked.

You alright Arthur?

He swallowed and nodded. I guess so, he said. I guess it's just one of those mornings.

I know how that is, she said.

I brought you something.

He reached into his greatcoat pocket and withdrew a small photograph and handed it across without looking at it.

What is it?

He nodded at it. Have a look.

She took up the photograph and held it out in front of her as if at something she dreaded to see. Then very slowly she smiled. Is that me with Callie? Where did you find this? She glanced up at him but he said nothing and she stared again at the picture. We must've been down at the breakwater. Look how young we were. What were we doing down there? She set the photograph upright in a slat between the keys of her cash register. He had said nothing and she glanced at him now. You always thought there were more secrets than there were, she said.

Well.

It drove her crazy.

She turned then and took down a jar printed Carib Special Blend and measured out and bagged and weighed and wrapped in paper the loose black tobacco. She had been a model for his wife's sculptures and later a friend and when he saw her now he saw a door that was closing but was not yet closed. She was ill and rarely left her chair behind the counter and the old man knew that one morning the shop would not be open, and what that would mean.

Anything else? Her eyes flicked down to a stack of papers beside the register. She waited with a finger curled above the register and the old man shook his head no.

I think I already read that one, he said.

I suppose at our age not many surprises are left, she said.

I wish I was old like you're old. I'd be running marathons yet. Go on.

The old man smiled a little, the wrapped tobacco caged in his open fingers. He turned his face and studied the street outside but made no move to leave and the tobacconist took up a cloth and wiped at the counter.

He said instead: Aza? Did you feel something a minute ago? Just before I came in?

Like what?

I don't know. Like an engine starting up underground.

She looked at him a long moment. You mean like an earthquake.

No. Yes. I guess I do.

She shook her head. It's got so I don't even hardly notice them anymore, she shrugged. My mother lived here eighty-nine years and she swore she never felt one. That's just fine with me, I say.

I hear they're good luck in the mornings.

Tell that to the broken dishes.

The old man smiled again.

In the yard behind the shop a dog was barking and barking but it fell suddenly silent.

The sunlight thickened.

A slow spackled dust was drifting in the shafts of light above the door and the mobile was turning faster in the display window. The old man closed his eyes. Opened his eyes. His legs were trembling. The tobacconist was still speaking and there was no sound and he watched her mouth and then all at once there was a great roaring in his ears. Car alarms along the street began to screech. The glass jars were rattling. Then his knees buckled and he grabbed at the pitching countertop, he looked out in time to see a car leap in the street beyond and the asphalt crest like a wave and then like that it was upon them.

He felt it in the small of his back, a sort of shiver. As if the cold teeth of a zipper were swiftly undone down his spine.

His fingers began to ache.

It came on.

It came on and pulsed shuddering up through the woman's feet and knees and up through her hips and ribs and the woman where she stood leaned pitching in it like a figure in a storm. The café countertop rippling in her grip like so much ribbon in a wind.

The cups and cutlery were rattling in the shelves. And it came over the boy in a roar and he reeled where he sat and the heavy table bucked and the walls began to sway.

Mom, he shouted.

Through the glass he could see the oak thrashing the cobblestones.

A crack sundered the drywall and dust sifted down and glass jars were shattering around the tobacconist where she had fallen to her hands.

The café ceiling flexed and sagged and flexed and sagged.

And her son staring at her terrified and the light fixtures blooming and dimming and then the storage room door behind the counter was banging shut and banging shut again.

Stay here, the old man was shouting. Don't move.

Mason, Mason, the woman shouted.

The old man crawling past the overturned shelves cut his hands on a shattered frame and his fingers fumbled at the door to the basement. The floor billowed under him and he leaned into it with a hand on the trim, the pipes in the walls groaning. The door opened onto blackness, a dry dust smoking up out of it.

The café air thickening with drywall dust.
    Mason, his mother was shouting.

Then the old man stood in that door frame with his hands held to either side as if to hold that building upright through his strength alone. He could see the tobacconist screaming at him. The blood from his upraised hands was dripping warm into his shirt cuffs.

Then the floor buckled and the boy could hear the hardwood ripping apart around him and he breathed deeply in the dust and sawing heat. Watching from the great distance of his heart the window glass clouding over as if rimed in ice then pushing out into the street.
    And all of this silent, slow.
    Glass. Exploding into the sunlight.

The woman grabbed her son, pulled him to the storage room doorway. She held him there. She covered his head with her arms and she held him.

His mother was crushing him to her chest and he could not breathe.

She held him.

As the ceiling lifted, as the floor gave out, as the world hurtled in
with a roar.

When it ended it ended roaring and engulfed them in a white brilliance and it seemed their very bodies burned and then for a long while was nothing but silence and darkness. The woman lay with her son breathing in that new strangeness and then someone was weeping, and she knew it was her own voice, and she hefted a shoulder and sobbed thickly: Go. Now.

And her son wriggled gasping out from under.

In the blackness she told herself she must be calm. She choked and coughed and tugged at her left arm but it did not give and she could feel nothing in it.

Are you hurt? she asked. Her voice shivering. Mason? Are you hurt?

When the boy did not answer she brushed at his nape, his forehead. He felt hot.

Try to keep still, she murmured. Let me think for a moment.

I can't see anything, he said.

I know honey. It was an earthquake.

She flexed her legs, her ankles gone bloodless and just beginning to ache and the chunk of brickwork above groaned deeply. It's alright, she told her son, hush, it's fine. The walls clattered and rapped and fell still. In the darkness with her limbs twisted as they were she could not turn her face and she lay very still, blinked wetly. She coughed.

Listen to me, she said. We'll get out of here. Don't be afraid.

I'm not afraid, he whispered.

The old man snorted and spat a thick clot of dust and blood and he turned his head gingerly as he came to, his eyelids shut fast. The air was grey with dust.

In his ears a white roaring. His head ringing.

He could just make out the slats of the ceiling stoven in around him, loops of wire, a wall leaning wildly. In the ruins of that small tobacco shop he groped about, seized a tin, struck at a girder angrily with shaking hands. Nothing. He kicked his legs and something, broken mortar, brick, shifted loosely. When he shut his eyes he was still plunging through that darkness.

In his left hand he was holding the tobacconist's wrist.

It was not moving and he understood she was dead. He let her go and tried to sit up but just slumped to one side, his head spinning. The cuffs of his shirt were crusted with blood. The old man felt a terror coming up through his body as if it were not his own but coming from someplace deeper. The darkness under him pulsing like a great blood-chambered heart. He turned his head and shut his eyes and he stoppered his ears with his hands.

She could not be certain which wall had collapsed. She did not know how long they had been buried and she wondered then if the entire building had fallen. Likely only the floor above them. Rescuers would be coming soon. They would phone her daughter.

Kat will be trying to reach us, she said in the darkness.

Kat's mad at me, her son murmured.

Oh honey don't say that. She's not. She won't be when we get out of here. I promise.

I don't care. She can be mad at me.

And remembering then her daughter, small, bird-wristed in her bedroom. She wondered if her daughter had tried to reach her yet. Shook her head weakly. Returned instead to a vision of her daughter three years ago, them sitting parked in the driveway at her middle school in the rain. The old school hazed through the windshield, the engine idling smokily in the grey light. The other children in their uniforms running stooped and blurred through the courtyard. And her daughter crying because she felt she was ugly and because she did not want to go in to class. A lump rose in the woman's throat as she remembered. She had sat with her hands on the wheel not knowing what to say as big drops of rain flecked the glass and shadow-flecked her hands, shadow-flecked her daughter's beautiful dark cheeks.

Kat'll find us, her son said quietly and she felt him nodding to himself in the black.

He did not remember clambering free.

There was no sound. The old man stumbled into the square, hands dangling at his sides. Dust billowing and smoking about him. He saw a child's shoe and glinting tins of beans and he saw bits of clothing and drapery wrapped tattered around bricks and pipes and shredded under slabs of masonry and he picked his way between these and the smashed grouts of furniture scattered there.

Then he was crouched on all fours in the manner of a beast and panting. His clothes hanging off him. He stood shakily, staggered into the ruined street. Everything was very still and white as after a snowfall and the stillness moved very slow. He could see others stumbling in the smoke.

Then a high sun, warm and dry on his neck.

Then nothing.

Then his bare skin, trembling. His lips tasted of dirt and steel and he gagged and spat and doubled over hacking. Clawed two fingers into his mouth to clean it. When he straightened he ran his hand across his face and noticed as if from a long way off that he was crying.

The woman coughed and could not stop and then she was gasping long slow ragged gulps of air.

Oh honey, she said. Oh I can't. My arm's stuck.

The air was sour and an oily wisp of gas was seeping in through the walls and a line of sweat slid itching down her ribs. She turned her head this way and that in the darkness, she tilted her chin, she forked her free elbow birdlike behind her and she dropped her hip and rubbed at her legs. Her calves bloodless and prickling there. All at once she froze.

Mason, she hissed into the blackness. Mason do you hear that?

A voice, very faint. Unwinding through that labyrinth of pipe and hairline fracture: *Is anyone in there? Hello? Can you hear me, hello?*

Yes, she cried, yes oh thank god, we're in here—

Her voice, burned hoarse and crackling from the dust and heat and pain. We're in here, hello, get us out of here, she shouted and then her son was shouting also in his own high scream: Hey, hey, hey, hey.

After a moment the voice echoed again down to them but softer now, less distinct. *Hell, anyone, can you hear.* Then it faded and was gone.

I think he heard us, her son said. I think he did.

She reached for his hand.

The old man's ears were bleeding as if the earthquake thundered yet within him and he shook his head slowly to dispel the noise. Cries were coming to him out of the drifting dust, distorted and slow.

He saw the figure of an old man stagger up out of the smoke, face streaked with dirt, and then the two old men approached each other as if stepping towards a reflection.

What happened, the old man whispered. Still shaking his head.

The door, the other was saying, the door, the door.

And then that figure too was gone. The old man walked, turned, walked. Thought vaguely of going to his house and then thought in alarm: *Where's Callie?* although it did not make sense, his wife had been dead almost forty years, and then he leaned against a grimy mailbox and began to tremble. There were people in the street now, standing with arms folded in shock and murmuring to themselves, and now the old man could hear sirens very far off.

A silver motor scooter came wending through the maze of rubble with a low whine and the sunlight flared off its fuel tank. Poles were downed along the sidewalk and there were figures half-naked and shouting. The smoke was lifting. Many buildings had slewed or collapsed entirely. He stood at the corner where the bank once stood and stared down the side street at the houses behind their rows of dahlias and rhododendrons and at the white wood fences and wicker arbours still of a piece and standing. The front yards strewn with bits of glass and with plastic chairs fallen on one side and with twists of clothes hurtled from clotheslines and from the buckled houses themselves. As if all along that street occupants had been evicted in force.

Then he saw the dead girl. Rolled onto her stomach and lying bonelessly on the hot asphalt. Her dress was rucked up over her waist. He sat down next to her socked feet, his face slack. The rubble was moving, there were figures coming out. The old man peered around him and the light in that narrow street seemed suffused with a fiery stillness and all that it fell upon appeared to burn.

Mason, the woman whispered with strain. The counter. Go over to the counter. Can you?

Her son was silent, breathing beside her. She ran a finger lightly over his face.

Mason? You have to get outside, you have to tell them where we are.

He was very quiet and then he said, sleepily: Why is it so dark in here?

She swallowed down her sudden fear.

It was an earthquake honey, she said. You know that. You asked that already. Right?

But when she bundled a dishtowel and lifted the boy's head onto the makeshift pillow he did not stir. As she turned her left arm spasmed with a black spiking pain and she cried out. Her son's thin chest rising and falling under her palm. She rested next to him in that darkness her legs throbbing and her ruined arm spectral beneath her and it seemed almost as if she had dreamed her way to this place, so much was the darkness around her like the darkness within.

She felt herself beginning to drift. Thinking: *Oh god, Kat.* She choked and coughed and spat up a great mouthful of phlegm to keep from crying. A reek of gas still pricking her nostrils, as if the stove lines were punctured.

After a time she could hear a scrape of iron and then the slab overhead shuddered.

She shook her son by the elbow. They're getting closer, she whispered. Mason? Can you hear them? They're coming.

She shut her eyes hard and spots of light flared up and faded before her. So loud was the digging that the woman braced herself, it seemed the slab overhead would peel back any moment, that sunlight would come flooding in upon them, sleek silhouettes bending down to fold them in their arms. But it did not come. And then she could not hear any digging at all.

We're down here, we're in here, we're people in here, she screamed.

The darkness shuddering, the dust sifting down over them.

Her son was awake now and breathing.

They're coming for us, she said.

But then her voice choked and she began to cry silently and when her son held her she cried the harder for it. His dark hands in her hair years ago like small birds, soft, cool, savagely clever. Pecking manifold and dexterous her tight braids. His sober eyes the colour of slate.

The woman lifted her wrist to her mouth, the saliva and dirt and tears smearing there.

The old man stood twisting a brown cardigan in his hands as if to wring it dry. He did not know where he had found it. When he heard a voice mutter something familiar he turned, dazed. Thinking: *What was that? What was that he said?*

A kid with a patchy beard was staring him down. Dressed in stained baggy jeans, clutching a crowbar.

I said, are you Arthur Lear?

His teeth were very yellow.

The old man was shaking his head like a fool. Do I know you? he asked.

The kid frowned as if he did not understand the question. You dropped this, he said after a moment, holding out the old man's billfold. I mean I think you dropped it. And then, uncertainly: Didn't you drop this?

The old man took it and stared at it strangely. And then he was remembering the black woman from the café who fainted in the square, and her son in the window, his hand pressed to the glass, and all at once he was shaking.

Hey, the kid said. Hey, easy there. You alright?

What's wrong with him? a girl asked, drifting towards them. She kicked aside a twist of metal with a clatter and stared down at the old man. Is he hurt? Are you hurt?

Where the old man's hands pressed to his knees they left soft bloodied palm prints and he stared at them uncomprehending and then at the kid's knuckles whitening on the crowbar.

After a moment the kid gestured with the crowbar at the ruined building across the street. You came, he said to the girl. I hoped you'd come.

But she just ran both hands along her skirt and sat beside the old man with her knees pressed together and her bottom lip sucked in and she did not meet the kid's eye.

Aza, the old man tried to say. Aza's in there.

What did he say? the girl asked.

The kid's face was grimed black and his eyes were red-rimmed and raw and he wiped at his nose with the back of a hand. He stared at the old man a long moment. He's in shock, he said.

Did he say Aza? the girl asked. Did you say Aza? The cigarette woman?

The old man nodded.

He thinks she's alive too, the girl muttered.

She *is* alive, the kid said quickly. How does he know Aza?

Rory lives right above her shop, the girl said to the old man very slowly. I mean, he lived above it. He thought he could hear her after it hit. Her and some others. How do you know her?

The old man looked blearily from the girl to the kid and back to the girl but said nothing.

We got to get her out, the kid said again.

They'll be sending crews for that. The girl looked at the old man. Tell him, she said. Tell him they'll be bringing crews in to do that.

You tell me, the kid said. Who do you think is coming?

I don't know, the police. The army. For god's sake Rory. You go in there it's just another person they have to save.

No one's coming Sara.

Stop it.

The whole fucking city's gone. What if it was your own family in there? What if it was Mickey, Sara?

He's in Toronto.

The kid looked a long moment at her as if he might say more.

Just say it, the girl said.

The kid looked at her then at the old man and then back at the girl and after a moment he spun around and picked his way through the rubble in the street.

The old man watched the kid climb the bank of the ruined café and cross over to the stoven roof of the tobacconist's, others already in the wreckage there. Sunlight was sifting down through the oak leaves above the old man's head and glancing off the asphalt and the fenders of cars. He pressed a bloodied hand to his eyes and he saw again in that darkness which was not darkness his elbows pinioned under bricks and glass and pipes and he smelled again the clot of dirt in his nostrils and he felt the ground lurch and give way underneath him and he feared he would be sick.

He got to his feet with a groan.

The girl stared at him. What. You too? Are you kidding?

I'm not going back there, he said.

But to his surprise he stepped out into the square anyways. He stepped out and then he was swaying unsteadily and the ruined buildings were swaying too and all at once someone was shouting and the shouting seemed to be coming from under his feet.

He looked out. The sky pitched to one side. And then he understood.

It was another one. A second tremor, swimming up from under.

In the rubble across the square the diggers stood suddenly with their tools held wide for balance, the metal winking in the sunlight. Their raw hands outstretched red in the dust. The girl at the curb was crying, Oh god god it's another one, and then the old man was shouting foolishly, No it isn't, it isn't, and then the salvagers across the street were running, shovel and pick and pail and axe all pitched aside as they fled skidding downward, some leaping from block to block and others with arms flailing and others yet sliding on hands and haunches and hard boot soles down. And then just as suddenly the low thunder had rolled on outward under the ground to the east and was gone.

The square in its sudden stillness righting itself. The trees shirring greenly over them.

The old man stood breathless. He lifted his head, he opened his eyes. In the sunlight he listened to a quiet rasping around him, like rusted scissors hasping through cardboard, like insects chewing through grass.

The boy held tightly to his mother's wrist. He could no longer feel his right arm and pebbles of glass crunched as he shifted, turned a small shoulder.

Mom? he whispered. Mom who are you talking to?

He kicked a dislodged pipe and it rolled clanking at his feet. Now his mother coughed into her arm, her body very still. As if having talked herself out, as if awaiting some word. The blood flooded back and he shook his right hand out and pumped it open and closed. He dragged the towel to his chest and twisted his face to one side. His hand went dead again almost at once.

Are you hungry? his mother murmured. Her voice dry, strained.

He wriggled closer.

Stop it, she muttered. Sit still, it's starting. You don't want to miss it, do you?

He parted her fingers, the web of skin between each. Mom? he said.

She did not seem to hear. If you're hungry you can get a popcorn. Use the five dollars I gave you. But no butter, mister. Kapeesh?

He lay in the dark beside her their hands touching and she gabbled on under her breath.

Mom, he said and now he was crying. Don't be sick Mom. Please.

If you're interested in the light, you study the shadows. My grandfather used to say when he was hearing a case, he'd watch the people sitting in the row just behind the defence. When someone was talking, he'd watch their eyes. When they were staring him down, he'd watch their mouths. He told me that what you want to be seeing is never what you end up looking at.

I don't know if the same kind of lessons still get passed on. Seeing how things are these days, I'd guess not. But maybe we're not so different from how we were. I don't know. My grandfather took me out to see the whale when I was five years old. It's just about my earliest memory of him now. It was winter, near the gravel pits in Colwood. You could stare across the water and see the low roofline of the city. I remember the carcass was huge, though when I think about it now I suppose it probably wasn't more than a young calf. Caught inshore during a storm, beached up. It happens now and then. There were lots of people standing around, huddled in the chill, like they were waiting for something to begin. It was my first encounter with the ineffable. My grandfather poked a stick at the hide, then gave it to me to try. It was like pushing into water-logged wood. And the grey sand sticking to its flanks, the swarm of sand-flies. I was looking for its eyeball but the head just seemed featureless, except for a slash of baleen half-buried in the sand. I don't know what I felt. I guess it was astonishment. This creature whose element was darkness and cold. I asked about its parents and my grandfather gestured out at the flat grey waters. They're out there, he said, they're watching.

I could see a bed of kelp drifting in the dark current. I shivered. I peered a long time but I never did see anything. I wonder now if that was his point.

Callie always thought he sounded like a hard man. He wasn't. Certainly no harder than the world. My parents were killed in a street-car accident in Vancouver shortly after I turned four. That was in 1936. My father had white hair, even as a young man. That's what I remember of him. My mother smelled of raspberries. Well. I don't know. My grandfather was the only parent I ever knew and he never once made me feel unloved.

I was ten years old when I found the bodies in East Sooke. This would be in the spring of 1943. I remember how the light in the cedars along the roadway fell on my cousin. He was riding on the handlebars because we had only the one bicycle. I remember the crunch of the tires in the gravel. A smell of dust and rain in the air. We found the three bodies in a small depression behind a log. Their wet clothes were in strips and sunken with mud and their bones had been pulled apart as if something had been into them. I'm sure something had. My cousin poked a stick through an eye socket, lifted one of the skulls. It turned out they were Japs who'd feared the rounding up of the internment camps, fled to the woods. Poisoned themselves. The newspapers called it cowardly, called them spies. I was proud of what I'd found and wanted my picture in the paper. My grandfather belted me for that. It was the only time he ever did.

I don't know why that comes to me now. Callie used to say a person never speaks except to conceal what he means. She was probably right. Talking about a thing never helped. I've been muttering to myself fifty years now at least and it's never helped me.

The first cadaver was exhumed in the hour before noon. Dragged smokily up out of the splintered bricks and dust feet-first and stinking, a blonde woman her lungs crushed, her soft limbs swollen. A yellow dirt was stuck in a film to her eyes and to her flaxen hair and her torn jaw slapped loosely as she came up. Her throat was opened and had dried to a black pudding.

The old man regarded her squinting as if to see her very clearly and not forget her and then he turned away. Someone had salvaged bedsheets and as the body was drawn out from its hole a white shroud billowed and draped across its features. A brown stain was seeping into the sheets. The figures bearing that soft thing in their gloved fingers moved stiffly along that weird sun-lit cliff and then a sudden quiet fell, the dark onlookers clasping their shovels and buckets. The old man wiped angrily at his mouth with his shirt cuff, his plastic shovel blade clicking in the rubble. The air was cold. He felt ferociously, luminously, tired.

He thought: *Arthur Lear you could have died in this and you would not have minded it.* His eyes were sore and he rubbed at them. Then he straightened, a lean grizzled figure with his shirt-sleeves rolled and his wiry forearms bloodied.

The sun was burning a high white cylinder through the dust. Something had been going out in him more and more often now, and he'd find himself stooped, unmoving, like a clock that had wound down. And then his elbows would bend, his head would lift, he'd begin again.

There were not many of them. Some he saw for a time and then did not see. They worked carving out tunnels by pick and blade deep into the ruins and as they laboured others shored up the narrow openings with salvaged timbers and pumps rummaged from a hardware store two miles distant. The sun was savage in its whiteness. Buckets of dirt and broken masonry were lugged by hand out of the buildings. Some few were willing to crawl in to listen for voices or stirrings of any human kind. But only a few. Two men had already been crushed by collapsed tunnels.

The old man was one such willing. Squeezing in to peer about in the dusty blackness with a wet rag tied to his mouth and the lamp on his helmet shining whitely. He had found only bodies so far. It took some time to dig free the dead and what emerged was greeted always with silence. Several hours after the first corpse a severed leg was unearthed and he watched a woman carry it streetwards. She bore it wound in a sheet which hung and trailed underfoot, the thing in her arms like a swaddled child.

Out of that conflagration none objected to his going in. There seemed no order and the salvagers did what work they chose. He did not know what drew him below. It was not goodness, he understood. A kind of exhaustion, a kind of fear, rivering under his skin, leaving him scoured and trembling and numb. He thought at first none objected because they did not want to go in themselves. Then he thought perhaps they did not realize his age. Somehow he had been mistaken for a doctor and what he had supposed was trepidation was in truth a kind of deference. But then he understood it did not matter. To be willing was enough.

The hours passed. Under a bathroom door frame, the bodies of two emaciated women were found. Kneeling in each other's arms, heads bowed in the manner of the penitent or the condemned and their mouths plugged, their eyes sealed fast with plaster.

Seeing them the old man began to shake. He sat on a broken slab and stared out at the city around him and the fires burning there and he shook. He did not know why these bodies over any others should affect him.

He shut his eyes, he opened his eyes, he ran a sleeve across his face. It was still afternoon when he stood. He passed lumped and beggared diggers in their dusty clothes and one raised her seamy hand and he nodded and the light off the wimpled steel in the ruins dappled across her face and flared in her turning shovel like sunlight on the bed of a shallow stream. He looked at her and he wondered what she would look like dead.

He turned away. Stumbled painfully down the far slope. There was something wrong in his stomach and he looked to be sure that he was alone and then ducked under a pinioned block of concrete, fumbled with his belt, hauled down his trousers. Still shaking. He squatted and voided himself painfully into the rubble. The air was cool and the sharp bricks pressing into his thighs felt cool and he could hear the faint murmur of voices on the other side, the distant scrape and clatter of masonry. And slowly, as if emerging out of a mist, he could hear something else, a thrum under all of that. He leaned forward. The sound disentangled and wavered and sharpened.

It was a child's voice. Singing in the earth.

It was there and then it was not there. The old man listened, very still. Then crawled with his face low to the crushed bricks and dust. He did not hear the child again and he thought he must be imagining things. Fussing with trousers still unbuckled and one long ropy arm holding him upright. And then he heard it again, unmistakably. A boy, singing.

He began to shout. Shouted down into the earth. Hello! Son! Are you in there, where are you? Son!

Crawling and shouting like a madman.

Then he got to his feet and staggered grimly back up the incline and called to a man dragging free a television. The man clambered across.

I've got one, he said, breathing hard. It's a boy. He's alive.

He led the digger down to the outcropping, waved him to his knees. The digger looked at the mess from the old man's bowels in its murky puddle and he glanced away ashamed but the digger just kicked a broken sink over top of it and then kneeled. They listened.

I don't hear anything, the digger said at last. You mean that?

Not that. Listen.

You sure he was here?

Just listen.

And then, very faint, the boy's voice reached them. Garbled and strange, like an aria from some other world.

Jesus, the digger said. Jesus he's in there deep. How're we going to get to him that deep?

I can't tell if he is. Voices carry strangely down there.

Well he's sure as hell not close.

You can't tell.

No. He sounds pretty deep in though.

The old man was peering back up at the crest of the rubble. He got achingly to his feet, one knee at a time. Where do we go in? he asked.

Listen, the digger was shouting, hey, kid. We're going to get you out. Just hang on.

He can't hear you.

The digger shrugged. Pike will know where to dig, he said.

Pike?

Pike. The engineer. Hey, you alright?

He was not alright. His throat was hawsing and rattling and his breath was coming thin and flecked with spittle and he leaned over and shook his head. I'm fine, he said.

The digger was watching him. I know who you are, he said quietly. I saw you pull out that dead woman.

The old man squeezed his eyes shut, said nothing.

Why don't you take a rest. They're giving out sandwiches in the street and we won't be ready here for a while. Take a minute. I got to get this started. Poor damn kid.

He cleared his throat and spat. I'm alright.

The digger pressed a dusty hand to his shoulder and a quiet sift of dirt dislodged and trickled from out of the seams there. We'll need you soon enough. Go on.

You'll be alright?

We'll be alright.

Come get me when you're ready.

The digger was already moving away. Get a sandwich, he called.

The old man nodded. He felt so tired. The shadows were lengthening and he could make out in the grey street below the slinking shapes of dogs or what he took for dogs at the edges of the sunlit buildings, their orange tongues slack, spines bristling. He understood that very little of what he had outlived mattered. He could see the swaddled corpses laid out in the street below and the mourners like spectres themselves wending past seeking their dead and he thought numbly that they should not be in the sun. The afternoon sky beyond hung like a drapery of flesh flensed and shuddering. The old man saw all this and realized that whatever his life might have been before, it would not be allowed to be again.

He felt hungry, grisly with hunger. His joints shivered with a lightness for the pain of it. He made his way down the slope of the ruined buildings and stopped when he got to the street and peered back up the way he had come. His stomach was a small hard stone squeezing itself smaller. He shook out his arms, brushed the dust from his clothes.

All was confusion down below. There were people standing alone or in small groups and others moving purposefully off down side streets. There was much shouting. The air pale with dust, dust on the abandoned cars stopped in the street. The buildings that still stood looked sorrowful and ghostly with their dark windows blown out.

He moved hungrily through. He stood in line at an old flatbed truck where sandwiches were being distributed and bottles of water and he waited his turn but when he took the sandwich and tried to eat it he spat the food out and found he could not eat it. He drank a little water and turned aside and sat down on the curb near the cab of the truck. He felt a hand on his shoulder and he turned in surprise but there was nobody there.

The doors of the flatbed truck were standing open, the radio was on. He could hear a reporter's voice, a woman's voice, crackling from the tinny speakers in the doors. Cutting into static then back out. Shouting to be heard over the rotary *whump* and roar of her helicopter's blades. We don't know very much for certain, she shouted, nothing's been confirmed, but early reports are saying the tremor registered at 8.7. The epicentre was somewhere off the coast, oh just a moment, yes, that's right, somewhere off the coast.

He raised his head. Others were standing or crouching in the street with heads lowered as if in prayer and with arms idle and some wore bandages or slings and others had blood in their hair. The radio station's helicopter was passing now over the city and the reporter within peered down describing a vision of hell half-medieval in its imaginings. She might herself have been in some horrific torture chamber as she shouted of the smoke in black columns funnelling up into the air and of the great low clouds of dust drifting over the city and of the fires in the street grates. She sucked in her breath as the helicopter approached Chinatown, Market Square. All of it blown inward, lone walls left tottering in the dark air. There are people in the streets, she was saying. I can see people in the streets but I can't tell what they're doing. They seem to be just standing there. I don't know. Oh god some of them are crawling out of the buildings.

He listened, grim. It seemed to him where he sat in his exhaustion that the vault of his skull was floating and a great dizzying absence filled his brainpan and he could not think.

And now followed a litany of destruction as the reporter postulated on further ruin unseen by the human eye. On ruptured telephone cables and power lines and water pipelines. On leaking gas and imminent explosions. She spoke of streets with little or no damage though these were few and remarkable for it and as the helicopter nosed onward the harbour came into view. She told of the Empress Hotel leaning violently backward but not quite fallen over and she told of the Parliament Buildings undamaged to her eye and of the great crowds gathered on the provincial lawns. The tide in the harbour was strangely low and she spoke of boats keeled over in the shallows and passing now over James Bay she told a tale of such unrivalled ruin and horror that at times her voice did fail her.

The curb where the old man sat was rubbed smooth like soap and as he leaned back on it he felt it again. A hand on his shoulder. And this time when he turned a woman with a bandage over one ear was crouching over him, her eyes very dark.

It's time, she said.

Under the watery afternoon sun he donned a pair of heavy calfskin gloves given him by a youth and then a man unpeeled a name tag onto his shirt and a fletched rope was tied to his ankle. He was given a headlamp, a hammer, a chisel. Then a slender girl with a soft yellow bruise on her forehead warned hoarsely of the lay of the tunnel and what would be found within.

Pike's already in there, she said. You know how this works. Just follow the ropes in. You'll want to check that lamp. Alright?

He nodded. He hitched his trousers high and toggled his headlamp.

Then went in. In through a jagged gash in the rubble. Twisting his hips and torso aslant and ducking his head and sliding his left thigh and forearm in first, into a small cavity of light. A low tunnel no taller than his knees. It sloped downwards and he laid himself out and crept forward following the engineer's rope, wriggling in filth and finning forth on his elbows like some worm-like beast. The stink of gas was strong and the strewn battery lamps hot in the dirt where he crawled. His safety line dragged at his ankle. The *tchink* of hammer and mallet in one fist as he went.

The girl had warned him of a corpse crushed over the hole and he could smell the rot in the tunnel as he neared it. A dead man trapped by a slab above. The corpse was pressed into the ceiling of the tunnel half-visible with his arm dangling there, his fingers curling earthward. The dead hand swollen and hard and hanging putrid before him.

He flattened himself as he could and crept on.

The tips of the dead man's fingers brushed through his hair, brushed his neck. As he passed it the cadaver bloated with gas hissed eerily. His right elbow seeped into something soft and cool and he rolled it squelching out and kept on.

After a time the tunnel turned sharply and he approached the edge of a vertical drop and he could hear the crunch of digging from below. He eased himself over and peered down and called in.

Hello, he called. You're Pike?

A man drenched in sweat and wearing a thick dark beard glared up out of the darkness. Begrimed and stout and brazen like a coal miner. A lamp pinned at an angle under his boots. He was folded awkwardly over a low girder and he twisted around to see the old man and then he grimaced weirdly.

I guess the doctor's in, he whispered. Come on down here doc. Keep your voice down. The kid's just through here. His name's Mason.

The old man slid very carefully down into the hole. The engineer's eyes were shining in the lamplight and the old man could feel the heat coming off the man's skin as if he were very sick. They were pressed up together at the bottom of that narrow shaft among the pipes and debris.

The engineer called softly into a crack in the wall. Hey, Mason. Hey you still in there buddy? He looked at the old man. I told him you were coming. He's been quiet.

The old man held his breath.

Come on in there pal. Don't go falling to sleep on me. Hey. You can hear me, I know you can hear me. I got a doctor out here to help your mom.

His mom?

She's buried in there with him.

The old man shifted his weight. The engineer blew dust from a deep crevice no wider than his thumb and he peered in and cursed. His voice bashing off the wimpled rocks overhead, rippling and fading up the tunnel.

I'm not a doctor, the old man whispered.

The engineer studied him. My name's not Pike.

He wondered if the engineer were joking. He regarded him a long moment then wiped the sweat from his eyes and called in to the boy. Mason? Mason, are you in there son?

They sat in silence for a long moment, listening. The old man could hear a hollow drip of liquid obscene in the depths, like water or blood or some darker grease. The creak of rubble all around them as in a ship's hull.

He's not doing so hot, the engineer muttered.

He'll make it. If he's in there.

He's in there. Unless I'm a fucken idiot. The engineer pressed one eye socket to the crevice, wet hair in curls at his nape. And you can fuck right off if that's what you think.

The old man's breaths came quick in the bad air. He rolled his forehead against a slab of warm concrete, dust in his throat, dust searing his eyes. He raised his head. A wet half-moon where his forehead had been. The heat was worsening.

Did you hear that? he hissed suddenly.

The engineer waved him quiet. His blood loud in his ears.

And then up out of the dirt and battered depths it came: a
small voice. She's sleeping, the boy whispered. She can't hear
you, you have to be quiet.

The engineer was grinning angrily in the ghostly light. What
did I tell you?

The old man knuckled his eyes shut. Thank god. Jesus.

God didn't do shit, he said. And then, into the darkness: We're
going to get you out of there buddy, just hold on.

I could hear him from up top. He was singing to her.

You want to lower your fucken voice?

The old man froze.

What?

What do you think? The engineer turned back. Hey, bud, he
called in.

I'm thirsty, the boy was saying. You're getting us out of here?
He started to cry.

We're going to get you out, the engineer called in. Can we
speak to your mom?

A long silence.

She won't wake up, the boy said. I can't wake her up.

It's alright, the old man called. Just hold on in there, okay?

Another long pause.

Okay, the boy said.

She's dead, the engineer muttered. She's gone and fucken died.

I was dead too. I got out.

The engineer looked at him. She's *dead*, he said flatly.

They began carving with a toothed trowel into the facing wall.
Banging and splintering off the rubble. Scooping the debris clear
into a bucket and grunting softly as they worked. The engineer
hoisted the filled bucket to the old man who raised it up to the
tunnel overhead and lowered down a fresh bucket. The shadows
sluicing crazily. Over the din the old man spoke to the boy telling
him of the work being done and of the nature of their excavations

and of the brief time left before their breaking through. While he spoke he dipped a black rag into a pail under his boots and sprinkled water upon the debris to settle the dust but nevertheless the air went bad and then was worse and despite the damp cloth tied to his face the old man soon sat wheezing. He ran a palm along his unshaven jaw and it came away black.

One of the buckets lowered from the tunnel held a water canister with a long plastic tube attached and in a folded handkerchief a rubber stopper and a sliced orange. The old man sat with that clean handkerchief open like a white lily in his lap and he stared. It seemed miraculous to his eye. He knew in that moment that he had been underground too long.

He called to the boy but there was no answer and he called again and he waited. Feeling always that wild insensible terror as his voice seeped into the rubble and was lost.

We've got some water here for you son, he called. Are you still thirsty?

He shifted nearer to the crevice and a pain seared his left leg and he sucked in his breath, he stamped and rubbed his calf until the blood again moved. He felt old and angry and useless in his anger and he leaned again nearer and he fed the thin tube into the crevice and his thick gloves jabbed it deeper in. He wafted it back and forth with his headlamp shining in and he called out to the boy to move towards the light. He did not know the hour.

Son? Can you reach it?

The boy did not answer. But all at once the hose dipped and tugged like a bite on a line and the old man's heart surged and the engineer wiped at his face and nodded soberly and turned back to his digging. The old man held the canister over his head and squeezed it gently and paused and squeezed again and its sides slucked gruesomely like some awful bellows.

How is it? he called in. Is that reaching you?

It's good.

When the boy had drunk his fill the old man set the canister upon an outcrop near the crevice and wrapped the sliced orange in a damp rag and affixed it to a coil of fish tape.

He told the boy he was sending in some food. But eat slowly, he cautioned. Just suck at it if you can. If you eat it too fast it'll make you sick. Okay?

Then he turned and his headlamp cut the smoking air.

They send down any of that for us? the engineer asked.

He shook his head.

I'm joking.

I know it.

The engineer had stopped digging. He had unearthed a kind of concrete girder many inches thick and now he flexed his fingers and rocked onto his heels and studied the thing.

The old man coughed uneasily. What do you think?

The engineer traced a finger along the girder. The rubble around him groaned, fell still.

I can't cut through this.

You can't cut through it?

No. It won't cut.

He slashed at the girder once, twice, as if to make his point, then slewed scrabbling up to the edge of the tunnel. The old man waited observing him quietly until at last the engineer peered down and met his eye. He slid back down.

The old man said, We can't wait. We don't know his condition. Or his mother's.

We know her condition.

We don't.

The engineer lowered his head and picked at his blackened gloves.

A long ragged crack had splintered out across the girder from its centre towards a lower edge and a second crack began not two inches from the first and the engineer tapped a forefinger gently between them.

This is where you'd have to hit it, he whispered. His eyes bloodshot in the dust, his raw throat grimy. But I'm worried about the sparks. They could ignite the fumes, the whole goddamn tunnel would go up. He spat then wiped his chin.

Do you think it will?

What?

Blow up.

The engineer shrugged. Fucked if I know. He was staring at the old man with a savage look in his eye and smiling sickly and then he said, Aw fuck it. Fuck it. He picked up his chisel.

Isn't there another way?

You should go doc.

It's just Arthur.

What?

I'm not a doctor. I told you.

The engineer regarded him queerly. You should go, Arthur.

The old man nodded but made no move to leave and after a moment he shrugged wearily and said, I guess I'm too old to be climbing these damned tunnels all night.

Right. Alright.

The engineer hefted the chisel and the mallet and he drew one fist back and splayed the other palm angular and fierce against the girder and he swung down hard. A flurry of sparks bloomed up into the dust and the old man suddenly felt light-headed, sick with dread. There was a great steel ringing in that hole and the sound shivered through his bones and teeth and the sparks arced incandescent and burning.

Nothing happened.

The engineer looked across, his eyebrows raised. Son of a *bitch*, he grinned.

The old man let out his breath.

And then the engineer swung and struck, swung and struck. After a time the old man took over and his blistered fingers felt thick and bruised and bloodied in his gloves as he hammered away. At each blow the bones in his arms shuddering. The heat swam in his eyes and he paused and wiped his forehead against his sleeve and glanced up at the engineer above him hauling struts in a clanking armload down through the spirals of blown dust and the old man's eyes ran.

Then they were through.

The old man at the engineer's elbow, the engineer grunting and the chisel clinking hollowly then punching past and in and through. The girder gave way. The engineer smashed an arm-hole, a leg hole, a hole the width of a child. A great fetid whoosh of air walloped past them and out up the tunnel and the old man coughed in the black reek and the headlamps were bending weirdly off the bricks and broken furniture beyond and the shapes wavered in the glare and then the light steadied and the old man squinted to see what lay within.

It might have been the back of a café counter once. He was calling in the roiling dust for the boy and he saw the mother's corpse on its stomach with its legs upraised and braced as if to bear the weight of the destruction. Her braided hair in tangles down her back. Her face turned from him. He saw she lay naked to the waist, her left elbow bent downward, the hand pinned somewhere underneath. The fold of the elbow was marbled with blood. He did not see the boy.

Son? he called in. Mason?

He called again and then the engineer beside him called also and their headlamps sliced along the haunted cavern walls and met and crossed and slid back.

Jesus, the engineer murmured. Jesus fucken christ.

Slowly, from the hidden side of the woman's body, a grey face lifted. Austere and terrible in the grey dust. The old man and the engineer both fell silent. Their headlamps glinted in the boy's eyeglasses and flattened and shone back and then the boy was blinking and regarding them from the deep well of his fear.

Come on, son, the old man was saying. That's right. This way.

He was tiny. He came out bent double at the waist and he climbed free and as he took the old man's arm his entire body began to tremble. He was wearing a red sweater coated in the white dust and his thick eyeglasses hung askew on his nose but he did not seem to be hurt at all. He was filthy and coughing and his face was streaked with tears. A small black boy with dark eyes. The old man knew him at once and the woman dead within.

I can't wake her up, the boy was saying in a small voice. She won't wake up. I think she's sick. Can you help her? Please?

The old man said nothing but held him very hard as if to crush the fear from him and the boy in that eerie white light burrowed his face into his shirt and then the old man was murmuring, Alright, it's going to be alright. Over and over, in a kind of incantation. As if it might really be so.

I wouldn't know where to begin. You get old. But it's the magnificence you don't expect. You're prepared for how the past pulls up short, for what burns off in the long heat of a life. We get ugly and soft like molten iron. I don't suppose any of us are spared. Well. I guess Callie was spared.

A woman at a gallery show once asked me about happiness. I gave her a peculiar look at that. I told her anyone who makes happiness the point, won't ever know it. Maybe that's not what she was asking. I don't know if you're born with joy inside you, or if it's a kind of choice you keep making as your life goes on. I really don't. I suppose joy and happiness aren't the same thing. I do believe I might have been more than I became. Callie used to say disappointment was what you held in your hands whenever you made a fist and then opened it. Then she'd make a fist and punch me on the shoulder. I don't know that I ever understood that. A lot of the things she said I didn't understand. I guess that's the thing about a life. No one makes you into anything except that you go along with it.

I met Callie at my first gallery show in Toronto. It was a small basement gallery. She was the tallest woman in a crowded room and she wore heels just to be sure. Her black hair in a bob over her ears. I don't think I took my eyes off her. When she smiled I thought of the sea. I don't know the connection myself. She held out her cigarette for a light and I asked her opinion of the paintings. She told me art and illustration weren't the same thing. It amazes me, how young we were. She touched my arm and told me I needed to learn to paint with my eyes closed, to learn how the paintings looked to my fingers. Her palm left a print of plaster dust on my sleeve.

Those early works were street studies. The city streets at dawn, at dusk. The light in those paintings was about a kind of searching, I guess. I didn't know exactly what for. I don't believe I ever found it. It took me a long time to see the light itself was the mystery. Callie used to say light was God to Giotto, and because of that light was God for the next six hundred years. Shadows came to stand in for knowledge, earthly understanding, for what makes us most human. I don't believe there's any contradiction in that. If you go into a dark room, your eyes adjust. They adjust and find what light there is. We're built to accommodate the darkness.

Listen to me. Thirty-six years on and my head's still trying to understand what my hands have always known.

His wife did not die in autumn and yet autumn was when he'd dream of her.

He came up out of that tunnel into the grey light coiling his safety line in the webbing of one thumb and slapping it forward and his legs stiffening in the late air, hamstrings cramped, back aching. And this was the dream: his wife shyly drawing her hand across the shiny knee of his trousers. A digger in the rubble held out a bottle of water and he took it from her. And this was the dream also: the steel-dark of his wife's black hair against his skin. The cold ropy weight of it after she had bathed, through the open door the clawfoot washtub gleaming. Something was in him and he did not understand it. It was not quite grief. He thought it was what happened to grief after a long time in a person. He thought: *The boy will know it too.*

He shook his head, pulled off his gloves in disgust. *You are going to pieces old man*, he thought. *There will be nothing left of you in an hour.* Only when he opened his eyes did he realize he had spoken aloud. He looked at the digger looking at him there.

You're alright, she said. Sure you're alright.

I'm not alright, he said.

His hands were sore and his arms streaked where the sweat had run. He leaned up against a slab and passed a hand across his eyes and then loosened the cloth at his throat. He felt nothing. They had brought the boy up out of that rubble and the woman lay dead below and he felt disgusted thinking of his part in it all.

After a moment he bared his teeth in a carious grin and drank the water then lowered the bottle with his chin sunk to his chest then raised it and drank again. He rubbed his eyes, looked up. The sun shivered orange and watery and huge under the low western sky like some terrible omen in the late blue light.

Where did they take him? he asked at last. His voice was hoarse.

The digger looked up. Who?

The boy. The boy they just brought out.

She nodded at the street below.

The old man studied the digger. She was a short woman with wide shoulders and big strong-looking hands and she wore stiff trousers that crinkled when she shifted her weight. He supposed they had been soaked and dried during the day. He did not know what they would have been soaked in. Gasoline perhaps. She looked very tired.

After a moment she said, It'll take them a while to cut her out.

Yes. Where will he go?

I don't know.

They won't make him see her body.

Somebody has to.

It's his mother. They won't let him see her like that.

She said nothing to that.

That boy needs to get to a hospital, he said.

Now she brushed a strand of hair from her face, looked at the old man. Her eyes were deep-set, dark. The hospitals are wrecked, she said. Nothing's left. He's got to go to a station.

A station? Where are they?

I don't know. The big one's at the Vic General.

You mean at the hospital?

She nodded.

He stared at her a moment then shook his head and looked off up the street then stared at her again. Well, he said slowly. That's where he'll need to go then.

There'll be trucks along soon.

When?

Soon.

When did the last truck come by?

She blew out her cheeks.

Have any trucks come by?

What's the matter with you?

What?

You got something you want to say just say it.

I don't.

Good.

She folded her arms grimly across her chest as if something had been settled and after a minute he got to his feet. He screwed back the cap of the water bottle and set it at his feet. He did not thank her for the water.

He scrambled achingly down the slope, hands fumbling with his gear. His wrists were black with grime and blood and he worked his fingers thickly. He did not see the engineer nor did he see the slender girl with the bruise at her forehead and both might have been apparitions of that horror for all that he would ever learn of their fates.

He could see a group gathered farther up the ridge and he knew there would be digging there but he did not go to them. He was sick, worn down, somehow ashamed. He had no intention of looking for the boy and yet when he reached the street he made his slow way over to where the digger had gestured. He saw a small group of survivors huddled together in the lee of an upturned Saab but he did not see the boy and he was surprised by how this made him feel.

He finally found the boy crouched alone against a mailbox with his knees pressed to his chest. His strange squinting eyes. Someone had scrubbed his face clean and draped a blanket across his shoulders and the old man stood over him peering down from his great height. He saw again the window of that café, a dark hand pressed to the glass. The boy's eyeglasses were bent at the nose-piece and he pushed them farther along his nose in order to see.

Mason?

The boy peered up at him.

My name is Arthur. Do you remember me, son?

The boy did not reply but only looked up at him with his burned stare and there seemed nothing at all in him that the old man could speak to. He gestured to the bent eyeglasses. Wondering what it was about this boy.

I can fix those for you, if you'd like. Do you want me to fix them?

The boy slid his eyeglasses under the ruff of blanket.

Well. Okay. His voice was gruff. He glanced off down the street and then back at the boy. Is someone taking care of you, son? he asked. When the boy said nothing he did not know what to say and after a moment he said: I've got to go home now. I'll come back in the morning if you'd like. To check on you. Would you like that?

The boy squinted up at him.

What is it? I can't take you with me. He grimaced suddenly, hearing himself say it. He had not intended to say such a thing. You don't want to come with me, do you? he asked.

No, the boy whispered.

He waited but the boy said nothing more and the old man reached down and very gently, very awkwardly patted his shoulder. The boy did not stir. After a moment he straightened and turned and began to make his way up the street. The buildings felt blown-out, emptied, shells of what they had been the morning before. The red sun was nearly down and the shadows were lengthening.

At the corner where the old pub still stood he stooped to tie his shoe and then paused with one hand on his knee and he crouched breathing like that for what seemed a long time. He was angry with himself for frightening the boy. He glanced at the sky, glanced back the way he had come. The dark streets strewn with rubble and stalled cars. Then he breathed in sharply. Someone was crouching in the shadow of the bank across the way, watching him.

He looked at the huddled figure and said nothing and then looked at the figure again.

Mason? he called. What are you doing? Come here son.

He got to his feet and stood very still in the road but the boy did not approach. He watched the boy holding his eyeglasses to his face, studying him with dark eyes.

Mason? he called again, more gently. You don't want to walk with me?

The boy said nothing. Mute and fierce with that blanket clutched at his shoulders.

At last he shrugged and turned and went on. As he began to walk the boy began again also. When he would slip too far ahead the boy hurried to catch him up, then hung back until he had moved on.

In this manner they went. The boy following. Or being led. It did not matter which.

They went.

Sometimes I'll hear her speaking in the next room, or calling up at me from downstairs. I don't know. I thought for a time it was grief. It wasn't. It was just my outliving her.

My grandfather used to say time has a way of worrying in. I guess he meant everything is in a state of decay. Painting isn't any different, it's like music in that. Its element, too, is time. You move through a painting quickly, or slowly. The eye takes in nothing at a glance. There was an expression I struggled to capture for years. It wasn't a large canvas. I dreamed it one night fifteen years ago and became obsessed with paint-ing it. It was of a young woman sitting in a silver car in a parking lot, her face just lifted towards the windshield. And on her face was an expression of just-flourishing sadness, a kind of serenity. I saw it with terrible clarity. I've never forgotten it. I never could get it right. Always it was complicated by regret, by apology, by blame. A face is a fluid thing, it's like the surface of the sea. It's never still. Even in sleep. I don't know, when you add the play of light across it it becomes near impossible to hold. Even photographs fail in that. I have a half-dozen photographs of Callie but none of them are her. I know it's strange to say it.

Not a day goes by I don't think of her. I wonder sometimes what my grandfather would have made of her. I didn't quit painting because of her. I don't care what anyone says.

A couple of years ago a woman came by to interview me for a book she was writing on Callie. I didn't want to do it. But I sat with her for a time. She pulled out a small blue notebook and scribbled down curt notes when I spoke. I didn't see how what I said could possibly be written down so quickly. I told her she could take a minute and get the rest of it if she wanted. I'd thought she'd smile at that but she didn't. She asked me if Callie left me because she couldn't complete her work with the pressures of being a wife. I suppose she wanted to know if I stifled her. I didn't know what to say to that. I told her my grandfather had been a judge and his favourite kind of sentence was a question. She didn't write that down in her little notebook.

I used to believe if I lived severely enough I might come to some kind of understanding about all of it. I don't know what I would have done then. I never did understand it. The heart's a dark room to me still.

THE LABYRINTH
AND THE THREAD

She could feel a wind on her sleeves, her shirt front. It was dark.

It was dark and the darkness was very blue and then she understood that she was staring into the sky and the sun was down. Something had happened. Something had just happened.

And then she was remembering her father's last visit, six months before his death. She had not known that he was dying. Her children adored him, this grandfather they'd hardly known. His great soft hands and the dark pitted skin on his face and the low rasp of his voice when he laughed. He had left Canada for his native Trinidad when she was six. Had returned after her mother's death only to vanish again into a small coffee shop he'd opened in Fernwood. His nation, his politics, his second life, these had consumed him. She carried always inside her that cold October day in the playground when she had realized he did not—did *not*—need her.

He was tilting the neck of the bottle towards her glass at the table and she came in from the patio and set her hand over the rim and shook her head no. The light was already deepening out in the yard and she looked at her father's face in the grey and thought he was still handsome. It was just the four of them there amid the clatter of dishes and the scent of dish soap and the steady running of the faucet. Her, and her father, and her two children. Her daughter sat on the counter with her coltish legs swinging loose and lifting her glass and holding it out.

Oui monsieur, she was calling to her grandfather.

Yeah right, the woman said.

Eh come on Jean-Paul, the girl said in her terrible accent. Toppa me off.

Jjjjahn-Pollluh, her son laughed.

Now look what you've started, the woman said. You call him Poppa.

Her father smiled and shook his head. I think one glass is enough, he said.

Come on. I drink more than that at recess.

The woman's father was looking now at his granddaughter's hair where she had cut it short and he waved a hand towards it. It looks nice, he said. Different.

Shut up, she smiled, then blushed.

Kat, the woman frowned. What's got into you? You want to go to your room?

What? I was joking. Kids say it all the time at school.

Listen to her. A little red wine and she loses her manners completely.

I got manners.

Right. Manners of speaking maybe.

Would you like anything more to eat, Mr Clarke? Could I fetch you a coffee, Mr Clarke?

The woman's father laughed. Ah yes. That is very polite.

Kat what did I tell you about sitting on the counter?

The girl smiled at her grandfather. See? Mom's driving us crazy.

You're not driving me crazy Mom.

Thank you Mason.

Her daughter snorted.

The woman crossed to the sink and banged open the cupboard and began putting the dishes away. Blue serving bowls emblazoned with asian fish. She squared the glasses of blown green glass. Oh your horrible mother, she said. However do you stand it.

Tell your grandfather how I beat you, how I work you like slaves. Oh you poor things.

You don't even know. You don't know how hard it is, it's not like when you were a kid. It's a different world. You think you had problems? We got problems.

The woman's father folded his chin onto his hands, raised his eyebrows exaggeratedly. I would love to hear, he said. These are the boyfriend problems? The drug problems?

She *had* a boyfriend. But Crispin Carter dumped—

Shut up Mason.

Hey? Language?

The girl glanced across at her mother. As if I'd talk about it anyway. She'd probably just ground me or something.

She has a *name*, the woman said.

It's Mom.

Thank you Mason. Aren't you awfully helpful tonight.

Yes.

Ah. She would ground you would she?

Poppa, you don't even know.

Usually I just lock her in a closet. With bread and water.

I used to send your mom out in the fields for the day. I think she should send you out to the fields maybe.

We don't have fields here Poppa.

Neither did we, honey, the woman said.

You could tie her to the rack, her father said. Or shave off all of her hair.

The woman laughed. I think she already did that.

You're both hilarious, the girl said, all at once distracted and immensely bored. She lifted the glazed head of the cookie jar and peered in, then slid lazily off the counter and sauntered out, a cookie in either hand, another in her teeth.

Can I have a cookie too? her son asked.

No.

I remember when you were that age, her father said.

No you don't.

He looked at her. Well. You were perfect. You were a perfect angel.

You said before that Mom was a little devil.

Hey? You want to be grounded too?

Her son shook his head. After a moment he looked up. Kat's grounded?

You get out of here. Go on. Go see what your sister is doing.

Her son scrambled down from the table.

She looked at her father. He's going right into his sister's room to tell her she's grounded. You know that.

Her father smiled. It is nothing. I had five brothers.

And two sisters.

Yes.

She said nothing then. She looked towards the sitting room. In the gloom its couches were lumped and misshapen, the old fireplace cold in the shadows. Embers of darkness coalesced within. The smell of the yard came in through the open window and she could hear a dog barking beyond their fence. She wiped the countertop down with the dishcloth and shook its crumbs into the sink. Filled her tarnished kettle with water, plugged it in.

Through the walls a thrum of music started up and the woman smiled grimly, regarded her father. The floor tiles under their socks shaking.

He stood. I will ask her to turn it down, he said.

You're great with them, she said.

I could stay longer.

No. You should go.

He nodded but did not move.

I could take them out on the boat on Saturday.

No.

Anna Mercia. What do you think I am doing here?

But she made a cutting motion with her hand and he went quiet.

He had always loved the ocean. When she was a girl and he would telephone on her birthday or on Christmas he would ask first about the changing light on the water. In the West Indies he had owned a small boat and it was one of the first things he purchased when he returned here, to this colder ocean. He had been famous in his country as a public figure. She wondered suddenly at how things alter.

She turned back to the sink. Standing there feeling slack and grotesque and old. She held a warm plate staring at it without interest and she set it again aclatter in the rack. She thought her father had left the kitchen but all at once she felt his hands on her shoulders and he turned her gently so that she was facing him. He took her chin in his palm.

He said to her very softly: They love you. You are their mother.

They need a father.

They do not.

She looked into his face. Everyone needs a father, Dad.

Everyone *wants* a father, he said. There is a difference.

She looked at his soft sloped shoulders and doughy face in the kitchen light and it seemed to her then that he was asking something of her she could not give. At first she did not recognize it and then she did and it was something she remembered from when Mason was very little. She felt all at once as if she were older than her father and feeling this filled her with a great sadness.

You were a good father, she said to him.

Even as she said this she knew it was not true and she knew that he knew it also.

There were many things else, he said quietly. But I did always love you.

No you didn't, she said, and looked at him. You didn't, Dad. That wasn't love.

She opened her eyes.

She was very cold. She felt something flutter across her face and it felt like a moth and the darkness before her was utter and absolute. Then she sat up, and the white sheet fell away.

She had been laid out in a field of the dead. She pulled the sheet away and got to her feet and her left arm was hanging at a strange angle from the elbow. All around her lay the bodies of the dead and some were covered as she had been and others had been rolled onto their backs and their sightless faces shone in the night. She was naked to the waist but she did not cover herself and in the darkness she could not see the bad shape her arm was in.

She staggered over the rolled corpses and down a grassy incline towards the street.

Her throat was dry and her lips cracked and her tongue felt huge and furred in her mouth. There was something not right with her and she cast her face slowly from left to right and then she knew it was her son and she lurched back up towards the bodies and picked her way among them. Gasping, her bad arm dangling. She could not think clearly and she stooped, peered, straightened, stooped. But she did not see her son.

She felt nothing. She did not think she could walk but even so her legs carried her down to the street and towards a yellow lantern where a man sat staring into the night. There were lights moving out in that darkness and she could not understand what they were.

He stood very quickly when he saw her.

Oh my god, he said. Oh god. Are you okay? Pike! Sit here. Pike!

She was trying to ask about her son and her ruined mouth worked silently and no words came. Then in that soft light she saw her crushed hand. The skin was mottled and black as if the rot had already set in and her fingers were half again as long as they should have been. Two fingers stood out at a weird angle. The arm was covered in slicks of blood and some yellowish grease that smelled of fat and she looked at it as if it did not belong to her.

Where'd you come from? the man was asking. And then: Pike!

Where is my arm? she said thickly. She raised her head and looked at the man. Where is my son? she tried again.

A second man came out of the darkness. He looked at her and kneeled down beside her speaking to her all the while and then he stood and disappeared again into the night. He came back carrying a case and set it down and unlatched and lifted its lid and he pulled from the box several coils of bandages and wrappings. He looked very tired. He pressed a pill between her lips and then lifted a bottle of water to her and she choked as it went down.

Give it a minute, the man said. He was a squat thick man with a black beard and his eyes were liquid and wet. He smelled of sweat and urine. His mouth was hard.

I know this woman, he said to his companion. I was there when they brought her out. We thought she was dead.

Christ. I thought she was a ghost.

The second man was wiping very gently at her face and the gauze was coming away black with dried blood.

My son, she said thickly. My son. My son is.

Try not to say anything just yet.

My son. He was with me.

The man sat back on his heels and looked at her. He did not smile. He said in a soft clear voice: Your son is alive. Look at me. No look at me. He's fine. We pulled him out hours ago.

Mason?

Yes.

She started to cry then and she bent over and cried for what seemed a very long time. She cried and then someone was draping a blanket across her naked shoulders and the bearded man was still talking.

What? she said through her tears. What are you saying?

Your son's fine, the man went on. He'll be glad to see you.

Where is he? she said. I want to see him.

What's wrong with her head? the first man said.

Nothing. It's just a small cut. But look at this. The second man lifted her arm with great gentleness. Each shift in position left her shuddering with pain, light-headed and dazed with it.

It's crushed, he said finally. And I don't know what else.

I want to see my son.

You will. Try to be patient. I haven't seen him since last night. He must have been taken to the relief station on the last truck. Which is where you've got to go yourself.

There'll be doctors there, the second man said.

You're a, she said and frowned. You're a doctor?

No. He did not look up from her arm as he spoke. I worked construction for a few summers. There were a lot of accidents. I don't know what else could be wrong with her, he said over his shoulder. She might be hurt internally.

She grimaced, her teeth clenched. Already the pain was subsiding and then it flared up again and then it seemed as if it were sifting through some sort of a mesh screen and when it reached her it was in very tiny points of pain and then even that was dissolving.

It's kicking in now. Look at her.

You feel that? the bearded man said.

No, she said dully. Yes.

Do you remember your name?

She stared at him and blinked and then she nodded.

What's your name?

Anna Mercia.

Do you know what year it is, Anna Mercia?

I need to find my son.

He began to wrap her blotched hand very carefully in a thick winding bandage and when he had pinned this he set her forearm as best he could and held it bent at her ribs and wrapped it firmly against her body and then binding it tight he pinned it off.

Who's her son? the second man murmured.

Little black kid. What was his name? Mason?

Mason.

As she said it she felt her thoughts clearing, hardening to a very cold sharp edge.

When is the next truck? she asked. I need to use a phone. I need to phone my daughter.

You won't get through to anyone. The lines are down.

She means a cell. Do you mean a cell? Some of the cells are getting through.

When is the next truck?

But they did not know. It could be an hour, it could be later, the second man told her. The two men slid a thick grey sweater over her head and very carefully worked it down over her dressings and she roped her good arm through a sleeve. Then the engineer with the black beard pointed to a light high up in the rubble and told her that she would find a young woman there with a badly stitched cut along her nose and that this woman had a working cell. He walked her to the base of the ruins and gave her a flashlight and held her shoulder briefly in his strong grip and then he was gone.

Anna Mercia went up uneasily. She found a heavy-set woman in the darkness sitting on an overturned crate and she said, Are you Aretha? I need to use your phone.

But the heavy woman shook her head and waved her on up towards a circle of light farther on. There were men sitting in the light speaking in low voices and a red-haired girl off to one side with a badly stitched nose and this girl's hands looked huge in the shadows.

Aretha? Anna Mercia asked.

The red-haired girl looked up.

I was told you had a phone.

The batteries are low.

I need to call my daughter.

The red-haired girl studied her a long moment. Two minutes, she said. That's it.

She nodded and took the phone and pinned it between her knees and started to dial her home telephone and then she stopped. Then she dialed her home anyway and listened for a moment to the dead tone. The girl watched with a furrowed brow. She quit the call and dialed her daughter's cell and let it ring.

On the fourth ring a man answered.

Who is this? she said abruptly. Where's Kat?

Who? the man said. His voice was echoing as if he stood in an empty room.

Katherine. My daughter. Let me talk to her.

Who is this? the man demanded.

Then the line went dead.

Hello? she shouted. Hello? Are you there?

The girl watched and bit her lip and Anna Mercia punched the numbers again, avoiding the girl's eyes. It rang and rang and this time no one picked up.

She stared foolishly at the phone for a long moment. She felt angry and then embarrassed and then very frightened.

It was the right number, she said.

What happened?

I don't know. A man answered.

She had not dialed the wrong number. She knew this.

Kat lost her phone, she told herself. *She just dropped her phone and somebody else found it. It doesn't mean anything. Anyone can find a phone. It doesn't mean anything.*

The phones are all a mess right now, the red-haired girl said. You could've been connected with anyone.

Anna Mercia looked away. The men were muttering among themselves and she sat then with her elbow on her knee and she closed her eyes, lowered her head. She did not want to think about what to do.

—at 8.6, one of the men was saying. And not just Seattle. Bill would know. Bill?

Anna Mercia opened her eyes, studied the men in the harsh light.

A short thick young man was leaning forward. His hands were badly cut up and he counted off on his fingers as he spoke. She watched the glint of his wristwatch in the lamplight. Electricity, water, hospitals, airports, most of the roads, they're all gone, he said. Airport's closed except to emergency traffic. Roads are a mess. If help comes it'll have to come by sea. But we'll be on our own for at least 72 hours.

She closed her eyes again. Her head felt thick and her arm had begun to ache. The voices rolled in and past her in waves and she could not quite grasp them.

I heard that too.

What does that even mean? Seventy-two hours from now? Or from yesterday?

We're just supposed to wait it out—

Until the weekend at *least*. Fuck this.

Take it easy.

Isn't anyone coming? Don't they have anyone to help?

Come on. Take it easy, Bill.

Shut off the gas. Conserve what water you've got.

You know what this means?

They got the army coming in. No fucking doctors. But the army? Sure.

Oh they got doctors. Just not for us.

Vancouver'll get the attention. You wait and see.

We're the fucking capital.

You think that matters? Wait and see.

What you need is a radio. You don't got a radio, you're fucked.

I said take it easy.

You tell me to take it easy one more time.

She sat for a long time in that darkness listening to them. The hour was very late when at last she stood. She crossed that small circle of light and paused and held her shattered arm and stared out at the darkness. There were no lights in the city. She shivered.

Men were bearing loaded buckets streetwards and their fore-arms passed back and forth in the darkness and their skins were slick despite the cold air. A wire handle snapped and a bucket fell skittering off the broken slabs with its rubble bursting in small clouds and she saw it tumble out of the harsh lamplight and heard it bang to a stop below and then a lady set up cursing. The bucket-bearer stood with the handle still in his fist and he met the woman's gaze and shrugged wearily and threw the wire aside and made his slow way down. Iron punch of shovels, the loose shale underfoot. She could just make out the shrunken heads of dolls, solitary bro-gans, sheets of music, a mattress split savagely with its steel coils bared like fish hooks and all of it bending spookily in the smokey white light. A choke of dust in the air and the sour smell of gas and rotting meat and she stood to one side eyeing the deepness beyond and there were fires burning up the street and figures huddled near them. She rubbed her eyes.

She rubbed her eyes and then she went down into it.

It seems a long time ago now.

We never did get to Karachi. It was the eighties, nothing seemed to go right. Our train cut abruptly at the edge of a south Indian city, I don't know what the problem was. I felt old. You're never as old as you are at twenty. I'd been with David only eight months and we barely knew each other. I can say that now. We lugged our packs through humid streets, thinking of home. The offices there were built of glass and steel and too modern to evoke old Asia. Which of course was the Asia we'd come to see. The Asia everyone that age comes to see.

I don't know what we were looking for. I was a girl, a child, not much older than Kat is now. I think of her and I can't imagine it. All the old relics, the temples, the languages, they were going to change something in us. Malaysia's pure beaches, Cambodia's temples, Thailand's cliffs—all of that was going to force us into some hard understanding. So we were romantic and foolish. So what. I hope Kat and Mason both are like that. Epiphanies should come at you night and day when you're young.

Something did change in us in that city, when we got stranded. We'd found a small hostel and I remember how unexpected and perfectly ordinary it was when it came. David was staring at me from the bed. We'd been fighting. It was dusk and his eyes were black, his pale face angular among the mosquito netting. He looked suddenly Thai, he looked Vietnamese, Malaysian, Chinese, every country we'd passed through, every man I'd seen trailing me with his eyes that summer. It wasn't shame I felt, it wasn't desire. I watched him watching me and it was like some part of my heart had been left behind. Like that train had arrived at a possible future. I feel foolish talking about it. David said he didn't know where we were. He had a map in his hands but he wasn't looking at it. I wanted him to find me inside myself, to guide me through. I didn't say it. My eyes didn't say it. Three nights we spent like that. We were poor, we survived off rust and water, and all that time a child was being made.

We didn't know it then of course. It happens so fast. You're a daughter at nineteen, at twenty you're a mother. I look back on my life before Kat and Mason and it seems almost like it was lived by someone else. A shadow self.

What was the name of that city? Jesus.

It's the little things. The sun at the curtains, the fear of being together, the fear of being alone. Maybe that's all being young really is, in the end. I felt David's bones through the sheets and how frightening it still was to be so close to a man. I felt outside of my own life, beyond absent fathers and sullen mothers. It wasn't the first time I had felt that but it was the strongest. I told him about my father, who had left us when I was still a little girl. How he had returned to his native Trinidad for some government post. I was six. I remember going down to the kitchen and finding my mother in her white nightgown sitting in the dark and when I asked her where he was she looked up at me with a very surprised expression in her eyes and said, Who?

I told David about my mother. I don't know what I was trying to warn him against. He just held me. He held me like some lost and awkward bundle he'd found at a train station, something not his own. All the while it felt almost like a third presence was listening, like that tiny person on the verge of becoming already had her ear pressed to our hearts. It stuns me even now when I think about it. She wasn't any kind of reason yet.

You know what it is being a mother? Nothing's in your hands. Everything's accidental and unexpected. Sometimes I get so frightened for my kids I don't know what to do. Because you can't make the world safe to walk through. You can't stop what's coming.

Where she walked the sun did not rise. It did not rise and the steel-grey light gradually dissolved and paled and a sickly white sky burned off to the east and then the day was thickening and she walked on into it hard and afraid and utterly alone in her fear.

She walked in the road avoiding the dark buildings on either side and all morning it seemed to her that a figure trudged behind her. Her mind kept straying to scraps of memory but would not stay fixed on any one for long. When she sat to rest or find her bearings the shadow sat also and when she stood it stood also and together they went on.

She would walk for blocks through deserted streets, past low-lying buildings, crumbled shopfronts, crushed cars, seeing no sign of life. Then she would come upon a crowd shouting and pushing in the rubble and these groups she would slip uneasily past. And then for another long while she would see very few people. But always she felt eyes on her, figures watching from cavernous dark-nesses in the buildings as she passed.

The sky was still very white when she rested beside a small schoolyard. She stood at the fence watching the people at work, amazed. The gymnasium roof had fallen and the long corridor of the school had collapsed and firemen were picking through the wreckage there. It seemed so strange to her to see rescuers in uniform. Just two blocks back she had seen shop glass shattered, storefronts looted. As she stood a body was brought up on a stretcher out of the rubble and it looked very small to her eye.

A circle of people had gathered to watch. A helicopter chopped low overhead and turned and circled back and Anna Mercia raised a hand to her face. When she looked away her eyes were wet and she understood she did not believe her daughter would be at the house. Not truly. But she did not know what else to do. She lowered her face, cowled in her thick grey sweater. Kat was stubborn and clever and wilful and she thought this might keep her safe. But, too, when Mason fell into the lake, how Kat had plunged in to save him from drowning though she could not swim herself. How she nearly lost them both that day. Her daughter's catlike body on the dock, shuddering and wracking up great sobs of water, her hair in dark tangles at her face.

She studied the others gathered there in their loose shirts, their dirty shoes. Their faces in the haunted backlit day. Her chest ached fiercely. She knew she would trade any one of them for her daughter's life. The air smelled of charcoal in the brutal sunlight. She was remembering the sleekness in her daughter's stooped figure as she rinsed their sedan in the driveway in the late dusk months ago and how the girl had straightened and turned the hose upon the lawn and looked up at Anna Mercia in the window and she felt then a grief she had forgotten was within her.

There was a fury in the world despite everything and hope was never really possible. She watched the sun glinting on the playground bars, staining red the cedar chips strewn there and shivering against the grooved walls of the garbage bins. The firefighters' hoses deflated and dry in the courtyard. A swing twisted, untwisted on its chains.

Poor goddamn kids, one of the men was saying.

Anna Mercia hooked her fingers into the mesh-wire fence and rested her face against it. She closed her eyes. He might have been talking to her.

She left them then, went on.

As she walked she would catch herself muttering. Running old conversations in her head in a soft shadowing voice: *You damn well better get those dishes done mister.* Or: *Kat honey I only got two hands, if you want something it'll have to wait.* Conversations without meaning. Looping them over and over. On her knuckles a tattoo of dirt and dried blood, her bad arm bound tight against her ribs. A darkness pluming out of the southeast over the bones of the city.

After a time she found herself on the sidewalk of a small block of coffee shops, banks, a dry cleaner across the way. The day was turning warm. Her stomach seemed a cold coiled thing inside her and she knew this was hunger and though she did not feel any pain she knew she must eat. She began rattling the doors, going from shop to shop. When she looked up she saw two black dogs slip out of a bakery two doors down and the second dog paused and raised its snout studying her with hard flat eyes then lowered its head and vanished up the street. She approached uneasily. The glass door stood open on its silver hinges.

Hello? she called. Hello?

The interior was dark and she waited in the doorway for her eyes to adjust. The lights were hanging in long loops of cable from the ceiling and the tables were overturned, splintered, the chairs kicked wide. The door to the back ovens stood open and a sour smell was coming from there.

She righted a sofa and slid down feeling heady and strange. She sat for some time.

At last she got to her feet and kicked her way to the counter looking for food. The glass had been smashed and the pastries had been taken. Some small cakes had been crushed underfoot and she looked at the dark smear of them and then at the blacker kitchen beyond. It was a place utterly without light. *You're not that hungry yet*, she thought. She could just make out a shape fallen in the doorway and she thought then of the dogs and then she left the bakery and she did not look back.

By noon she began to encounter families camped in tents or tarped shelters built of chairs and odds and ends strung up between trees

on their lawns. Pale mothers in dusty jeans with children three or
four in a line staring bleakly out. Their houses largely undamaged. Foundations shifted. Garages crushed. She walked through
the unnatural glow watching children wash in steel tubs in the
yards or old women sit on canvas chairs in open doors and no
lights burned in the houses. Sometimes there were men with them
and they would straighten from whatever task and watch until she
had passed.

Her daughter would be waiting. Her daughter would be. *If
she is not there then she'll be somewhere else*, she thought. *If she is not
there then you'll go to Mason and then together you'll find Kat. That is
all you need to think about now. Keep your head. It's not far now.*

A short while later in the stark midday light a truck rumbled
past with figures jouncing in the bed of it and then its brake lights
flared and it turned around and came slowly back. There were two
of them in the bed and the paler boy folded his elbows over the
siding as they pulled smokily up. He was young and well-dressed
and his companion likewise. He held a crowbar crosswise in his
lap.

Hey, he said. Where you headed?

Anna Mercia stood in the gravel holding her broken arm
firmly by the forearm and wiped the grime from her forehead and
looked at their eyes and at the truck and at the road.

Nowhere, she said.

We'll give you a lift. Climb in.

It's alright.

You goin into town? We're goin into town.

The two boys were watching her intently.

No, she said.

Come on.

No.

She turned around and started walking back the way she had
come and after a moment the truck began reversing slowly behind
her.

Hey, the pale boy was calling to her. He sounded angry. Hey, where you goin?

She could feel herself shaking. She did not answer him.

Hey, he shouted at her. You fucken cunt.

His companion said something she did not hear and the boy laughed. Then he banged the flat of his hand twice on the roof of the cab and the truck started back up.

Over her shoulder she watched them go and then she slipped down into the drainage ditch and crouched in the bushes holding her knees and she waited. She could not stop shaking. She crouched like that for a long time watching that the truck did not circle back. The white dust smoking off in the gravel.

The hours passed.

And then she was stumbling along a street she knew, and then another, and she knew it was close. She passed a row of burned-out houses, the blackened shells of garages and iron railings twisted from the heat. Her feet in their thin black flats were aching and each step seemed to drag heavily. And she lifted her head, and slowed, and stopped.

Her street too had burned. A fire must have swept through after the earthquake hit for most of the houses stood charred and gutted in the high sunlight and her own house had burned along its eastern wall but for some reason the fire had not taken the house. The kitchen and the garage were gutted. But the bedrooms, the living room looked undamaged from where she stood taking in the sight and she was trembling. She stood at the bottom of the driveway for many minutes but no one came out to meet her and then she crossed the lawn and approached the house. She was moving quickly.

Kat? she hollered into the dim hall. Kat are you home? Kat! Katherine!

She left the front door standing open and her shoes drummed over the carpet into the hall. The house was a mess, the furniture kicked aside, the photographs and paintings askew or fallen. She saw her television had been taken and the stereo in the dining room also. The kitchen was burned out and blackened and she could see the sky and the next house through the far window. The sink was charred and filled with drywall and strips of cupboard. The walls smelled of grey water and ash and singed carpet. She could see no sign of her daughter.

Okay, she murmured. Okay. Okay.

The house felt very silent and strange and she did not know what to do. She could feel something in her throat and she knew it was fear and she swallowed it back down. She must keep her mind very clear, very cold. She stood with one hand on her head staring at the stained walls.

Then out of the stillness of the hall she heard something.

Boots. Scraping on stairs.

There were three sharp steps, then a pause. Then three more.

She left the kitchen and stood at the end of the hall and peered into the darkness and after a moment her basement door swung open. A man came through. He had black hair and wore a bandage wrapped around his temples and over one eye and he was sweating heavily. Hefting in his arms a box filled with jars of canned fruit and stewed tomatoes and tins of soup and when he saw her he stood dead still and stared. His knuckles were white where he gripped the box. The skin on his neck and arms looked red and sore and the hairs on his forearms were tacky with dust.

Who are you? she asked sharply. What're you doing in my house? Her eyes flicked to the dark basement behind him. He looked to be alone.

He was breathing softly with his one eye scrunched narrow and he said in a quiet voice: The door was open?

She did not know if he was explaining his own presence or asking how she had herself got in. Her head felt hot, gluey, light. Then it was cold and clear again. Are you alone? she asked.

Yes, he said. I was just getting a few things.

This is my house.

Yes.

I'm looking for my daughter—

No one's been here, he said. We came in after the fire.

We?

The house was empty.

We?

He blew out his cheeks. Me and my wife.

I thought you were alone.

He was silent a moment. Then he said, She's hurt. We needed somewhere to go. He shifted the box onto one hip and grunted. I got to set this down. See what there is in here.

That's my food.

I guess it is.

He brushed past her into the living room and set the box down with a clank on the upturned coffee table. He kept looking at her out of the corner of his good eye and there was something in his manner she did not like. An uneasiness. Or some other thing she could not name. He began to tell her of the quake as it had struck and how it had caught them just as his wife was in the shower. He was a barber and took Tuesdays off and so was at home and only just waking up when it hit. He said his wife's brother had been killed in the quake and he spoke in a low voice and said his brother-in-law had been a guest in their house at the time. Had gone out jogging when it struck and a car had driven up off the road and killed him. He had found him laid out in Henderson Field amid a great crush of other corpses all nameless and muti-lated. He wrinkled his brow as if surprised and turned his head and looked down the hall.

Henderson Field, she said. You mean the ballpark?

He nodded. It's terrible there, he said. That's where they're taking them. The bodies.

He did not ask about her. He did not ask about her daughter. He seemed not at all curious and sat darkly on the couch after he had finished his account and he reached one mottled hand up to his bandage and rubbed at his damaged eye.

What happened to your eye?

The barber glanced at her and his eye was dark but when she did not turn from him he looked away.

I walked all day, she said. I thought my daughter would be here.

You shouldn't be out there on your own. A woman like you. It's not safe.

A woman like me?

The barber nodded.

Where's your wife? she asked.

Anna Mercia followed him down the hall to her own bedroom. The floorboards creaked under his boots and his steps echoed along the blistered walls and in the half-darkness it did not seem at all the house she had lived in. She was suddenly very glad that her daughter was not here. He opened the door softly, peered in.

Aggie? Are you sleeping? the barber murmured into the gloom. We got a guest.

There was a muffled shifting of blankets, of sheets. The sound of uneasy breathing.

The barber's wife said something Anna Mercia did not hear.

He turned back and looked at her with his one eye. His head monstrous, swollen, a blood-thick thing in the darkness. She could smell his breath.

She's in bad shape, he said. I don't know. Come on in.

They went in. The bedroom light was grey through the sheer drapes drawn yet over the window and Anna Mercia peered around at the chaos of that room. Her clothes had been upended out of the mahogany drawers and the drawers stacked end on end and the wall mirror taken down and leaned up against the far wall. Her closet doors had been dragged off their runners and turned sideways and kicked into the opening and even her bed had been shoved up against the wrong wall, away from the window. She sucked in her breath and wondered suddenly just who these people were.

What happened here? she muttered. What did you do to my things?

The barber shrugged. It was like this when we got here. I mean we went through it again looking for blankets and stuff. You know.

I don't know.

He touched a hand to his head. Bandages and stuff.

Anna Mercia said nothing.

We didn't take anything. We're not thieves.

No. You just come into someone else's house and make yourselves at home.

Well.

The barber's wife lay shivering in the bed under a thin sheet and the sheet looked soft and brown with discolour from her wounds. Her eyes were glassy where she looked at her husband and Anna Mercia understood at once that the wife was dying. She was a heavy woman with brown hair fallen about the pillow and her drained face was etched by slices of glass.

What do you want, the wife hissed. This is our house.

The barber grunted. Aggie, he said. You know that's not true.

Anna Mercia swallowed and her throat was suddenly dry. I thought my daughter might have come here, she said to the barber. I hoped— She bit her lip hard.

Get out, the barber's wife said. Get out of here.

Her girl's lost, Aggie, the barber said gently. He was leaning over his wife and lifted a wet strip of cloth from a bucket and squeezed some water into her hair and she closed her eyes.

Who is she? his wife whispered. Is she alone?

She's alone, the barber replied.

Anna Mercia did not like the way he said this. I'm looking for my daughter, she said again. Do you have a phone?

The phone lines are down, the barber said.

I meant a cellphone.

The barber's wife opened her eyes.

What is it? Anna Mercia asked.

Nothing. We've heard stories. About some of the people out in the street since the quake.

What kind of stories?

You know, the barber said. Looters. Thieves. Kids driving around looking for trouble. Stealing cellphones.

You think I want to steal your phone?

He smiled but the smile did not reach his eyes.

They're just tired, Anna Mercia thought, watching them. And then: *No, that is not tired. That is something else.*

They were quiet for a moment and then the barber asked, What are you going to do?

She shook her head. I don't know.

You could stay here. Wait for your daughter.

She frowned.

You might as well stay. Shouldn't she stay, Aggie?

The barber's wife murmured something to her husband.

Aggie thinks you should stay.

Anna Mercia did not reply but looking at the barber's wife wrapped in her sheets with her yellow piglike eyes peering out at her she did not think this was what she had said.

She left them then and went to her neighbours' but found no one at home. *At least they are not dead*, she thought. And then: *No. Be precise. You mean they are not dead here.* As she was coming back down the street she heard a groan from the side of the yard and found the barber doubled over in her neighbours' rhododendrons, a crate of tinned soups overturned in the dirt. His hands were pressed to his face and she approached him carefully and when he looked up at her his good eye was squinched nearly shut in pain.

It's my goddamn eye, he said. It's my goddamn eye.

You're stealing their food, Anna Mercia said. Her voice sounded thin, impatient. They got two little girls. You think they won't need that?

Please, he said. You got to help me. Oh my goddamn eye.

What're you doing? Stealing food from everyone around here?

Goddamnit, he said.

She looked off up the road and then down at him where he kneeled.

Go on up there, she said.

He did not move and she shoved him with her foot as she would a stubborn dog and she felt at once sorry for it. But he unfolded and got unsteadily to his feet.

She went inside and found a pan and rinsed it with water from the tank behind the toilet and then she found some tweezers and a bottle of iodine and she held this up to the window and peered at it wondering how old it was and if it was still good. Then she went back outside to the front steps. Her hand was shaking as the barber kneeled in front of her and she took his jaw in her hand and tilted his head to the side. In the pale afternoon light she very gently began to unwind the bandage from around his head. A smell of ash in the thick air. The gauze was yellow and she peeled it softly from his socket and there was a watery pink blood and some clear fluid oozing out from his swollen eyelid. He was biting his teeth down hard.

What happened to you? she asked him.

His hands were gripping her knees tightly.

Easy, she said. Just be easy now.

She reached down for the water and ran it lightly over his forehead to clean the eye and then she took up the tweezers from the pan and she folded back the red flap of skin. The eye was scarlet and gruesome and it rolled wild and unseeing.

Something's definitely in there, she murmured.

He groaned.

Don't move. Try not to move.

She slipped the tweezers under the lower edge of the eye and he screamed and pulled away.

Do you want me to do this or not?

His head was lowered and he did not reply at once.

We don't have to do this.

No, he said. Please.

He set his head again into her lap and she slipped the tweezers in under the jelly of the eye and felt the tip tap against something hard. And withdrew in a single long strand of sticky blood a fragment of iron a quarter inch in length. She held it up in front of him and he looked at it wonderingly.

My god, she said.

It's a goddamn nail, he said.

And then he leaned over and was sick.

The afternoon passed. She did not know how it passed. She had some vague sense of drifting through the rooms of her house, sitting at the blown windows, standing on the lawn staring blankly up the street. She did not attempt to right anything, repair anything. The sun slid lower in the sky, the shadows thickened in the grass, the light faded. She thought of her son watching the sun descend somewhere out in the city and then she thought of her daughter and then she did not think of either for the terrible feeling was in her and she could not.

When she turned to go inside the house she saw the message in white paint on the door of the house: *Kat Mason I am alive and looking for you Love Mom.*

She had found the tin of paint in the basement and the brush in the wreckage down there where the fire had not reached and she was remembering this now where she stood. Then she was remembering the body pulled out of the gymnasium that morning and how the firefighters had lifted the stretcher clear with great gentleness as if bearing the injured and not the dead up into those slats of sunlight, slats of shade. How she had leaned on the low hood of a car and the sun-hot metal under her thighs. The firefighters' steel helmets burning like halos of fire.

Then she was inside again and there was a grey blanket on the couch for her to sleep under and the house was already dark. Down the hall she could see a light burning under the door of the bedroom where the barber and his wife lay. She made her way down to the bathroom but as she neared she could hear them speaking in low voices through the door and she paused a moment in the darkness to listen.

The wife was speaking quickly and then her voice grew louder and then she said, angrily: And what does she think? The girl was here and left?

She doesn't think anything. She's just looking for the girl.

Anna Mercia almost could not hear him.

His wife said something then that Anna Mercia did not hear and the barber spoke again, quickly. That's ridiculous Aggie. Why would she do such a thing.

How do you know she's not lying?

I don't think she's lying.

The wife's voice came again muffled and unclear. Then there was a creaking of the bedsprings as something shifted and then she could hear both voices very clearly.

—Cole. You know what I'm talking about.

Come on, Aggie. Her picture's on the floor there. It's her. She's trying to find her family.

You mean the girl.

Yes. The girl.

I don't trust her.

You don't need to trust her. How's your leg. Let me take a look at it.

You get her out of here. I mean it.

It's her house.

I don't care. Get her out of here.

The barber was silent.

The bed creaked again. You know what's going on out there, his wife said. You saw that family in the Volkswagen. You want that to be us? Is that what you want?

The barber said something more but Anna Mercia could not hear what it was and then she made her slow way back to the living room. She left the drapes undrawn. The sky outside was orange from the fires that still burned across the city and the room was bright as it had been on moon-filled nights before the earthquake and she lay with her broken arm folded carefully across her sternum and her face turned to the hall.

She did not understand what they had been saying about her daughter. It did not seem to her that Kat could have come here yet. She knew she was weakening but her mind remained hard. *That is good*, she thought. *Keep your thoughts very clear.*

She remembered how when Kat was a child her husband would hang a silver globe in their window in the days leading up to Christmas. Glinting as it turned in the slow light from the street below. She remembered this and how her daughter would lie in their bed staring up at it as the sound of carols drifted from the radio next door and the snow drifted in the darkness outside. The white flakes coalescing on the cold glass. Her little eyes opening, closing, and David laughing through the wall with his friends. A sweet scent of cloves as they smoked and smoked and her daughter asleep in the cot with her.

The silver globe in their window, spinning and spinning.

And too that last visit from her father. Pulling out of her garage in the car, late for work. As her father came hefting a garbage can in his big arms and setting it in the dirt at the curb. How she had thought he was coming to say farewell. The bag had come apart and scattered eggshells and coffee grounds into the low weeds and he stood a moment with his hand atop his white hair before stooping there. The lagoon below shining harshly in the early sunlight and the tide beyond draining out. Her radio had come on playing an aria of some old Italian opera and moved by this she saw a grace and sadness in her father she had not seen before. She slowed the car and her old father straightened holding in his hands the dripping trash, father and daughter regarding each other without expression through the car window and neither speaking. The father staring past his own watery reflection to find his daughter's face.

She opened her eyes.

All at once she was remembering the voice on her daughter's cellphone and she knew with certainty that it was the barber she had spoken to. She was shaking.

She did not know how long she lay there. After a time she kicked back the wool blanket and pressed her shoes to the armrest of the couch and her heart was thundering inside her.

She got up from the couch and made her way back down the hall, trailing her good hand along the charred wallpaper. She knocked softly on the bedroom door where she had slept all those years and then she turned the knob woozily with one shoulder to the wall to steady herself. When she opened the door the barber had already got up from sleep and was standing just inside holding a lit candle and she gave a start.

What is it? he said. The shadows strange in his bandages.

Anna Mercia could hear the barber's wife snoring softly in the gloom. She said, I need to talk to you.

The barber glanced back at his wife then stepped out into the hall and shut the door to the bedroom. They stood a moment in the candlelight, the wax melting slowly over his thumbs.

She's sleeping, he said. What's wrong with you. Are you sick?

I need to talk to you.

In here.

He opened the door to the bathroom across the hall and they slipped through. He set the candle onto the edge of the sink and then leaned back on the bathtub.

Sit down, he said. I thought you might come. What is it.

Anna Mercia watched him a moment then sat on the crooked toilet. The bathroom walls were black from the fire and the ceiling dangled in strips over them. The floor littered with pieces of masonry and small bottles and jars. She could feel the slick of sweat on her arms.

I know she was here, she said.

Who?

You know who.

He was looking at her and the light deepened and stretched in his face. The skin around his good eye looked swollen. Who are you talking about? he asked.

Katherine. My daughter.

The barber frowned suddenly and in the flickering candlelight his bandaged head looked grotesque and deeply ugly. Your daughter hasn't been here, he said. I already told you that. Jesus. He looked at her very hard. What do you want? he asked.

I want my daughter.

You're confused.

I'm not, she whispered.

Yes.

I called her cell earlier. You answered it.

He looked at her for a long moment.

How'd you get her cell?

He shrugged angrily.

How'd you get her cell? she asked again.

He was looking at her with a dark expression. I found it, he said. Here. In the house. But she hasn't been here, nobody has. You know there's nothing going on here.

You're lying to me, she whispered. Why're you lying to me? But then she leaned over and held her face in her hand and then her shoulders were shaking. She felt like she could not breathe and she gasped and she shook.

They sat in silence for a while, the candle burning down. At last the barber shifted his feet and the glass crunched under him.

That's enough, he said quietly. There was something in his voice. She did not hear it at first and then she did hear it and she looked up.

In the hazy orange light he was standing where before he had been leaning on the lip of the bathtub and she realized how much bigger he was than her. He said to her, Why'd you come to me really? What do you want?

She did not like how he was looking at her.

He said, You never thought your daughter was here. Did you.

She said nothing.

Come here, he said.

He unbuckled his belt and opened his pants. His penis was standing out.

Suck it, he said.

She blinked at him, uncomprehending.

He leaned across to her and gripped her chin hard. He said, Suck my fucking cock.

She glanced over to the door. Across the hall his wife would be sleeping. Don't do this, she said. Please.

Get on your fucking knees, he said.

He pushed her down. The bathroom floor was black with char and there were chunks of rubble and shards of glass from the mirror gouging her knees. She could feel herself starting to cry but she made no sound. His penis was warm and sticky and tasted of sweat when he forced it into her.

He was gripping her hair hard and he made small grunting noises as he went. Her good hand was thick and cold in the dirt and slapping there and suddenly there was something sharp under her palm. A slice of glass from the mirror. She was coughing and spitting. He was thrusting deeply and his coarse hair was scratching her nose and chin and all at once she took up the shard and pressed it under his scrotum. His fists were still on her head but he stopped abruptly. She could feel a line of blood opening in the folds of his skin.

She was crying and spitting.

What did you do to her? she cried. Her lips and chin were wet. She held the blade hard against him. What did you do to her?

He looked at her, frightened. Nothing, he said. I swear. I never saw her, she didn't even come here. I swear it.

She could feel his sticky penis withdrawing across her wrist where her hand was pressing with the blade of glass.

Please, he said.

She thought very coldly and very clearly of her daughter coming home and meeting this man and she stopped crying and she made herself look at him. Then she pushed the shard in with as much force as she could manage and twisted it sharply and it snapped off in her fist.

He screamed.

He screamed and still screaming fell thrashing against the side of the bathtub. There was something warm and slick running down her arm and the front of her sweater and she got to her feet and stood with her back against the wall and watched him. In the candlelight she could see the barber curling up under the edge of the bathtub in his shirttails and with his trousers tangled at his shins and he was gurgling in a strange, brutal, guttural agony.

Then she stumbled out. As she passed the bedroom she could hear the barber's wife calling for her husband but she did not slow and she stumbled for the front door breathing hard. She kicked the door wide and took the steps two at a time half-running onto the lawn. She could feel the shard of glass cutting into her hand and she threw it into the grass. Something was rising in her throat but she swallowed it back down.

Then she slowed. Stopped. Stood in the street under the pale burning sky and turned back and looked at her house dark in that undarkness. She thought: Kat could still return. Kat could go there still. She did not fear the barber any longer but she understood that she could not let the barber's wife find her daughter. She knew this suddenly and with a burning clarity.

She went back in. She went in and up the stairs and down the hall to her bedroom and in the darkness she turned the handle and the door swung softly open. The room stank.

The barber's wife was feverish.

Cole? she called weakly. Is that you? What's going on?

Don't turn on a light, Anna Mercia said.

The wife was fumbling in the sheets and then the flashlight flared on and cut a slow beam across the ceiling and down the wall and lit up Anna Mercia where she stood.

Oh god, the wife began to cry. Oh god what have you done to him.

She was drenched in the barber's blood. She stood in that doorway studying the barber's wife and then she felt suddenly sick. She could not do it. She knew this woman would not live out the week. She was trembling with the thought of what she had come back to do and she could not do it.

Where is he? the barber's wife was crying. What did you do to him?

Anna Mercia said nothing. The heavy woman could not stir from the bed. Anna Mercia went to the closet and sifted through the clothes on the floor there and stripped off the grey sweater and pulled on a shirt and made her way back out of the room, ignoring the wife's cries.

In the living room she stood for a long time staring out at the orange sky and she did not understand why she did not leave at once. She went to her phone and picked up the handset and listened but there was no dial tone. She put it back. Under a bundle of coats she found a pair of her hiking boots and laced them on awkwardly, holding the long laces in her teeth. Then went back down the hallway and into the burned bathroom and saw that the candle had smouldered down but was not yet out. The barber lay unmoving in his blood. The candle leaned unmoving in its wax. She looked at him and she did not blow out the candle and after a time she left.

The hour was late. She walked in the middle of the street along the dividing line. She had not walked twenty minutes before she slowed, and sat heavily, gulping air. *Don't you stop here*, she thought to herself. *Don't you stop, Anna Mercia. Don't you stop.*

But she just curled up onto her side and started to shake.

She closed her eyes. Then she felt the ground shiver under her, and she opened her eyes in fear, and saw headlights approaching very slowly. The asphalt was cool under her cheek where she lay and after a time she lowered her head and closed her eyes.

They wanted so much, our mothers. I think about it sometimes. I don't know how they did it. They wanted their lives back but still felt responsible for ours.

I miss having her to talk to, there's so much I'd ask. She was a secretary in a private school and I think of the paperwork and the staples, the dry air and the paycheque and the feel of a day's work behind her and how much she must have wanted it. I don't think my father liked it. But men get as much without judgment. Or so it seems when you're not a man, and you watch them pass freely from the breakfast table to their cars in the morning. It looks so easy. Of course it's not, it's not easy for anyone. But it's harder for a woman, the costs are physical. Men don't feel the pain of possibilities in the same way, the permanence of choice. At the end of her life, bed-bound by illness, my mother said to me, Don't let anyone tell you you can have everything. You can't. A woman has to choose.

I don't think she ever got over my father. I could see it as a girl even if I couldn't explain it. She met him at a swimming race in the Okanagan in 1964. He was the only black man there. He beat everyone in the race easily, everyone except my mother. She was famous for a while for winning that race. She had a newspaper clipping somewhere with her lifting a trophy, smiling. My father was standing beside her and you could just see his arm and shoulder cropped on the right.

I think sometimes about what my mother said. All my life I guess I was living under that. You don't choose your parents, you don't choose what they go through. I guess as a girl I understood I was meant to pick, that I couldn't have both as she'd tried for, couldn't have both a family and a career. That idea guided me for so long, the awful strictness of it. When I learned I was pregnant with Kat I cried for days. I hate to think about it now. I didn't choose to change. You can make all the decisions in the world, it doesn't mean your body will listen to any of them. Kat, Katherine. My beautiful Katherine. She was a hard labour. Mason came out easy as anything, like he just couldn't wait to get to know the world. Not Kat.

I don't know if anyone gets to have everything. But I don't know that you have to choose either. I was almost thirty before I realized that was my mother's life and not mine. I think about Kat and Mason and I worry what I must be pushing on them without knowing it. I know it's something. It's always something.

THE INTERRUPTED MAN

What is it, son? the old man asked. Did you hear it again?

Mason nodded.

From downstairs?

Yes.

The old man grunted and came into the study with the candle stub in his fist. It's nothing, he said. I hear things too. There's nothing down there.

Mason watched the old man set the tray on the edge of an up-turned chair. He was coming back to himself now and he could feel his thoughts righting themselves and he did not fear the old man as he had.

He had followed him to this place. An old house gabled and shuttered. A tall door below had opened into gloom, into a narrow dim staircase leading up to the landing, the banister creaking and rickety under his sore hands as the old man ascended before him. All this he remembered now as if it were not real. Above the wainscotting were photographs of worlds long vanished, and where he sat with his back to the wall he could just make out the ghostly half-eroded faces in their frames.

It's just the shock of what we've been through, the old man was saying. It does things.

But Mason knew it was not the shock. He lifted his head.

The old man was very pale, and very tall, and the folds of skin under his eyes were deep and grooved in the candlelight. He kneeled and with a small brush swept aside the crumbled plaster

on the desk and shook out the battered books and set out the tins
of food he had found. His big hands were trembling badly. Sometimes he would clear his throat and the sound reminded the boy
of ships in the harbour in the dark water. He remembered his
grandfather's small suitcase on the bed and the feeling in him of
farewell. He thought then of his mother and then he thought: *Kat
will never believe me and will never believe this but she will believe
Mom. I will find her but first I will find Mom and I will not be afraid no
matter what.*

It's getting dark, the old man said then. He leaned back in the
gloom picking at his hands and eyeing Mason aslant. We'll have
to hide that candle. I don't want people in the street to see it.

What about people in the house. Should they be able to see it?

The old man said nothing.

What.

The old man gave him a long look. You know what, he said.

Then he picked up a can of chili and opened it very slowly and
bent the lid back and passed it across. Mason took it but did not eat.

There was no glass in the big window frame and the evening
was blowing coldly in. A low grey ocean of light beyond the stoven
roofs and laddered telephone poles flared first a deep blue then
burned translucent and faded as if sucked down over the rim of the
world. The day was failing. He thought of his mother out there in
that city and then he tried very hard not to think.

The candle stub had been set melted into a broken-legged
stool and pooled now white and eerie in the hollows of his burnished hands where he sat and he watched the old man rise with
a lantern shutter and cover the flame with its orange shade, the
glare softening and smouldering on in the high, coved ceiling.

I grew up here, the old man said. In this house. Did I tell you
that?

No.

He opened and closed his fist in the bad light. A long harrowed
scar rode in the white flesh. He said, Well I did. I can remember

being your age and standing where you are now and watching my grandfather in the yard in the fall. You could smell the warm pies in the oven from right across the fields when the cook left the windows open. All this was pasture then.

I don't like it here, Mason said.

My grandfather kept a cow and you could hear her bell when she came near the house. The old man looked up suddenly. This is as safe a place as any, son. I promise you.

Mason was watching the darkness spilling in through the broken hall.

Aren't you hungry at all? the old man asked.

No.

Because you look like you could eat a horse. Are you sure?

Mason turned back to the window. A dog was barking somewhere in the twilight.

You can be happy in your life at a certain point and not be able to imagine ever being happier, the old man went on in his low voice. And then you get old and everything is different and it's a different kind of happiness.

Mason thought he was speaking now to someone that he could not see and he shivered. You should check again, he said stubbornly. You should go downstairs and check again.

The old man nodded but he did not move. This was my grandfather's house, he said. I know it as well as I know anything. There's nothing here but ghosts and memories. I don't mean real ghosts.

No.

My grandfather was a judge, he said. He was a wealthy man. I didn't wonder about it as a boy but after his death I did. This isn't a big house. At the time I supposed he'd donated his money to some charity or other. But that wasn't it. Do you want to know something very strange?

Mason rubbed at his crumpled sleeves, his fingernails outlined in dirt.

What, he said.

Fifteen years after his death I received a letter. It was from a woman in Italy, a very old woman, who wanted to meet with me. In her youth she had been an actress on the stage. It seems my grandfather had sent monthly cheques to her for almost thirty years. Nearly his entire fortune went to her. Can you imagine?

Mason said nothing.

In the letter she included a little ivory hairbrush, as if for a doll, and a faded blue ribbon. I have no idea what these objects meant to her. I don't know what she was to him. I don't know whether he met her after my grandmother died, or before. Love is a strange thing, son. It's judged harshly during its lifetime and then kindly afterwards. Mason watched the old man frown as if to think over this last statement and then raise his dark eyes. I returned her letters unopened, after the first one. I never met with the woman. I suppose she must be dead now. And now do you know I wish almost more than anything that I had met with her. It is almost my only regret.

Maybe she wanted money.

Maybe. But I don't think it was money she was after. Money doesn't mean as much when you get old.

Mason turned and peered out at the hall.

What is it, son?

You didn't hear that?

The old man shook his head.

But then it came again, unmistakable. A clattering from somewhere deep inside the house. The scrape of boots across a wood floor, kicking aside masonry.

That, he hissed.

The old man held up a hand and the sound fell away in a shirr of drapes from the room beyond. His dark eyes were doubtful. It sounded like the furnace, he said.

It wasn't the furnace.

Well. This old house makes some strange noises.

The wall where Mason sat was canted to one side and there was a buckle running along the hardwood floor and he thought, *It is not safe not here and I know that. I do not know what he wants but I will not forget no matter what. I will stay only as long as I need to and no longer. I will stay only until the morning and no longer.*

In the morning I'll go to look for your mother, the old man said.

Mason looked up, startled.

You don't have to come if you don't want to, son.

But as the old man said this he would not meet his eye and Mason all at once understood. *He does not believe it*, he thought. *He does not believe he will find her. But it does not matter what he believes.* He did not want to speak but then he looked up and then he spoke. You don't think we'll find her, he said. He could hear the hurt in his voice and it sounded like anger but it was not anger. She's not dead, he said.

The old man's eyes were leached and sad. Okay, he said.

Okay what. Don't say okay. You don't mean it.

No. I guess I don't.

Do you know where she is now?

No, son. I don't.

That's right. You don't.

The old man regarded him strangely.

Don't look at me like that, Mason said.

He had been speaking loudly and it was the most he had spoken since the tremor and he felt exhausted by the effort.

The old man turned his head towards the doorway.

Jesus Christ, he said.

He got to his feet.

Mason looked across in alarm.

A figure stood there. Lean and whip thin and wrapped in a white bedsheet unwinding like smoke in the dark hall. It wore heavy boots and stood in the doorway staring down at them and its eyes were as yellow as a dog's. In one fist it held a rifle.

Jesus Christ, the old man said again.

And then it was like some muscled thing was uncoiling inside the stranger and slowly raising itself swaying before them and then the stranger spoke.

You scared me, he said. His voice was very soft. I thought I was alone in here. You two are like ghosts. You are as quiet as ghosts.

There was something wrong with his eyes, with the way he studied Mason from the darkness.

This is my house, the old man said. You're in my house.

Mason could see the bones in the old man's back through his shirt and he felt very frightened. The stranger stepped through the doorway into the candlelight.

What do you want? Lear demanded.

The stranger's face looked very drawn and very grey. It is just the two of you? he said.

The old man frowned.

Forgive me, the stranger said. May I come in? I did not know anyone was here. I did not mean to startle you.

The old man had been standing to his full height and with his lean grizzled jaw set tightly he stared down at the stranger and finally he nodded and waved a hand at the oak desk. He said, We don't have much and it's cold but if you don't mind that you're welcome to it.

I am not hungry.

The old man held out his hand. Arthur Lear. The boy here is Mason.

Novica.

The stranger came in and he sat but he did not put down the rifle.

Mason was standing behind the old man and he had not taken his eyes from the stranger. He was a small man with rolled shoulders and a long sharp face and he tugged off the white bedsheets he had been draped in and then held them balled in his lap. Dressed as he was in a tight red sweatshirt with its sleeves rolled and double rolled back from his thin wrists and in greasy blue jeans and with his dark hair frayed weirdly on his head he seemed more a battered denizen from some strange carnival than a man like any other. In the candlelight his expression was unreadable.

I know you, Lear said. How do I know you?

The stranger smiled but the smile did not touch his eyes.

The old man was looking at him closely.

I am one of the gardeners at Union House, he said. I pass you at the Japanese bridge all the time. You go alone to look at the pond. You are an easy man to recognize, Mr Lear, he said.

It's just Arthur.

There was something about him Mason did not like. He was not sure what it was but the dislike was palpable and it rolled over him and then past in that small room like a bad air and the candle was guttering in its wax and then it stood tall and orange again. Mason frowned. No it was not dislike but something else.

What's the rifle for? the old man asked.

Does it make you nervous? I will put it down.

What's it for?

The gardener regarded him coolly. For shooting.

Shooting what?

Do not be afraid, he said. It is for protection only. You smoke, yes?

He took out a packet of cigarettes from his shirt pocket and shook one into his palm and passed the packet across to the old man.

Mason nudged the old man's arm.

What is it?

But he did not want to say in front of the gardener.

What is it, son? the old man asked again. Are you tired?

I'm not tired.

The old man gestured at the open door in the far wall. I thought we'd set you up on the couch just through there, he said. When you're ready.

Mason felt all at once a slow exhaustion pour through him like heavy sand. He shook his head. I'm not tired, he said again.

The gardener was watching with his yellow stare. You were caught in the earthquake together?

Yes, the old man said.

No, Mason said.

The gardener looked from the one to the other and the old man finally shrugged. We were in the same building, he said. I helped dig him out of the rubble. But we weren't buried together.

It is none of my business.

My mom's still there, Mason said. We're going back to get her tomorrow.

The gardener looked at the old man carefully. It is a nightmare, he said and he made a strange noise in his throat. I have been thinking it is not real. And then I know it is real. And then I think it cannot be real. It is a little crazy.

It's not crazy, the old man said.

I do not care about that. Do you know where I was when it hit?

I don't know. In the gardens?

In the gardens. Yes. I watched everything around me go up and go down and I could hear it. The whole ground was moving. I have never felt anything like it. The ground went soft like water and I was just watching it. That is what was bad. That I was not a part of it.

Yes, the old man said. We all felt that.

It was happening and I was not inside it. Even though I was inside it. Do you understand?

Yes.

The gardener rolled his tongue, picked at a bit of tobacco in his lips. All of my life my hands have worked in the earth, he said. I trust it. I trust it and listen to it. Do you know what the earth talks about? It tells us that the green things in this world do not thrive through care but through adversity. The earth is always eating, it is always hungry. You people do not understand that. In this country you think nurturing means gentleness. It does not.

The old man smoked quietly.

Children are also green things, the gardener said. They are more tough than we think.

Leave the boy out of it, the old man said. How much of it have you seen?

You mean the destruction?

The extent of it. Yes.

It is bad, the gardener said. It is very bad. But the destruction is not the worst thing.

The candlelight slid and wobbled among the dark objects in the study like a thing alive. Mason leaned back out of the light and felt his heavy eyelids closing.

The gardener said, I was born and lived all my life in the city of Visegrad. I came here just before the war broke out. It is in Bosnia, on the river Drina. I lived there with my parents and my little brother. When the war broke out he would have been about this boy's age.

Mason opened his eyes and saw the gardener looking at him.

Many men were killed on our bridge, he said. My brother used to bicycle past the soldiers during the executions on his way to school. They shot them in the head or cut their throats and kicked them into the river. I heard all of this much later. There was an old man who was forced to drag the bodies out of the river when they rolled up into piles there in the shallows. There were stacks of the dead. I try to imagine my little brother. We knew those men, they were neighbours. We are Serbs and my family was in no danger. I am not ashamed to say I sleep at night. But I could not go back there after I heard the stories. He stubbed out his cigarette and reached into his pocket for another and then as if thinking better of it he set his hands in his lap. I think of my brother daily, he said. He will be almost a man now. I have enough money to bring him over here but when I wrote to him he refused. I think of those bodies lying in the river. He shook his head. There is nothing worse, he said. There is nothing worse than to be lost like that. There is no worse thing.

Alright, the old man said. Don't get stuck in it.

Because of the boy? I think that he is stronger than you think.

Alright.

I expect he has seen terrible things.

The old man rose then and he seemed angry. I said alright, he said. Leave it alone.

The gardener said nothing.

You can stay the night, the old man said, but leave it alone. Do you need a place to sleep?

I have a sleeping roll in the truck.

You drove here?

The gardener nodded. He was holding his rifle again as he got to his feet. I will get my things, he said flatly.

If you're not afraid to sleep inside, the old man said.

The gardener gave him a long look. Do you mean from another tremor?

What else would I mean?

The gardener shrugged. He looked at Mason. I am sorry, he said. Do not listen to me.

They went out and Mason sat for a time in the dimming candlefire and the house was very still and then the old man was shaking him gently by the shoulder and he opened his eyes.

I wasn't sleeping, he said.

I know you weren't.

Where is he?

Novica? He's still down at his truck. He has a radio there. And look at this. The old man held up a flashlight and flicked it on and off and the beam cut across the wall.

The old man set to clearing the floor in the next room, righting the chairs, stacking and sweeping aside the broken mortar and books. A glass cabinet fastened to the corner wall had not shattered in the tremor though a long spidery crack traced the pane from handle to bevel.

We probably shouldn't be sleeping in here, he said. I think it's safe enough though.

What if there's another one? Mason asked.

The old man set a bundle of blankets on the foot of the couch.

There won't be, he said.

You don't know that.

No. I don't.

But you wouldn't sleep here either if you didn't think it was safe.

That's right.

Where will you sleep?

Right next door. Just through that door there. I'll leave you the candle but make sure you keep it away from the window. Okay?

I don't need it.

Are you sure?

Leave me the flashlight.

Alright.

Will he sleep out there with you?

Yes.

Arthur?

Yes?

What kind of a name is Novica?

I don't know. It's Serbian I guess.

I think it's weird.

Well. Go to sleep.

The old man went out of the room then and after a few minutes Mason could hear the gardener come back up and down the hall and go into the room where the old man was. The door had not shut completely and Mason lay very still in the darkness watching them through the opening and he could hear the gardener's soft voice rising and falling.

They did not want to go into the city, the gardener was murmuring. We went for food. I knew we would be hungry.

You keep going back to it, the old man said. Leave it. Put it away someplace until you're ready for it. Tell me about the gardens.

But the gardener did not seem to hear him.

In the supermarket we found a girl, he went on. A woman. No a girl. I thought she must be dead but she was not dead. The gardener lowered his voice. They did *things* to her.

All at once Mason felt very young. He thought about calling out to them and then he did not and then he just lay listening with a taste of iron in his mouth and he did not interrupt.

Why didn't you stop them? the old man asked. Why didn't you help her?

What could I have done?

The gardener lowered his hands and looked across at the old man and Mason saw with a shock that he was crying. His grizzled cheeks shining in the candlelight.

They burned her body after. In the parking lot. So nobody would be able to tell.

Why are you telling me this?

There was a silence then and then after a time the old man said in a low voice, Novica?

Yes.

I'm sorry. It's the tiredness. In the morning I have to go back to find his mother's body. Then I'll have to see where to take the boy. All of it's hard.

Mason opened his sleep-heavy eyes.

You think I am a coward, the gardener said.

I don't know. I don't know what you could have done.

They would have killed me.

Maybe.

A low orange glow was burning over the city through the broken wall or perhaps it was just the candlelight itself.

The boy said he has a sister, the old man said after a time. Maybe she will take him.

The gardener started to cry again.

Mason lay very still. He thought something fierce or angry or wild would come up in him then but it did not and he lay there in the darkness beginning to drift off and thinking quietly. *Tomorrow*, he thought. *Tomorrow I will find her and we will go back home and it will be okay. Whatever comes it will be okay.*

Then the gardener was leaning forward and in the eerie light his bright eyes shone.

You do not want to go back out there, he said.

Mason through his sleepiness felt suddenly afraid and he shifted in his sheets and the couch springs wheezed in reply.

For god's sake, the old man said. His door's open.

It is going to get worse, the gardener said.

Then Mason heard only the old man's shoes scraping on the floor and him shutting the door firmly and then he was asleep.

Tobey Blekkenmeyer said where is your poppa did he go back to Africa. I told him to shut up, he was not from Africa he was from Trinidad. Luke Mackey said did they eat bananas in Trinidad? I told him to suck on this banana. Jeremy Bindle laughed. I told them my poppa was kidnapped in the night by the Russians and tortured. My mom woke up and found Grandma sitting at the table in the dark. That was before I was born. Luke Mackey asked if he was a spy. I said I did not know if he was a spy but what did he think. How many people get kidnapped by Russians and tortured if they're not? I gave him a dark look. Tobey Blekkenmeyer said I was brown like shit because I was full of shit. That was when I hit him.

Teachers do not see it they think you just fight people. But I do not just fight people. Mr Owens told me fighting does not solve anything and did I want to grow up with friends or enemies? I said friends. He said well you do not get friends by punching them do you and I said I did not want Tobey Blekkenmeyer to be my friend and he said well you made that clear. He said did I want to spend my life in jail or have money and a job and a family? I said I did not want to spend my life in jail. He said that was good. Then he told me I would not be going on the field trip to the museum. I said what about Tobey Blekkenmeyer and he said you just worry about yourself.

How is that good advice, to just worry about yourself. I did not say it though.

When I think of my poppa he was wrinkled like a pair of pants. He had very white teeth and a thick moustache and when you hugged him *his big belly was not soft it was hard. I did not see him very much. His funeral was sad. One day after school Mom told me he was the cleverest man she ever knew. She does not like to talk about him usually. I said was he cleverer than me? because she is always telling me I am smarter than I look. Kat says I better be smarter than I look or there is no hope for me. When I asked Mom that she stopped stacking the cups at the counter and looked at me and said I don't know if you're clever like your poppa was but I hope you're not foolish like him.*

She gets sad sometimes. She thinks we do not know it but we do. I hear her sighing in the kitchen after we are supposed to be in bed. I think it is because she misses him. Kat says it is because she wanted another daughter and instead got me. Maybe she is sad because you're an idiot, I tell her. Kat says it does not matter we should not ask Mom about it.

But I would not do that. You do not ask about some things.

He slept a long time and he did not dream.

When he awoke his head was throbbing. A pale light was pouring in through the broken latticework in the high windowpane and the spiral patterns of dust on the glass cast strange grey shapes across the rug. Because his neck was stiff from the leather armrest and the headache had begun in earnest he turned and grimaced and did not get up. He lay there listening to the quiet house. He could feel where the seams in the leather had left deep marks in his cheek.

He was still wearing his sneakers though they had come untied and in the daylight when at last he got up the room looked sad and grey. He could see through the glass door of the study the blurred shape of the gardener and he crossed the room then paused. Stared down at his hand. The dark skin at his wrist looking crinkled in the light. Then he opened the door.

The gardener was crouched at the window with his rifle across his knees and he did not look up. Arthur went out, he said in his soft voice. He was asking for you.

He went out?

The gardener shrugged. He did not want to wake you. He said you should eat something.

Mason glanced across. A bowl of cold oatmeal, a can of warm juice on the desk. Sunlight coalescing in a spoon.

I don't believe it, Mason said. He wouldn't go without me.

I am sure you are right.

Did he really go?

Do I look like his keeper?

Mason went to the window where the gardener crouched and peered out at the street. A big wind was up and he watched a pail clatter and bang down the street and then nothing but the wisps of dust curling up in gusts. The rubble in sloping moraines, the early shadows long between the dark buildings there. He did not see Lear.

How long ago did he leave?

You slept a long time.

How long?

The gardener shrugged again. I have not been watching the clock.

In the early daylight Mason saw the gardener now with great clarity. He crouched now in a stained yellow undershirt and his chest and arms looked very thin and very strong. When he raised his hand to his face Mason saw the bones in his knuckles hard and sharp as stones. There was a dark mole with hairs growing from it just above his upper lip. *There is something in him too*, he thought. *It is something bad though it is unhappy as much as it is mean. But the meanness is still there in him. It is still there in him and I can see it.*

Do you want to see something interesting? the gardener said. Come here.

The gardener's thick black hair was flattened on one side where he had slept on it and when he turned his face in profile he looked crested like a lizard.

Look down there. What do you see?

They were three men in sweatpants and torn shirts and Mason watched them from the upper floor of that house as they turned into the street and began wending their way through the rubble, over the abandoned cars. The wind was pushing hard at their backs. Two of them carried a big television between them, the third swung a steel pipe and cleared their way.

You see it is already beginning, the gardener said.

What are they doing? Mason asked.

They watched the men disappear into the blue house on the corner. When they came out they were carrying empty backpacks and their faces looked serious. They kept to the shadows on the far side of the street their sleeves and pant legs crackling flat and they passed Lear's house by and they did not look up.

They have been doing it all morning, the gardener said. This is the kind of taking I do not understand. I understand it. But it does not make any sense. Food, water, yes. But this?

He stepped away from the gardener. The man smelled strange, of ashes and ink and of something sharply metallic. Did Arthur really leave? he asked.

The gardener studied him. You are angry with him.

Why would you think that?

He believes that you are.

He told you that?

He believes that you blame him. That he should have done more for your mother.

Mason frowned and looked away. It's not his fault.

That is what I told him. What.

Nothing.

The gardener studied him with his grey eyes. There is something.

Mason shrugged reluctantly. He left her, he said. He left her in there.

You are angry.

I'm not angry with him.

You left her too. You came here with him.

He was silent and then he got to his feet. Did he really go?

No.

Mason looked at the door and then back at the gardener. He didn't go?

Do not be angry. I meant it kindly.

Mason didn't understand. His head felt thick, blurred.

It matters, the gardener said, even if you think it does not. I feel terrible for you. It will be worse for you than it is for me or for Arthur. Has he talked to you about it? You should expect the worst. You should be prepared for the worst.

His head was throbbing. He blinked angrily.

I am sorry if it sounds ugly. I am only trying to help.

Just then there was a clatter in the hallway and the creak of a door opening and closing and then Lear came to the study and looked in. I'd about given up on you, he said.

Mason turned away, wiped at his eyeglasses.

What is it, son?

He believed you had left without him, the gardener said.

I wouldn't do that, Lear said. Are you ready?

Mason said nothing.

Mason?

He could feel a prickling sensation crawl up the back of his arms. He shivered.

I'm ready, he said.

Then his headache bloomed. It climbed up inside his skull like a flower and bent heavily back and opened wide its petals of light and pain. He watched the greasy hairs hanging down over the collar of the old man's charcoal coat and he squinched his eyes shut and stumbled and went on. A big wind was blowing. They leaned into it through the streets in that strong light and there were people lurking in doorways or crouched over mattresses they must have dragged into the streets the night before. Mason felt uneasy but did not ask. His mother combing her fingers through his hair, the rough creak of her dry voice. That. Oh but he did not think he would find her. *That is just Arthur talking*, he told himself angrily. *I know she is alive whether it is today or not does not matter. I will find her. I know it truly.* His headache had split its roots along the back of his skull and he could feel it now drilling down his spine. He stopped, shuddered, the old man trudging on ahead oblivious and he swallowed and shivered and with one hand held to his neck he hurried on. Thinking of his mother lifting a tray of shining mugs in the café morning, sunlight scumbling in the huge blue windows. Thinking of her sharp eyeteeth when she said his name. The sky over the city was very white. Then the wind overturned a plastic chair outside a ruined office and Mason watched papers skitter over the asphalt and slap flat against a building and then shake free and be blown on. His ears felt thick with water. The wind was pulling on him and the morning was passing and then he stood in the street where his mother had worked and the café was not there and there were men digging in the rubble and the old man took his hand.

How much do you remember? the old man asked. Do you want to wait for me here?

He shook his head no.

And so they went in. They went in and his mother was holding him and the wind was pushing hard on her chest. They went in and the old man turned his shoulder into the billowing dust and shouted to the men he met asking if any had seen her. They crouched behind a truck to eat but Mason could not eat and the old man made him drink deeply. His mother was clutching a fold of her skirt down against her legs with one fist and peering across at him in the wind and then the wind was in Mason's head banging about and he did not see the old man. He saw the old man. Then the wind was talking to a girl with long laddered stitches across her nose and the old man was pulling on Mason's sleeve as if to drag him into the street. The light did not scour his skin. The day was not ending.

And then it was done. The wind was down. It was down and the pain in his head was there, but less, and then it was not there at all. In the sudden quiet Lear was murmuring to him, She's not here, son, she's not here.

He stared hard at Lear's hands with their torn and bloodied nails and knuckles cross-hatched in scabs and at the black grease begriming his shirtsleeves and it all seemed very sad and very pure in that pale and burning hour.

When they returned the house was thick with a webbed silence. The drapes in the kitchen glowed golden and translucent in the late afternoon light and light poured in through the gaps in the bricks of the fireplace and the walls felt very cold and very still. Mason set the bag with a clatter on the counter and looked at the old man coming back down the stairs.

Novica's gone, he was saying. He didn't take his truck.

No.

Or his flashlight.

They were standing in the kitchen and Mason looked back at the front door as if the gardener might return even then. Lear had taped a black plastic bag over the glass and it had come down during the day and hung now like a shred of skin there.

Don't worry about your mother, son. We'll find her tomorrow.

I know.

It's a good thing that we didn't find her today. It's a good sign.

I know.

Lear looked at him carefully and then nodded. How's your head?

It doesn't hurt.

It doesn't hurt really?

He shrugged. His breathing felt ragged but clear.

Are you hungry? Lear banged through the cupboards, pushing aside what he could not use. Sandwiches? Crackers? I don't know what else. These cupboards aren't much use even when they're organized.

I don't care.

You might not, Lear said, but there's two of us here. He picked up a tray and led Mason through into the sitting room. A rabbit-eared television stood in a corner and there were potted plants still on wires. The walls were lined with canvases propped facing away and there were jars with paintbrushes and plates of glass and folds of cloth. But the furniture had been righted and the dust and broken things swept against the walls in tidy piles and Mason thought the gardener must have done this before he went out.

They ate dry biscuits and honey and tins of cold ham in water and slices of bread slathered in blackberry jam. And they ate off the old man's good china plates and Mason was surprised at how hungry he was. He drank warm grape juice out of a big glass bottle and the old man drank a half-cold beer and they did not speak while they ate.

When he reached for the last tin of ham Lear shook his head.

Not that one, he said. We'll save that one for Novica.

Mason could feel his head clearing. Do you really think he'll be back?

I don't see why he wouldn't.

I heard you last night. Talking.

I know you did.

I heard what he said about that girl. What they did to her.

I don't think any of that happened.

Mason was pushing the last crust of bread around his plate.

I know what he said, Lear added. I just don't think it happened.

You think he made it up?

I think he's been sick.

That was not it or that was not all there was to it, Mason knew. He thought about it for a time and then he could not think about it any longer. You're a painter, he said.

I was.

You don't paint anymore?

The old man said nothing, his face pale in the gloom.

You don't look like a painter.

The old man smiled wearily. Well.

Did you always live here alone?

Not when I was a boy. My grandfather looked after me. I think I told you that.

What about your wife?

Callie.

Yes.

Lear turned his head and looked at a picture hanging on a picture rail near his head and then he pulled it down and rubbed his sleeve across the glass to clean it. She was the tallest woman I ever saw, he said.

He passed the photograph in its cracked frame across to Mason who took it silently.

She was even taller than me, he said. She was six and half feet in heels. We used to laugh that she was the only person I could look up to. And she had tremendous hands. You can't see them there. They were long and as white as milk and when she held a teacup it looked like a thimble. I thought she was the most beautiful thing I'd ever seen.

The photograph was of a young woman's face in profile, the thick hair piled high and pushed back from her face in antiquated fashion. A very long, very pale throat twisted to the left. Her sharp angular eye glaring out of the frame impatiently, her dark mouth unsmiling. Mason thought her beautiful and cold.

You can't tell her height from that of course, Lear said. But you can see how beautiful she was. She had classical features. Look at her strong nose. She hated it, of course. He smiled a tired smile. She wanted to look like Veronica Lake. You won't know who that is. Lear turned his head to the ceiling. Did you hear that? he asked.

What.

Novica? he called.

They waited but the gardener did not come down and there was no sound more and after a while the old man frowned and said, I guess it's my turn to be hearing things.

I wasn't hearing things.

No. I didn't mean you were.

He took the photograph back from Mason and looked at it. He said, Most of the time it's okay but then it comes up in you. His smile was tight, pained. She died on the hottest afternoon of the year. It was July. I wasn't with her. All that was a long time ago.

How did she die?

A car accident. Her taxi hit a streetcar and overturned. She was in Toronto on her way to see her father. That was years ago. It was so long ago your mother wouldn't have been born.

Mason did not know what to say.

Do you know it should feel like another lifetime. He did not seem to be speaking to Mason anymore. That's what people say about it. But it doesn't. It's this thing that stays with you always and that's how you know it's real. And everything afterwards is just a kind of waiting.

Oh, he said.

Lear cleared his throat. It's like when you're waiting for something to come in the mail and you check the post each morning and it never comes. It's that feeling. Except you have it all the time.

Mason nodded uneasily.

You have it all the time and the postman is your own death. That is what it's like.

You miss her.

Not a day goes by that I don't.

All at once Mason felt assailed and he lowered his sharp chin in the half-light and glared stubbornly down at his shoes. So she's dead, he said. It was abrupt and hard and he did not know why he said it.

Lear looked at him. Mason, he said gently.

Mason said nothing.

Mason.

What?

Callie's not your mother.

He glanced up at the old man and he could feel something ugly in the room with them.

Your mother isn't dead, Lear murmured.

You don't believe that.

It doesn't matter what I believe. You hold on to a thing as long as you can. That's all there is to it.

She's not dead.

Good. Then we'll find her tomorrow.

But there was something wrong between them now and Mason felt it and did not like it.

Lear cleared his throat and twisted across the sofa to hook the photograph of his wife back in its place and when he turned back his face was dark. I'm sorry, he said. I'll be fine in a minute. I just need a minute.

Mason left him then and went out into the kitchen and stood for a moment feeling the house settle in the twilight. The floor under him seemed to shift and he felt as he did on the big ferries that crossed the strait to the mainland. His stomach lurching uneasily. He went out into the dim parlour and kicked his way through the books littering the hardwood and he could see the old man through the doorway, standing at the window, staring out into the darkening street. Then he noticed the door.

It stood closed beside the dead refrigerator that had started to smell and he tried the handle and found it unlocked. He peered back out towards the living room but heard no sound and then he picked up the flashlight from the kitchen table.

A kiltering stairwell led downward. The floorboards groaned under his weight and he paused and in the flashlight beam he saw tracked in the dust underfoot the scrape and slide of boot prints.

Hello? he called down.

He slipped softly to the landing and stopped every few feet listening but he did not hear any sound. He thought of the men he had seen out of the window that morning. He knew there were those who would use the destruction for their own ends. That evil was real and existed.

Halfway down he waited with a hand on the balustrade peering down into the darkness. He had left the cellar door standing open and the stairs shivered under him and the rubble clinked quietly but there was no sound from below. A faint grey dusk slanted in through the holes where the windows had been. The ghostly forms of rubble and broken things. Dust everywhere.

He could just make out the silhouette of a man seated behind the washing machine. He was bowed forward as if in repose and then Mason saw the rifle between the knees and the scoop in the back of the skull and he lifted his eyes and then too the dark slide of bone meal and blood and brain down the far wall. His heart was beating very fast.

Novica? he whispered. Novica?

The man did not move. Mason glanced quickly into the shadows then stepped closer.

He crouched beside the body and stared into the flat dead rooms of the eyes. The spatter on the wall bloomed outward to the left and he saw now that the gardener must have flinched in his last moments. Mason did not touch the face in that dust.

After a while he pulled the rifle from the dead man and the body came heavily forward then fell back with a thunk against the wall. Mason checked the chamber and he slipped two fingers into the gardener's pockets and withdrew the box of ammunition. He was careful not to touch the cold skin. Then he took the flashlight and went back up.

He left the rifle leaning against the couch and the box of ammunition tucked under the stock and when the old man came in to check on him it was the first thing he saw.

Where did you get that?

Out by the truck, he said. And blushed.

Why did I say that? he thought. *What was it that made me say that?* He wondered suddenly if it was in him now too whatever it was he had seen in the gardener. But he did not think so. The heaviness that was in him from before was still in him and he thought maybe it came from there.

The old man had picked up the rifle and was looking at it and he checked the chamber and then set it down again. It doesn't make any sense, he said.

Mason felt suddenly sick. He did not want to think about the gardener. He did not want to think about what he had found. When are we going in the morning? he asked.

Whenever you're ready.

I'll be ready early.

Okay.

I need to sleep now.

The old man gave him a strange look. Okay.

I just really need to sleep.

Okay. You have the flashlight?

Mason did not reply. He was noticing how filthy the old man's clothes were. He still wore his grey shirt from the day before and it was streaked with grime and torn and the shirttails hung long on his long frame and Mason thought, *There is something wrong in him too and I know that it is there though I do not know what it is.*

Mason? What is it?

Mason looked away. He said he saw my mom.

Who did?

Novica. He saw her.

He didn't see your mother. He's mistaken.

He said he did.

Listen to me, Mason. He didn't see her. Go to sleep.

He wanted to tell the old man what he had found but just lay there quiet and staring stubbornly down at his hands. Instead he asked, Do you think he's going to come back?

Novica? I don't know.

What do you think happened to him?

The old man wet his lips. I expect he just went on his way.

Without taking any food?

I guess so.

Or his truck? Or his gun?

Well. I guess he wasn't thinking straight.

I don't think he was either.

No.

Arthur?

Yes?

I didn't like him.

The old man got to his feet. You get some sleep, he said. If you need me I'll be right here. We'll fix your glasses in the morning, okay?

Okay.

The old man paused at the door and looked back at him. He was carrying the rifle.

I didn't like him either, he said.

In the hour before dawn the old man awoke, and Mason heard him, and he rose from the couch and carried the flashlight in to him its light cupped in one hand. A sour odour curdled up out of the bedsheets, out of the old man's flesh. As Mason came in Lear turned his head and his dark eyes were glassy and wrong.

Arthur?

What.

You were shouting.

The old man swallowed. His eyes darkened, he peered at Mason. Picked up the clock beside him and rubbed at his unshaven face. Jesus, he said roughly. Mason. Go back to sleep.

My dad gave me an air rifle for my birthday. It was dark and thick-stocked and the pellets were tiny and dangerous like real bullets. When you put your nose to it the barrel smelled like hot chalk. Kat did not like it but it was my rifle, I told her she better watch out. Kat said if I even thought about it she would paint the rifle pink with nail polish. Mom told me I could not take it out of the yard. Kat said tell him don't point it at anything that moves. What about a tree? I said. Kat said a tree does not move and I told her it does so in the wind it moves. Then don't point it at a tree either Mom said. And don't point it at the house. That will leave nothing to shoot at I said. That is fine with me she said.

I phoned my dad to thank him but he was not there. I left a short message because you have to pay to talk long distance. Next day was a Monday and I snuck the rifle to school down the leg of my pants. It was hard to walk but if I took very little steps it did not look like I had an air rifle down my pants. I was late for school. Mr Owens made me stay in at recess. At lunch hour I showed it to Luke Mackey behind the sandpit, he wanted to shoot it but I did not give him any pellets. He said it probably could not hurt a fly. I said it could it is very dangerous. He said what have you shot? I told him I had shot two crows and a squirrel. I thought that sounded believable but he said Mason Clarke you're a goddamn liar. Shut up I said. He said have you shot any Russian spies with it? Shut up I said again.

After school Luke Mackey and me took the rifle down into the empty lot where the high school kids smoke. No one was around. The sky was grey and I said it is going to rain but Luke Mackey said give me the gun *let me try it. But I did not want him to try it yet. I loaded the rifle and sighted along it and lifted it towards the sky and pulled the trigger. The rifle bucked and punched back against my arm. I lifted my head and looked at the sky like I had just shot a hole in it. I felt still inside, the way you feel when you go into an empty classroom. Like you expect somebody to be watching you.*

Cool, Luke Mackey said quietly.

A crow started up when I fired but it came back to the litter of a sandwich in the grass and I lifted my rifle and aimed at it. You can't hit that Luke Mackey said. I aimed a little bit high so that I would just scare it but when I fired there was an explosion of feathers and a horrible screech then the bird was just lying in the grass very still. I was so surprised. I stood there not believing it.

Holy shit, Luke Mackey said after a minute. Holy shit you killed it. You cannot know if it is dead, I told him, maybe it is just stunned. Because sometimes they are just stunned. You killed it, you killed a crow, Luke Mackey said again. Shit. He was running over to it.

There was a wetness in its feathers that must have been blood. One wing was outstretched, its feathers frayed and wild. Its beak looked very sharp. I was still holding the gun. It was very interesting to see it though I was a little sorry for the crow. It did not understand, it had not done anything. I peered around to make sure nobody had heard us shooting. When I looked at Luke Mackey he was crying.

Who is the liar now I thought.

They climbed down from the house after breakfast and crunched through the rubble to the gardener's truck where he had left it half drawn up onto the lawn. The street was cool with shadows from the ruined buildings. When Mason opened the passenger door his palm left its print in the white dust on the glass. He climbed up and in and Lear held the door open for him and then passed in to him an orange cloth satchel stuffed with sandwiches, bottles of water. He handed over the gardener's rifle last. Mason could see in the side mirror where Lear lifted the door of the canopy and tossed in the crowbar and blankets and then the gym bag they'd filled with two flashlights and batteries and a portable radio. The old man had changed his shirt and put on a pair of stiff jeans and he looked both calmer and more composed to the boy's eye.

Mason leaned across and wiped the inside of the windshield with one sleeve. The light burned coldly in the quiet street. When Lear banged the canopy shut the echo carried flatly between the buildings like the report of a rifle.

Lear came around and climbed in. He reached under the seat, coughed thickly.

Where are we going? Mason asked.

Lear turned the key, adjusted the rearview. They said they were taking her to the station at the Vic General, he said. I thought we'd start there.

You're not worried he'll come back?

Who?

Novica.

Lear gave him a long look. Are you worried about that, son?

What if somebody comes looking for his truck?

Who would come?

I don't know. He could come back.

Lear sat looking at him. You want me to leave him a note?

Mason said nothing.

Lear leaned forward, punched the truck into gear. I didn't think so, he said.

Their going was slow through the ravaged city. Lear stopped often so that he could climb out and shift rubble from their path. In the middle of some streets they saw mattresses thrown down, figures sprawled in sleep across them. No one woke or called to them or tried to stop them.

At the overpass they could not get down to the highway for the broken asphalt and Lear turned the engine off and climbed out and Mason climbed after him. He sat on a traffic divider in the webbed blue shadow of a Douglas fir, hands between his knees. The concrete was cool under his thighs and he sat with his head lowered remembering the night before the earthquake and the lighted kitchen and the blackness of the yard. The apple tree's roots like a great dark secret flowing there. When he had poured the peelings into the compost he turned and saw his mother and sister talking at the table through the split-framed glass. His mother went to the sink and began to rinse the dishes and stack them to dry. He could see plates shining in the light. A stink of cut grass and rotted matter swirling up around him as he breathed. The slop bucket clicked and swung on its wire hinge. He had stood there without the words for it, feeling astonished, and grown-up, and somehow very sad.

On the highway a route had already been cleared by heavy trucks. Traffic was backed up close to the hospital with the injured being brought in from all over the city and Lear pulled to one side and parked at the crest of the road overlooking the hospital grounds and he stuffed their provisions under a blanket in the canopy and locked everything carefully.

Just in case, he said.

Mason nodded. He was looking down at the crowded tents in the parking lot and at the huge crumbled edifice of the hospital itself and he felt something darkening inside him. The faces of entire wings had sheared off and the central building looked to have stoven in upon itself.

A hand on his shoulder.

Come on, son.

Look at them all, he whispered. There's so many of them.

He looked at Lear and Lear nodded.

She could be anywhere.

Yes.

Mason could feel a lump in his throat and he swallowed it down.

The crowds were sluggish in the heat and the eyes of those they met seemed dulled with pain. They clambered along the shoulder of a roadway filled with abandoned cars, their shirts dampening in the sunlight as they went. And then they were half-sliding down a grassy hill into that sprawling city of tents, and shouldering on, through the crowds, seeking word.

Underfoot was asphalt, painted white lines. There were figures squatting on boxes, leaning up against tent posts, clutching bundles of clothes to their chests. Everywhere tarps were strung up on thin ropes or wires as if to build small enclosures and in these spaces a strange assortment of electronics, suitcases, cookingware, packages and parcels, their owners glowering watchful over them. Mason saw a woman leaning at a bucket, washing her hair. A group of men in bandages regarded the old man trudging past and Mason watched their etched faces feeling uneasy. When one glanced at him he looked quickly away. He could hear babies crying, men shouting. The air was sour, dark with the stink of open food and unwashed skin.

Lear shoved his way through the crowds, a head taller than most, his fierce visage turning hawklike in the sharp sunlight.

This isn't the hospital, he said abruptly. He stopped, ran his tongue along the inner wall of his cheek. He was sweating.

Mason said nothing.

We're in the refugee tents, Lear said. We need to get over to the hospital.

Is that where my mom is?

The old man's grey hands were scarred and blistered and thick. He reached out, took Mason's hand.

But Mason was studying a girl in a green dress who stood half-obscured by a strung-up sheet. Her face begrimed, her blonde hair chopped savagely short at her collar. She was staring at him with dark ringed eyes and she said nothing and she looked very abandoned and very alone.

He felt sick. He felt sick with the fear of it.

They were directed towards a blue tent marked *17-C* but they found themselves turned around in the winding alleys between the tents and had to retrace their steps and ask again before they found it. The refugee chaos gave way to a maze of vast green tents and tarped amphitheatres and it was here the old man furrowed his brow and studied him and said, I don't know if you should come in.

Mason peered past the old man at the dark entrance. He could see nothing beyond it.

There'll be a lot of hurt people in there, Lear said.

I'm not stupid.

No.

I know what's in there.

The old man studied him and then nodded and they went in.

Inside all was shaded purple as if the very light were bruised. Mason peered about. He did not understand why they had been sent here. Outside was crowded and busy and draining but here in this place all felt uneasily still.

It was a big tent. There was a line of nurses still masked and scrubbed sitting on a wood bench with their heads bowed, arms folded. Flood lamps had been ratcheted into the posts nearby and other lights stood on small steel tripods and all had been shut off and three plastic-sheeted operating tables stood scrubbed and vacant. A radio was playing softly in one corner.

Mason saw dark splatters on the tarps hanging nearby which he understood at once to be blood. He thought of his mother and then he closed his eyes. When he opened them one of the seated nurses was very slowly lifting her head, as if just coming to. Her skin was almost as grey as the old man's but her blue eyes were clear.

Lear cleared his throat. We're trying to find the wards, he said. I think we're a little lost.

She gestured tiredly back the way they had come.

Just keep walking towards the ruins, she said. You'll find them easy enough. Go to where the soldiers are. You do know it's all wrecked, don't you?

Yes.

She nodded and seemed as if she might say something but then she did not.

We're looking for his mother.

The nurse looked at Mason. I hope you find her.

Mason said nothing.

She was brought in yesterday, Lear added. We just don't know where.

The nurse watched them from under her heavy lids but said nothing more.

They went out. The morning was already hot and there was little shade and they walked in the direction the nurse had suggested.

When they reached the edge of the destruction Lear raised a hand to the crown of his head. Where the hospital should have stood there loomed only cliffs of rubble, collapsed medical wings, the gutted walls of buildings tottering like bombed-out ruins.

My god, Lear said under his breath.

Mason said nothing.

There were fires burning amid the rubble and in the blasted sunlight a faint roar of trucks and cranes and a distant clatter of stones like soft applause. Mason thought he would feel something like he had felt the day before but he did not. He saw diggers drifting from heap to heap and their shouts carried to him and he saw wending up the slopes of the rubble antlike columns of men. He lowered his eyes. His shadow and Lear's shadow in the earth.

And then he started to cry.

He was surprised to be crying. He stared across at Lear in alarm and he was gulping air but he did not stop crying. Lear did not go to him nor did he speak and Mason stood with his hands loose at his sides and cried silently. He knew his mother would not be here. He knew it with the same clarity that he had believed the night before.

After a time he ran a sleeve across his eyes.

Feel better? the old man asked softly.

Mason shook his head.

Well.

It's not fair.

No. It's not.

She didn't do anything. She didn't do anything.

We'll find her.

You don't even believe that. You don't.

The old man said nothing to that.

They turned back. Mason followed the old man past a low-slung tarp under which a young woman sat distributing water and then the old man turned and studied the cloudless sky and then he trudged heavily back. He took the proffered water and lifted his chin and drank deeply with his eyes on Mason as he drank. Then he passed the bottle across. Mason was parched and tired and drank for a long time then wiped his mouth with his sleeve.

The young woman turned her face towards them. Her pitted cheeks long scarred over, her milky eyes unmoving. She was blind.

The sun climbed a pale sky. The light blurred, shimmered. They trudged down into the mess of the wards and went from tent to tent through the drifting crowds. Mason felt a growing dread inside him. At last Lear led him into a vast ward and they stood at the edge of that darkness waiting for their eyes to adjust, the old man rubbing his face with his hands. Mason was remembering his mother with her ruined hand, the old man so serious in that smouldering dark. The tent they had entered was crowded and clamorous and Mason saw the old man lift his head, peer angrily at the rows of the wounded.

The beds were hospital beds with bars on their sides and they went slowly down the aisles. Mason tried not to look too closely. The bloodstained bandages. The haunted eyes. The groans and weeping and crying out. The air was very bad and he was afraid he might be sick.

She's not here, he whispered. Arthur? She's not in here.

No.

Then they were standing at the far side of the tent watching a nurse approach.

Can I help you? she asked.

No, Mason said.

The old man frowned. We're looking for someone. Her name is Clarke.

Is she supposed to be here?

Is anyone?

The nurse looked at him wearily. I beg your pardon?

Is anyone supposed to be here?

She shrugged. After a moment she said, If you don't see her, she's not here.

Where would we find her?

The nurse was pressing the back of her wrist against her forehead and Mason saw the pinched lines around her mouth, the red skin where her collar was rubbing.

You looked in the other wards? she asked.

Some of them.

She smiled bitterly. There's no order here, she said. No one's keeping any records. I'm sorry.

It's alright. Thanks.

She nodded, went on her way.

The old man looked at Mason. How are you holding up?

I want to go.

Okay.

They slipped back out into the crowded alleys between the tents and the old man led him across to a makeshift counter and they waited in line there. A young man was distributing sandwiches and they each took one and found a seat on the ground nearby. The sandwiches were wrapped in a greasy brown paper and when Mason peered about he saw crumpled brown wrappers all over the ground. He felt very tired.

What do you think is in these? the old man murmured.

Mason had not taken a bite.

The old man peeled back the top piece of bread, studied the mess there.

It's not chicken. Jesus.

Arthur?

Mm.

Arthur.

What is it.

What if she went back home. Back to the house.

The old man chewed and studied him with shadowed eyes and swallowed slowly. She was hurt, son. You know that.

She could have gone home though. Maybe she's waiting for me there.

I don't know. I don't think so.

Mason stared at his dusty shoes.

The old man cleared his throat. Well. Okay. Do you want to look for her there?

Kat could be there too. She could've gone home too.

Mason. There are a lot of wards here. We haven't even been through half of them. You don't think we should finish looking here first?

Mason said nothing.

What is it, son?

He shrugged.

The old man got to his feet. Well. We won't find her sitting here.

They found a smaller ward to one side of the main tents and made their way across to it. The old man looked defeated, disappointed in something Mason did not quite understand though he felt it too. It was not sadness, not exactly. They went in and stood next to a low folded table and stared in exhaustion at the rows of cots. A nurse and a doctor with white hair were speaking nearby.

The arm's shattered in the second quadrant, the doctor was saying. I don't know what happened to her.

Mason stared at the wounded in their cots.

They found her in the street, the nurse said.

Lear turned to them. Who? Is her name Clarke?

Mason's eye slid down the second aisle, up the shadowy recesses of the third.

The nurse turned her head. Excuse me?

Bed after bed of blanketed figures, unmoving.

Who are you? the doctor asked.

And then Mason was no longer listening. He felt tense, electric with some kind of fear he did not understand and then Lear's hand loosened in his own and let him go. A stained cot, a shifting body under sheets, an arm heavily bandaged and held up out of the bedding. She was still. She was so still. Her haunted face a disc of burnished light.

Something kicked inside his chest.

And then he was pulling away from the old man and running towards her.

You have to be careful with what you have got. Or else you will lose it. Or somebody will take it when you are not looking. That is what people are like. Tobey Blekkenmeyer is like that.

Yes Kat is pretty. She is a horrible singer though her voice sounds like a crow being tortured to death. Tobey Blekkenmeyer said she was a lesbian but he does not even know what a lesbian is. He just said it because she dyed her hair blue once. I know she is pretty because she looks like Mom, they both have green eyes. Once after supper Kat drove us to the old mall that is going to be torn up next year, I said what are we doing and she grinned and parked and got out but she left the keys in the ignition. It was in July and the sun was still red in the sky. She came around to my side and opened the door and told me to slide over. Why should I slide over I asked. If you do not want to drive well that is fine with me she said. Drive, I said. For real? Don't make me change my mind she said and I smiled and said Holy shit.

It was hard to see over the steering wheel. She showed me where to put my feet. I had to stretch to reach. You have to push down one pedal and slowly let the other up to get the car to go. It kept jolting to a stop. Don't laugh I said. Okay okay she said take it easy, don't be mad. Then I turned the keys and stalled again. I started laughing too. We did not tell Mom about me driving, it was our secret.

Another time Kat and her friend Leah drove us out to the caves in Langford. Leah is tall and plays basketball and her arms are very strong. Kat parked by the blackberry bushes we used to pick over for Mom's pies and followed a path up the hill towards the old trestle. Leah led us down through the long grass and along a ravine and up another path to a dark narrow opening. There were pop bottles and plastic wrappers in the grass. Leah went in and Kat went in and I hurried after them. I said Kat? but she just hushed me. Inside it was very dark and the air was cool. Where are you? I whispered. Hello?

Hello hello hello hello hello hello, said Kat beside me.

I could not see her but I heard Leah snort close by. The rock walls were wet and cold when I brushed them. It is not funny I said. I could hear her sandals moving around. Kat told me that every month three kids get lost and die in there. Shut up I said. Leah said that it was the truth she knew one of them. Kat said yeah that was right it was Billy from math class. I said I did not believe them but then I imagined my voice echoing down over the bodies and I shivered.

I felt a sudden cold hand on my shoulders.

Why don't you go in and find them? Kat whispered at me and then she pushed me in deeper and my feet went out, the floor dropped. I screamed but it was just a small step I did not fall. There weren't any bodies. I could hear Leah laughing and laughing outside. I do not know why Kat did that. What is wrong with her. I would not have done that to her.

MEANS AND ENDS

Then the old man felt the boy pull away and in the slow darkness he turned slowly and then he saw her too.

She lay bundled in white sheets and gauze at the end of the third aisle. Her slouched cot barred, the rails folded up and locked in place. It was her. Not the woman he had met on that dark morning and not the woman he had left in the earth for dead but someone lighter, more translucent, startled out of herself. She lay with her face crushed into the pillow, the sculpted hollow of her clavicle pooling with light, and he watched the boy's bony shoulders rise and fall where he bent above her. The shells of her ears were white from the dried plaster dust that stuck to everything.

What's wrong with her? the boy asked as he approached.

The old man scraped a plastic milk crate from under a nearby bed over to the woman's cot and sat wearily. The floor under the cot was bare asphalt, slashed by the white painted lines of a parking lot.

I don't know, son, he said. Let her sleep.

Is she sick?

I don't think so.

Her cot smelled of rust and blood. The walls of that tent were orange and cast a cool orange light over all and when the old man peered up he saw netting had been slung overhead between the posts and in the netting were bundles of clothes, bedsheets, bandages. His knees had begun to ache. *Well and what did you think would happen?* he grimaced. *Old was twenty years ago. Old was Callie just in the ground. Get used to it if you are going to.*

He started to get to his feet.

Where are you going? the boy asked.

I'll find out how she's doing. Do you need anything? Water?

You're coming back?

He gave the boy a strange look. Of course.

What if something happens?

What would happen?

What if she wakes up?

Well, he said. An oily light glistened and slid thickly down the boy's eyeglasses. If she wakes up call for one of the nurses. That's what they're here for. Okay?

Okay.

But he did not move. He was thinking how little the boy betrayed in his face and how complicated that was. He stared past him then at the battered steel bars of the cot, at the rumpled folds of bedsheet sagging loosely there. The woman's throat where she lay with her head twisted sharply to one side was pulsing with a weird light. Thrumping shallow and rapid like the breast of a small bird. He glanced up. Her eyes were open.

Mom? the boy said. Then he smiled.

The woman turned her face and looked at her son.

Mason? she swallowed. Mason?

Hi Mom.

Oh god. God.

She was holding him and her good hand was in his hair.

I knew you were okay Mom. I knew it.

The old man watching them felt a thickness in his throat. He knew he should not be there. He glanced across the aisles and after a moment got quietly to his feet.

Mom, this is Arthur, the boy said. He drove me here.

The old man turned and curled his big-knuckled hands over the bedrail at the foot of her cot and stood uneasily there. He could feel himself blushing as she stared at him.

Her irises burned green and gold. I know you, she said. You dug us out.

He cleared his throat.

But she was staring hard at her son again and holding him fiercely. How did you find me? she asked him. Kat? Is she with you?

The boy shook his head.

Her feverish eyes absorbed this. Have you heard from her? Anything?

The boy glanced at the old man, adjusted his eyeglasses.

Nothing, he said.

The woman leaned back, the paper pillowcase at her neck crackled. She shut her eyes.

Don't worry Mom, we'll find her. She's probably at home.

Yes, she said, though something had gone out of her. What day is it?

Thursday.

Thursday. She opened her eyes and looked at the old man. It's Arthur?

He pulled the crate forward and sat close to her and nodded. Yes. Arthur Lear.

Thank you for finding my son, Arthur.

He could see then her deep exhaustion. She reached up and brushed a braid back from her face and the skin on her good hand was broken, the black-ringed fingernails ragged and torn. He said very gravely, You're welcome. Mason's a brave kid.

She coughed wetly and the corded knots in her throat stood out in stark relief.

Let me call a nurse, the old man said. He could feel the dappled bruises along his ribs aching steadily and somewhere just beyond that point a ghostly tingling. As if he had lost some part of himself he had not known of.

The woman reached her good hand out, stroked the hair of her son.

Mom you're crying again.

I'm not. She blew out her cheeks and glanced aside and her eyes when they met the old man's were glassy.

Mom?

Mm.

We'll find Kat. Don't worry.

I know we will, honey.

But she was slipping heavily back into herself now and the old man watched her struggle to keep her eyes in focus and he said to the boy, I think your mom needs to sleep.

And then she was asleep.

A nurse appeared, went away. A second nurse appeared, pulled gently back the bedsheet, dabbed at the bruises on the woman's belly. Her skin was lumped and yellow and brindled badly. The old man looked away. His left hand was still beside her pillow and he could feel her breath pass over his knuckles like smoke. At one point she opened her green eyes and held his gaze a moment and then she was gone again. He felt as if a lamp had been turned off, his skin left cooling.

He took his hand from off the bedsheets, the print of his palm impressed there. He thought how strange it was to encounter people you worried for. How it could happen anytime and how there was no way to prepare your heart for it.

While the woman slept Mason drifted like smoke around her, leaning over, fussing with her bedsheets. She was slighter than Lear remembered her or seemed that way asleep and in pain in that ward. He wondered how long she had been under the earth after he had pulled the boy out. Then he thought that the boy's sister must be out there still. He did not know if she would be hurt or not and he hoped not.

What are you going to do? Mason asked him. He sucked at his lips as if on something sour. His small hands gripping the metal railing of the bed.

What do you mean?

Mason shrugged.

Lear shook his head. I don't know, son.

Kat will find us, Mason said. If we go back home she will find us for sure.

Your sister?

She has a car.

I think your mom needs to stay here for a while.

Lear watched the boy's eyes darken at that and wondered just what was in him. He had found the gardener's body that morning while locking down the house. Last night the boy had squared his jaw and looked him in the eye and lied. He did not understand it. He did not know if the boy was in denial or feared to think about it or if some other darker reason were in him. The old man had covered the gardener's body with towels from the overturned linen basket by the dryer, not feeling anger but something else while standing there, a heavy sadness, a heavier regret. But now when he looked at Mason he did not feel it. He understood that in times of disaster what is true and what is untrue are sometimes one and the same. That the light we see by is a different light and the places we know change with that light. He thought: *The boy is trying to live like any of us are trying to live and he did not do any harm.*

After some time an attendant approached. And how's Mrs Mackenzie? he asked. He reached gently under her and folded back her sheet and adjusted the pillow and checked the IV.

Mackenzie? Lear said. You mean Clarke.

The attendant was a young man with very black hair fallen across one eye and he glanced at the clipboard in his hands. He wore jeans, a blue checkered shirt. Clarke? he said.

Clarke. Anna Mercia Clarke.

You sure? The attendant peered from Lear to Mason and back to Lear.

Yes, Mason said sturdily.

It's his mother. I'd say we're sure.

This goddamn manifest. They're supposed to be keeping records of who's where. They send us these lists but they don't have a clue.

What lists.

From the Records Desk. That's not how you found her?

No.

We just searched through the tents, said Mason.

Well. They got her down as Mackenzie so it wouldn't have helped anyway, I guess. How is she? Any changes?

No. She was awake for a bit.

She was awake? The attendant looked at her sharply and then at the old man. Has the doctor been by?

No.

I'll get him. Jesus.

The attendant turned but then he turned back and he gave Mason an open cardboard box. Somebody left this, he said. You're welcome to play with it.

Mason took it wordlessly. It was a chess box. Inside was a wafer-thin folding board, small magnetic pieces.

Then the attendant was gone.

Mason looked across expectantly and Lear grunted. Not me, son. I'm a little rusty.

I'll go easy on you.

You will, will you. You're awfully confident.

Just one game?

I don't think so.

Mason's spectacled eyes shifted over to his mother where she slept. His hands knotted between his knees. He put the chess board aside.

Hell, Lear thought. *What is the matter with me.*

Alright, son, he said. Give it here.

He fumbled with the carved figures and held out his fists and the boy tapped his left fist and pulled out the black pawn. He turned the board carefully and looked at the boy and together they set up the pieces and then he sat back and opened. They played slowly and they did not speak as they played. After a while Mason frowned and moved his queen.

Check, he said.

Lear moved his bishop.

Check, Mason said again.

Lear moved his king.

He saw a sheen of sweat in the woman's hairline and Mason looked across and then ran the corner of her bedsheet over her face. A few minutes later Lear was leaning on his fist, intrigued. Sawing at his chin with the back of his hand. The stubble rasping.

Now why would you do that? What are you up to?

If Kat isn't at home she might be at Leah's, Mason said softly. Or she might still be at her school. She could still be there.

Lear looked up, his hand hovering over the pieces. I guess so, he said.

He waited but Mason said nothing more and did not look at him. At last Lear took up his pawn and crossed the boy's queen and held two fingers on his chess piece and peered around it on all sides as if some opposing piece might be concealed there. At last he lifted his hand from the board.

Well, son, he said. Do your worst.

Mason slid his pawn to the outer edge of the board.

Lear looked from the board to the boy to the woman where she slept and back to the board. What was that?

What?

That.

Mason peered down as if he might have made some error. It's checkmate, he said.

You'd think I'd know when I'm being hustled. Was that even a little bit hard for you?

A little bit.

Sure it was.

Kat showed me that. She calls it Mireau's Gambit.

Lear shook his head. She's a good player?

Yes.

You're not so bad yourself.

Want to play another?

I don't. I really don't. You'll go easy on me again?

Yes.

Then I definitely don't.

The woman was muttering and then she fell back and slept on. Mason pulled off his eyeglasses, rubbed his eyes.

Lear reached across, dumped the pieces into the frayed cardboard case with a clatter and slid the board inside and folded the flaps shut. Through the tarp doorway figures were moving very slowly and the long shadows stretched their long fingers over the brown asphalt. He was thinking of the attendant who had not returned and of the error in the names and then he got to his feet and ducked his head to avoid the overhanging netting.

The boy peered up at him and he looked all at once like the boy he was.

I'm just going for a cigarette, Lear said. I won't be long.

Okay.

I mean it.

Okay.

He stepped out into the sunlight ducking his head and squinting and he walked slowly across the pavement. There was a smell of motor oil and softening apples and as he shouldered his way through the crowds of refugees he caught his hands trembling and he slipped them into his pockets. He was thinking of the attendant's words. If a Records Desk existed perhaps some evidence could be found of the boy's sister. He made his way to an open space lined with desks on all sides. Small tarped shelters where rows of tables had been set up. He could see on one side of the square a group of volunteers pulling bundles of clothes from black garbage bags, passing them across to the desperate crowds. Ahead of him a large handwritten sign indicated the Records Desk. The crush of the desperate was restless, thick, hot with the stench of unwashed bodies. The old man wiped his face, his neck. There were tarps and tents tacked up at strange angles and wide crooked lines of figures making their way between. He pushed his way in.

When he felt a hand on his shoulder he swung around.

Arthur? Arthur Lear?

He screwed up one eye, stared down his interlocutor. He did not know him. It was a grizzled old man in rumpled blue coveralls. His wrinkled skin was loose and dry under his jaw in the sunlight but his voice was powerful in its soft darkness and seemed not of his own devising. As if it rumbled out from some space just behind him.

The old man stared. Struggling to revive a world and time long past. Then it came to him.

Brady? he said. Jesus. I'd never have known you.

This man from his distant past. This man who had been a sculptor years ago, whose wife had known Callie in Toronto. Lear sighed. Something heavy and dark was rising in him.

Who're you looking for? the sculptor asked.

What do you mean.

You're not here for the Records Desk?

Lear frowned. It doesn't matter. I don't know if she's even here.

The sculptor nodded, set a scarred hand on the old man's sleeve and drew him out of the crowd. I'm with the salvage units here, he said. We got updated lists. I'll take you.

Lear shook his head. You came in from Toronto?

No. Why?

I just thought.

I've been living here for fifteen years Arthur.

Of course.

But then the old man fell silent. He reached into his pocket and withdrew a stained handkerchief and dabbed at his face and at the back of his neck and then stuffed the rag back in. He felt light-headed, weak in that heat. How's Suzanne? he asked.

The sculptor took off his cap and clawed his fingers through his white hair and put back on his cap. She died two years ago, he said. No, it's okay. It was a long time coming.

I'm sorry. Callie always liked her.

She always liked Callie.

Well.

The sculptor unbuttoned and folded back the heavy blue sleeves of his coveralls baring his forearms. The old man studied the run of faded ink covering them. There seemed a thing wild and frightening in his old acquaintance. He wondered at it and then at what he must have seen these last few days.

The sculptor put an arm around his shoulders. You doing alright, Arthur?

Lear did not know how to answer that. After a moment he said uneasily, I got out. I guess that's something.

You were buried?

He shrugged.

Were you alone in it?

Yes.

The sculptor regarded him strangely. They were walking around the perimeter of a great heap of rubble and Lear peered up at the slope, at its huge tumbled blocks of concrete.

We got dozens of people still trapped in there at least, the sculptor said. God only knows how many others. He shook his head. It's a mess. We keep trying to get in there and the army spends half its time just arguing with us. We know what we're doing. You move the wrong piece and the whole thing comes down. It's got to be done right. But the army's got teams trained for it and they just don't listen to us.

Well. It's hard, I guess.

The sculptor pointed at the ruined collapse of some outbuilding to their left. Yesterday a guy got up in there looking for survivors. I guess he could hear someone and he went in. Came out with a kid in his arms. But while he was getting the kid out he saw another kid in there and so he put down the first one and went back in and as soon as he was inside the opening came down behind him. We were starting to get him out when the army stopped us. They said it wasn't safe.

Lear said nothing. He pinched his eyes shut.

We still haven't found his body.

I'm sorry.

I heard you stopped painting.

What?

The sculptor was looking at him.

Lear grimaced. I don't know. I guess I did.

The yellow air was hazed with dust and a sour daylight was bleeding through and they wandered in that smokey wasteland for a time in silence.

At last the sculptor said, I just keep thinking this can't be all of it. Suzanne used to talk about it. How much you can't give back. Your hands learn things they can't unlearn.

The old man ran a hand through his hair.

Where are those lists?

Just up here.

The sculptor led him towards a kind of communications shelter and two soldiers nodded to him as they passed but did not break stride. There were soldiers wearing headsets and working dials amid tall racks of instruments. A wall of television monitors showed various scenes of destruction and the sculptor left him watching them. The old man could see on the screens tall fires burning unchecked in the streets and he saw ambulances and police cruisers weaving slowly through the wreckage. He saw a bloodied woman bearing a child in her arms. Two men dredging a body from the Inner Harbour. The Empress Hotel sunken and tilted onto its back. Houses with collapsed chimneys filmed from the air, their families milling in the streets. And then he was viewing what seemed a crater of destruction ringed by tarps and asphalt and he saw it was the Vic General and he could see ragged silhouettes picking slow paths down and a crowd was gathered in the grass and then he looked away.

There are more coming in all the time, the sculptor said.

Jesus, the old man muttered. You hear about this. But it's another thing to see it.

The sculptor nodded. He handed a clipboard across thick with papers.

Is this the list?

It's all in alphabetical order. That was good as of this morning. There's a new additions list somewhere around here. Let me find it for you.

Lear flipped to the C's but he did not see a Kat Clarke. Nor did he see an Anna Mercia Clarke. He put the clipboard aside.

The sculptor had come back and he handed across more loose pages and the old man looked for Clarke and again found nothing. He flipped to the M's and saw there three distinct listings for a Mackenzie and he closed the papers and then he opened the papers again and looked again. Just under Mackenzie he saw an entry for Maddin. Aza Maddin.

Lear could feel his hands trembling and he wiped his palms on his thighs and he regarded the sculptor where he stood. What is this list? he asked slowly.

What do you mean.

What does it mean. Does it mean they're alive?

No. I don't know. That's the arrivals from today. Is she there?

But Lear's tongue had thickened. What does 2D mean?

Second Division. Those are the tents we passed on our way up. What is it?

Lear shook his head.

Arthur?

Nothing. It's nothing.

He left the sculptor then. He made his way back through the shouting crowds and he ducked his head and entered a Second

Division ward with his heart heavy inside him. As he stepped in he let the tent flap fall back into place. It was dim and hushed within and he paused, rubbed his eyes.

He could hear a soft weeping there and then he could make out the stooped figures of nurses among the cots. An old bulb swung on its naked wire and sent his shadow sliding weirdly up the tarp walls and over the upturned faces of the wounded in their cots. Sleepers slept on pallets in the crowded aisles and he picked his way among them with care. A boy in bandages studied him with dark eyes. From a bed in the corner a young man lifted his long wet face from his hands. A wispy moustache ghosting his upper lip. He had lost both of his legs. The bedridden regarded him as he went past with their feverish eyes and one called out to him but he did not stop. Fans in their silver cages were turning the slow air in the tent, the rotors ticking noisily.

He stopped at the rail of a rumpled cot. There was something wrong in his chest and he could not breathe.

Oh god, he said.

It was her. Tiny and boneless and bruised where she lay. Her mouth had been badly torn along one cheek clean to the ear and the flap of skin had been stitched roughly there. Her nose was heavily bandaged as if it had been crushed. Both of her arms were gone. But it was her.

Aza, he said. Aza?

And then his voice gave out and he was crying.

He sat with her. After a time he stood and lifted her intravenous drip and dapped at the bag with his fingernail and then he unhooked her chart from the foot rail and stood reading it. He could make no sense of it. He sat again.

He wet a strip of cloth with a bottle of mineral water and he sponged it over her bloodied lips, her raw eyelids, he drew it in streaks over the translucent skin at her nape and the damp grey hairs plastered there. She trembled at his touch. As if the temblor were within her still. Some aftershock shuddering up through her flesh. The old man leaned over her and washed her, washed her, thinking of the woman and of the boy asleep beside her and then of the gardener dead in his cellar. A dark figure came to the tent doorway and the old man could not quite make him out and he stared and shook his head and swore softly to himself. It looked like the gardener and the old man knew his mind was not well.

Don't you go to pieces, he thought.

A nurse rose from somewhere nearby carrying a tray of bloodied rags and as she walked past she was crying. He was remembering the boy. His hair tufted and grey with grit. The weight of him in his big hands. The red brick dust and the hot lamps beating down upon them where they dug. Lifting the boy up out of the ruined ground and then the men with blankets rushing in to swaddle him and him crying out for his mother in the still-pulsing earth.

He ran his big scarred hand through the tobacconist's hair and she groaned.

Aza? he murmured. He set the back of his rough hand at her cheek.

But she did not wake. He leaned his ear in close, as if to hear whatever horror had taken hold in her, as if to hear her crying deep in that darkness, and in this way find her, and perhaps bring her back.

In the early hours of the evening he felt an eerie lightness come over him. It seemed under his own grimed skin a second skin was growing, all burnish and shine. He could feel some part of himself which had come away while he had been buried beginning, slowly, to attach itself again. He sat there with the tobacconist, filling with an immense light, as if the clothes he wore and IV standing beside her cot and the sickening groans of the ward itself were all afire and yet unburnt. As if grace were real, and with him as she slept.

No. My god no. I hardly knew Aza back then. She was Callie's model, not mine. I don't know if we shared ten words between us.

I'd see her some mornings from the upper bathroom. I'd be shaving, and turn, and catch a glimpse of a girl in a bathrobe smoking in the doorway of the shed. She'd be barefoot among the weeds and I'd wonder always about broken glass. I remember she had black hair with a strand of grey tucked behind one ear. I guess she dyed it that way. Callie would drift like smoke just inside the doorway, her dusty hands pale in the shadows, and then Aza would turn to her and smile and I'd blush, like I'd just witnessed something shameful. I don't know.

Aza told me her friends never liked Callie. I guess I can see that. Callie was brash for back then. And loud. She laughed with just about the least ladylike laugh I ever heard. She couldn't keep her hands off anything. She touched and caressed and fondled and fidgeted, she ran her fingers lightly over countertops, stroked her friends' thighs, patted their shoulders, fingered the fabric of their blouses. Hefted and squeezed and set back whatever was near her. She had a nervous way of coming down stairs too. Always clutching the banister, shuffling her feet, like she was terrified of falling. I wonder if she suffered vertigo. It wouldn't surprise me if she did. Not much to do with Callie would surprise me. She didn't like to talk about where she was from. She had no interest in my past. When my grandfather died we took the train across the country, back to the island. I stood at the curb staring up at the house and said to her, Well here's the old puzzle. And she just shrugged and looked at me and there were lights in her eyes but no curiosity.

I never did understand how she could capture such introspection in her figures. I guess she took the world in through her fingertips. I didn't see that then. I guess there were a lot of things I didn't see. Aza asked me once, if I were to meet another Callie, now, would I still be attracted to her. Would that interest still be there. I didn't know how to answer that. I'm not so foolish as to imagine there aren't any other women out there like Callie. But they wouldn't be Callie. It's not the same thing. It's not the same thing at all.

As he made his way out into the crowds something came over him and he turned and stared back at the ward where the tobacconist lay. A man jostled him, pushed past. He felt a sourness rising in his throat like fear and he swallowed it back down. She need not die. Death is a tide that rises and slackens. The dry grass on the hill beyond the hospital stood long and yellow in the late sun and he wandered slowly over to it and up into it thinking of nothing at all.

Overhead he heard the creak and hinge of geese in formation moving south on heavy wings. Soon they were but elongated shadows and too far distant to be heard and they passed like that into the deepening blue sky and he stood for a time feeling that long grass rippling around his knees. He had left the gardener's truck just beyond the rise and he made his way towards it feeling an enormous weariness. He remembered how his wife would grip his elbow with her pale calfskin gloves and lean into him pretending to be very old. Her heels clicking over cobblestones in Montreal and a trumpet playing in the streets at dusk. The cold air stinking of rain and boiled cabbage. He did not know where this memory came from.

He made his way up the slope above the grounds and turned at the crest of that hill and stared back over the smouldering ruin, the sheets of yellow dust rising in the wind. The refugees drifting among the slouched tarps looked very small. He crossed the uneven grass past the shade of a small tree, turning his battered face to the late sun.

The truck had not been molested. He checked that the doors were locked and then he opened the canopy in the back and shifted through the clinking bags until he had found the rifle and he double-checked that the bullets were safe. He straightened and peered out at the road but he did not see anyone approaching. He and the boy could sleep in the truck that night, he knew. Though he would be stiff in the morning.

He was thinking of the nurses he had seen in the wards. How tired they seemed, how thin in their own skins. He wondered if they were local and what they must have lost in the quake. He thought how goodness will burn of its own accord. How a soft light shines in a hard darkness. He banged the canopy shut and locked it fast and sat alone in that high grass and rested his eyes and he could feel the earth shuddering gently under him as the heavy trucks worked in the ruins below. He thought in amazement that there is real goodness in people and when it rises it rises no matter what. He did not include himself among such people.

What you take to heart, he thought with a tired smile, *is always just the warning*.

After a time he sat up and shielded his eyes and stared back at the road beyond him. There were still trucks wending their way down towards the hospital, still figures limping or staggering along seeking some requisite kindness. The good feeling in him was easing and pouring off and then he felt very old and very tired and he got to his feet with a groan.

He thought he would check on the tobacconist again but instead made his way down to the ward where the woman lay. The air among the refugee tents was pungent and thick and he breathed shallow breaths as he went. His left shoe was coming apart at the toes and he could see a slash of sock sticking through, comical and awful like an old-time slapstick tramp. At the woman's ward he lifted the sagging tarp and stepped through into the half-light and the high muffled groans carried through to him. A nurse nodded wearily as he entered.

He found her dressed and sitting up in her cot, her bandaged arm folded at her stomach. She cracked a swollen eye, her blood-thick face peering up at him.

Mason said you'd be back, she muttered. I didn't believe him.

Mason sat beside her with a bottle of cola balanced in his lap, a chewed straw standing aslant in it. Mom, he said.

Is everything alright? Lear asked.

She gave him a long look.

He glanced at the boy then gestured at her clothing. She's dressed.

She says she's feeling better.

But the woman raised her hand from the bedsheets with its palm facing outward as if to fend off further query. I'm not feeling better, she said softly. She lowered her hand onto her son's head and rested it there a moment.

But you're leaving? Lear said. He furrowed his brow and then he sat down.

I need to find Kat. It can't wait.

He nodded. He nodded and glanced at the webbing strung up overhead, at the bundles of clothing and bedding there as if some answer might lie above. Then he said, It's almost dark. You can't mean to go out in the dark.

Why not.

With Mason? With your son?

She was silent.

I don't care, Mason said quietly. Mom? We can go.

They need the bed, she said after a moment. There are people worse off coming in.

Did someone say something to you?

No. It's not like that.

Lear glanced at a harried nurse across the tent leaning over a tray of bedclothes and he watched her run a backward wrist over her forehead and he frowned sadly.

They're doing so much, he murmured. He saw in his mind's eye the tobacconist with her crushed body and then he shut his eyes sharply. *Jesus, Lear*, he thought in disgust. *Pull yourself together.*

When he opened his eyes she was watching him.

Mason says you took him back to your house, she said.

He nodded. I didn't know what else to do. I thought you were dead.

It's okay.

We were going to look for your girl next. Kat. If we hadn't found you.

She smiled sadly at him. Mason says you have a truck.

No. Yes. It's not mine. It belonged to a man we met.

Belongs, Mason said. It still belongs to him, Arthur.

The old man glanced at him.

That would be Novica? she said.

Yes.

Where is he now?

Lear wet his lips. He saw the boy's dark eyes boring into him and he met his gaze and did not flinch. How much did you tell her? he asked.

For a long moment Mason said nothing. Then he stood. He did not look at his mother and he did not look at Lear and then he turned and stalked off out of the tent. The old man watched him go.

He's tired, she said.

We're all tired. That's something else.

What.

He looked at her, looked away. He cleared his throat. It's none of my business, he said.

She was still looking at where her son had stepped out. She said nothing.

He went on, The nurses said you were picked up in the street. Covered in blood.

Yes.

It was someone else's blood.

I don't remember any of it.

None of it?

What else did they tell you?

Nothing.

Nothing else?

No, he said. But something in her voice made him pause. Like what? he asked.

She held his eye a long moment and he felt his scalp prickle.

She looked away. She picked at her bandages with her good hand and smoothed out the fabric in her lap and the old man felt an old heaviness thicken in him.

He said, Mason thought you'd be here. I mean, we were told you'd be here. That you'd have been brought here after they pulled you out.

He was looking at her carefully.

I don't remember, she said angrily.

Well, he said. It's none of my business.

Arthur.

He looked at her.

I need to find my daughter.

Lear's mouth tightened but he did not know what to say. A long brown shadow fell aslant from the boy's cola bottle and stretched crookedly over the bedsheets and a wasp crawled out of the mouth of the bottle trembling and it circled the rim and then flew off.

Will you help us?

But he was shaking his head.

Please.

I can't.

Of course you can. Why can't you?

He slipped his hands into his pockets. The cries of children could be heard drifting in from the crowds outside and the old man saw through the ward doorway a plastic chair where an old woman sat in the sunlight, elbows on her bony knees. Blinking and working her gums and peering about at the passersby. Curled up under that chair lay an old honey-coloured mongrel dog. The old man felt a line of sweat creep down his rib cage.

He said, Because there's someone here I need to take care of. He looked at her for a long moment and then he said, You can have the truck if you think you can manage it.

She lowered her face back into shadow and the old man saw all at once just how fearful and tense she had been. I was afraid you wouldn't offer it, she said.

She lifted her head and her dark braids poured about her. She said she had seen nothing in that blackness under the earth to tell of. But that she had heard things. She raised her hand and held his wrist gently a moment and her skin felt cool against his own.

After a time he said, You must be so tired.

I'm not tired, she said.

They were silent and the old man felt something welling up in him again and he ducked his head and crushed his eyes shut but he could not clear it. Something was not right in him.

I was buried too, he said. I was buried with someone too.

But you got out.

His lips whitened and he bit down hard on his words. She's here, he said.

Here at the hospital?

Yes.

That's who you have to stay for.

He leaned into his forearms and knees and his hands were thickly scarred where he held them in the half-light. Out of the drugged whorl of the hammered darkness he peered and peered. Lord the long pitch and roll of the earth. I could not stand it even if I never. The woman was looking at him as if awaiting some reply and he stared at her helplessly.

I said, where were you when it hit.

His tired shoulders rose and fell.

It's alright if you don't want to talk about it.

He picked feebly at the scabs on his knuckles and he wet his lips and he said, I knew her from before. She was an old friend of my wife's.

You don't have to tell me.

We were in her shop when it hit. I remember telling her, *It's just an earthquake, it's nothing.*

Yes. I thought that too at first.

I remember the glass breaking. There was a lot of glass. The doors were banging shut. I wasn't afraid. I remember the fire alarm went off and the lights flickered and went out.

And you could hear all of it very precisely.

Yes.

And everything seemed to slow right down.

Yes. He was staring hard at his big sore hands. She wanted to get out into the street but I stopped her. I don't know what I was thinking. I think I was looking for a table to climb under.

You stopped her?

If I hadn't—

She might be dead now.

She might be alive.

She *is* alive.

The old man flushed and did not meet her eye. He could not seem to explain to her just what it was he meant. The words were right and yet he could not get the sense of how his wife hung over all of it, he could not convey this to the woman.

Nor could he describe rightly his glancing from Aza to the door shuddering in its frame and again to Aza nor him shaking his head nor her face twisting in fear. *The street*, she had shouted,

Arthur the street. None of that. Nor his seizing her wrist and pulling her back from the lurching floor nor the building screeching eerily as they held their ears though he knew the woman must have heard that too. Aza's wrist was in his hand and he did not let it go.

He lifted his face then in that tent and it seemed that the shadows were draining off him like water and he rose uneasily out of it. She watched him as he stood.

I need to get back, he said. She could be awake.

She nodded.

He thought she looked very beautiful and very gentle. Where will you sleep? he said. If you're giving up your cot.

Where were you going to sleep?

He shrugged. At the truck, I guess. There's room in the cab and in the back.

That's fine. We can get an early start.

I can't go, he said. I can't.

Maybe you'll change your mind.

I won't.

She nodded. After a moment she said, Send Mason back in if you see him.

He could think of nothing more to say and he turned then and made his way out. The boy had been sitting with his shoulders slouched against the sun-hot wall of the tarp cleaning his eyeglasses with the underside of his shirt and he got to his feet and called out to the old man as he emerged.

Did she tell you? the boy asked.

She told me.

So you'll take us?

No.

The boy studied him with his burnt eyes.

He looked at the boy then and then back at the tent where the woman lay and then he shook his head. It seemed so much to explain. I told her she can take the truck, he said instead. I can't go with you. Not yet.

The boy nodded but he did not move.

What is it, son?

Nothing.

He gave the boy a long look. Either you tell me what's troubling you or you don't. But I don't think I can handle all of these looks you keep giving me.

The boy bit his lip and stared with hard flat eyes at the old man. It's her.

What about her?

The boy shrugged.

Mason.

I don't know. She's different. She's not the same.

The old man studied the boy. Give her time, he said. She's been worried about you and she's still worried about your sister. Just let her get through this.

What if she isn't?

Are you the same as you were?

The boy blinked and regarded him and the twin dark coins of his eyes flipped over.

The old man nodded. But you will be, right?

The boy said nothing.

The old man wondered if he should say something about the gardener. *No*, he thought at last. *Let the boy have it. Let him say it or not say it but give it to him to hold on to if he needs it.*

She said to send you back in if I saw you, he said.

When he returned to the Second Division tent the tobacconist's cot stood empty.

He felt suddenly frightened.

A nurse came past and he stepped forward and grabbed her arm roughly.

I'm sorry, he said. Please. I'm looking for the woman who was in this bed. She was here just a few hours ago.

The nurse, clutching a roll of towels to her chest. Peering narrowly up at him.

Who? she asked.

Maddin. Aza Maddin. She was badly hurt from the quake.

She glanced at the cot, furrowed her brow. Just a minute, she said.

I just need to know where she is.

I said just a minute.

The nurse went away and she came back.

You're a relative?

Yes.

I'll need some identification, please.

He looked at her.

I'm sorry. We can't reveal anything without proper identification.

He turned out his pockets. I don't have any, he said. Please. Is something wrong?

The nurse bit her lip and glanced behind her and then she studied him with soft brown eyes. Okay, she said. Look. Mrs Maddin was taken into surgery just a little while ago. If you hurry you can catch her.

Surgery?

Yes.

Is it serious?

Elizabeth will take you. Elizabeth!

A thin young woman with rolled shoulders and a lean face came over.

Elizabeth, take this man to 5D. He's looking for Mrs Maddin. She just went in.

They went quickly from that tent through a warren of back tents and in and over staked guy wires and they did not talk as they went. The waiting room of the surgery tent was small and cramped and badly lit and the old man stepped through quietly and when he turned his guide was already on her way back to the ward. The room was empty. He ran a hand through his hair and went through the plastic sheeting and found himself in a tall bright tent. Nurses in stained gowns were hard at work over an operating table and he could not make out what they worked on. Against one wall stood a contrivance of buckled steel poles screwed together into a frame bearing above it a huge square lamp. It had the look of an antique camera or drilling tool.

He found the surgeon scrubbing his hands at a basin in one corner, the shadows falling slantwise across him. He was holding his hands up and his skin looked very white and the water ran down his forearms in brown rivulets as he shook them dry.

You shouldn't be in here, the surgeon said. What are you doing here?

I'm looking for a, the old man began. Then he fell silent.

Two of the nurses had moved away and he could see now on the operating table a figure laid out half-naked and exposed, her stomach swabbed darkly with iodine. A nurse was carefully unwrapping the stump of her left arm.

Do you know her?

He nodded.

The surgeon looked wearied. Nurse, he called. And then to the old man: We'll do what we can. She's hemorrhaging bad. You can wait through there.

A nurse led him back through to the closetlike entry and left him. It was quiet there. A small metal folding table, two chairs by the entrance. He watched her disappear back into the operating theatre and the plastic strips over the door clattered and cut softly and fell still.

He stood a moment listening. Picked up a clock on the metal table to wind it and propped it back in place. Upon a white cloth unfolded there lay various weird implements hooked and toothed like articles of dentistry or the refined instruments of some torturer's bag. He could hear the surgeon murmuring in the room beyond. The click of scalpels. A high whine and sluck of some fluid sucked clear. He sat and leaned back and crossed his ankles to wait. Pinched his eyes shut.

Sometime later he rolled one eye groggily open. He looked at the clock to see how long he had slept. He rose and looked in the basin and saw silver forceps soaking in the clear water but otherwise all was as it was before. His own watery reflection stared out at him.

He crossed to the door and looked out. The heat was baking up out of the earth and the old man squinted and ran a hand along the inside of his collar. The tarps were lifting and shimmering but there was no wind and he felt uneasy seeing it. Something had awoken him and he thought perhaps he had heard the tobacconist cry out in pain and then he thought perhaps the surgeon had come in and stood over him while he slept but neither seemed likely and there was a scent of the sea in his nostrils and then he rubbed his eyes for he recalled his dream.

In the dream he had been standing on a sandy log and a tide was going out and out but it was no tide he had known. In a yellow inflatable raft his wife and grandfather were being carried farther out and they were laughing. He heard out of the grey sky the bellow of a ship. Dark ropes of kelp and shining rocks and rippled banks of mud sat exposed to the air and still the tide went out and the old man began to wade out across it. He wore gumboots in the dream and the going was hard in that mud.

The sky above the tarps looked blue and pure to his eye and the sun was still sinking at that hour and on another day this would have passed for great beauty. Standing there in that sunlit doorway he thought the world of man ineffable and fiery and blessed. And he saw the boy pulling a rifle from a corpse and then his dead wife holding a black umbrella at a curb and he saw a sliver of light in a blackened hall. He saw the tobacconist lifting a glass of water to her lips and drinking in the white stillness of her shop and her slender eyes were upon him and he saw the black woman with the bandaged hand laid out in the cot. A yellow rope was tied to the low brass ring of a tarp sheet and he watched its canvas billow and roll and it seemed to him that he stood at a window staring in upon the world, so removed was he from it.

Then a nurse was standing beside him and she pressed a hand against his shoulder. She told him the tobacconist had died. She told him she had not regained consciousness and she did not suffer in the end. Her voice was soft and tired.

The old man stood breathing. Is that it? he said at last. Is that all of it?

I'm sorry.

The old man looked down at the nurse's clean white hands and up at her face and he nodded and turned and left that place. Under the dying red sun his heart felt cerulean and cold.

She said I played the victim. I expect there's truth in that. She said there was no space in our marriage for her anger. That she couldn't be justifiably angry ever. Well. She'd smash dishes, throw crockery. She was difficult and sensitive and there wasn't any right move to make with her. I don't know. I think this city stifled something in her, the drab buildings and miserable parties and the silence in the streets after dusk. Maybe it was me. It didn't help that we didn't have any kind of friend except a Polish mechanic who lived across the alley. He'd stay up late smoking cigars and getting drunk on a brandy he brought over with him. Then he'd close his eyes and get to muttering in Polish and Callie would just give me a look and go to bed. I wouldn't say we were lonely. Not that. But tying on an apron and cooking and cleaning was never the fate for Callie. I can remember one night she hurled a casserole dish out the kitchen window into the driveway. The raccoons got into it, the metal pan clattering and scraping over the gravel while we tried to sleep. I was a little frightened of her. I think sometimes I argued with her out of shame. She had strong hands and when she hit me it hurt. But she was also kind, and generous, and she tried not to let her unhappiness infect anyone around her. So what do you do with that? It's been more than thirty years and I don't pretend she was something she wasn't. She made me sick with anger sometimes. But I learned more from her than from anyone. And I include my grandfather in that. It's a hard thing living with a debt that can't be repaid. I guess that's what guilt is. I've felt it a long time now. I don't know that I'd take back any of the fights if I could. They were a part of what we were. I suppose Callie'd say otherwise. I do *wish we'd been gentler with each other. I do wish that. I could've been a better person. I know it.*

Well. If somebody could invent a machine that told you happiness when you were in it, I guess they wouldn't have to eat potatoes ever again. I guess not.

Is there no coffee? he grimaced. Tilting the steel canister.

A table of nurses glanced up from their trays.

Hang on, the counterman said. Ladling up grey scoops of potato. Scraping the mess towards him and banging the spoon on the dish and wiping his fists in his stained apron. Coffee?

The old man nodded.

Can't sleep, eh?

A flurry of muttering from the nurses' table. Sad frowns his way.

I'm not much for it myself. Some people just want to roll over and go to sleep when something like this hits. The rest of us just can't. The counterman swung the shining canister down and lifted a second from near his shoes. Flicked a red switch along one side. You a doctor then?

No.

Well. You got that look.

Surgeonlike himself in his apron, sleeves rolled high past his elbows. Doffing his white cap. A tall and stove-chested stranger in a pair of yellow galoshes, rumpled clothes, two dirty adhesive bandages set crosswise low at his throat and puckering outward as he dropped his chin.

The old man watched him at his work. Scraping and stacking an empty silver tray, wiping down the server's counter. Hefting a pail of watery soup into place by its handles. A brown fluid slid down the walls of the pail, hissing. He watched it, thinking of Aza with Callie long years ago, the soft sepia light in the parlour windows where they sat laughing softly, dark-tressed heads bent together, and then Callie's wide angry mouth lifting towards him as he came foolishly in and saw too late that they were not laughing but crying. He glanced around.

What?

I said, are you hungry.

The old man blinked, a cup of coffee in each hand. Some pink meat sore-looking and inflamed in its dish of thick grease. Pale noodles slick with mucus. Platters of fried eggs sweating under heat lamps, beans leached and grey.

He took a step back. I guess not, he said.

Well, said the counterman. If you are.

Thanks.

He set down one cup and pocketed a handful of creams and packets of sugar. An old cook coughed in the kitchen beyond, his shadow in the door's light. Ropy black loops of electrician's wire overhung the crossbars of that dining tent and the caged fluorescent lights were buzzing softly overhead by whatever miracle illumined their lives. He slid between the rickety tables and out into the warm night.

He made his way along the dirt path, ascended the grassy slope. The coffee hot through the paper cups, the deep smell of it rich and fine. He could just make out the gardener's truck, the tailgate standing down where the woman sat with her legs swinging slightly.

Arthur? she called softly. Is that you?

He came up to her in the darkness.

Mason's sleeping, she said. How are you holding up?

He sat next to her, held out a cup. White dust rising in the rubble below, men standing about tiny and shadowy against the halogen lamps.

Regret giving up your bed yet? he asked.

No.

How's the arm?

She said nothing, blew on her steaming coffee. Then she frowned. You want the truth?

I guess so.

It hurts.

The old man nodded, grunted at the crews far below. I see they're still at it.

I keep thinking it doesn't feel real.

He lit a cigarette, straightened, breathed out. I was just thinking the opposite. It's so real I don't know what to make of it.

Yes, she said with a nod. That too.

He knew that she was thinking of her daughter and after a moment he said, Mason was sure he'd find you. He never doubted it for a moment.

He's like that. He's always been like that.

He was so sure.

She scratched at her bandaged arm. But you weren't.

No.

She gave him a searching look and he saw this but said nothing and then she was picking at the frayed white threads in her jeans. Out of the floodlit ruins a caravan of trucks was passing. The old man shifted on the grooved metal tailgate and watched their windshields flare and vanish like halos in the false light.

Arthur? the woman said.

What.

I wanted to thank you.

He sat staring at his hands and they were trembling faintly. Then he twisted around to see through the dirty window where the boy slept with his face dark against the pale leather seats and he said, very softly: He was just a rumour down there. Both of you were. I could hear him singing to you.

Her dark fingers cradling her shattered elbow. The slouch of her shoulders in silhouette.

I'm sorry, he said. You wanted to know.

I do. I do want to know.

It was another man who did most of the work. Pike. He was digging all night. If you want to thank somebody you should thank him.

He thought I was dead. He left me in there.

So you do remember.

She shook her head, uncrossed her legs. Gazed unseeing at the broken taillight by her knee. I can't make any sense of it, she said softly. I don't think I'm the same as I was.

No.

It scares me.

There was something in her voice as she said this and he did not ask and she did not say.

He wet his lips, drew long on his cigarette. He was thinking of the tobacconist polishing the brass railing in her shop and the glint of silver in her mouth when she smiled. He winced in the darkness.

I wonder if we could have known this was coming, she said. If there were signs.

He sipped at his coffee. What do you mean. Like warning tremors?

Maybe.

Do you mean signs from God?

An inky black shine in her eyes as she smiled at him. I don't mean from God.

He held her gaze a moment. You're being so polite, he said.

I'm not being polite, she said. It wouldn't even occur to me. God doesn't even come into it for me. I can be rougher if you want.

Be rougher.

You believe in God?

The old man drew deeply again on the cigarette and lifted his chin and blew out the stars. The tobacconist in her shirtsleeves in the sunlight, peering up at him. Her leathery spotted hands.

I don't think that's the sort of question anyone can answer, he said. Not honestly.

No?

You don't agree, he said. You think you can answer it.

She said nothing.

You think you can. But you can't. That's the trouble with it. I don't know how to make sense of what happened today. Was I given a chance at goodbye? Or did I just fail her twice?

You can't think like that, she said softly.

The cigarette burning between his grazed knuckles. The smell of that surgery tent and the sharp cloudy stink of the iodine. I'll tell you a story, he said. This happened in a small town in southern Alberta. Just east of the Rockies.

Is this a true story?

It really happened, if that's what you mean. He brushed at his trouser legs and then waved his hand large-knuckled and knotted and white at the darkness to dispel the smoke in the air. He tipped the ash from his cigarette into the dirt. He said, There was a teacher in the local high school, a good man. But not a lucky one. Some years earlier his wife had been killed in a car accident and in his grief he'd turned to drink, and then, drunk, he'd turned to God. I don't know how exactly. But in the end he was reborn, he was saved.

Saved, she said.

Yes.

Is this how you answer my question? Or how you avoid it?

He cleared his throat. I don't know, he said. Maybe both.

So this man, he went on, this teacher. He kept a faded pocket bible buttoned in his shirt flap and he consulted it often. He came to believe it the word of God given to men for safekeeping and that all things written in it were true. That all men are brothers in that they are sprung from Eve and that God in his goodness created the world in six days and on the seventh day he rested. This man's faith in such creation stories became his compass, and he guided his life by it. A good life, lived among his fellow men, and he didn't drink or walk in temptation.

The woman rolled a sore shoulder, frowned.

But this faith influenced his teaching, and his teaching influenced his students. As will happen, I suppose. One of his students wrote in her graduating essay that only the church had been brave enough to challenge the scientists. She wrote that evolution is an attempt to take people away from God and the truth. She thought it was sad that so many people in the world today do not want to know the truth of their origins. This man, her teacher, wrote in the margins of that essay: *But the real evidence has been suppressed and most people don't realize it.*

You'll think I'm making this up, the old man said. I'm not making this up. All of this was printed in the newspaper when the fighting broke out. There were more examples. Another student argued for the necessity of teaching all theories of creation in the classroom, and in this way allowing the students to decide whether they came from apes or not. An honour-roll student acknowledged the global conspiracy of scientists to discredit facts that proved the earth to be not even twenty thousand years old. Scientists, they argued, should not be allowed to brainwash people any longer. It was clear to them that all evidence confirmed evolution to be impossible. The scientists needed to be stopped.

He gazed fixedly at the white storm of lights below, the shadowed wicker of bent girders and gaping masonry and the men trudging through it. He touched the paper cup gingerly to test its heat but did not lift it nor move it. Then he grunted deep in his throat, tapped the ash from his cigarette. Our inclination to believe begins early, he murmured. We all of us have to rely on advice, on opinion. That's how we learn.

What did the parents think of all this? the woman asked.

The parents of the students? You'd expect them to be outraged?

I don't know. Yes.

The old man grimaced. This man, this creationist, entered his classroom one morning to find the principal and a school board official waiting for him. The three men sat facing each other in the small desks and while the principal spoke the creationist folded his hands before him on the desk. He had big scarred hands, a strangler's hands.

It seems complaints had been lodged. Newspapers had been notified. On the evening news in Calgary a segment had been aired and the teacher was now to be fired and a replacement from the city brought in. You must understand, the old man said, how difficult it was. These men were friends. All three attended the same church and all three believed vehemently in the literal bible. But to the creationist, there could be only the one moral path. God allowed for no half measures. And so he cleared out his desk that very morning and carried his possessions—pens, paperweights, books—in a cardboard box out to his truck and set them rattling down on the floor and slammed the door shut and he didn't teach in that town again. It's an old story. The man of God set ablaze in his beliefs suffers the more for them. Had he believed less fiercely or lived less admirably he'd have met with less misfortune. Can I help you with that?

The woman shook her head. With her good hand she was prising off the lid and then she blew the steam from her coffee and drank.

The old man continued. And so a replacement teacher drove out from the city that very week. He arrived in an old sedan and rented a room in a local boarding house and there he shelved and drawered his few books and clothes. There were news reporters from the city staying nearby who wished to interview him but he asked them to leave. He was a tall man with a wind-pitted face and hard black eyes and he was very thin. A man more voice than flesh who in his spare time was something of an amateur geologist.

I think I can see where this is going, the woman said.

You think so?

What happened to the geologist?

Well. He was a man of science, of course. But he believed the true value of science lay not in the opening of nature's secrets, but in the opening of men's minds to such secrets. He believed truth holds no value except to the extent that it leads us back to ourselves.

He doesn't sound like much of a scientist.

No? He understood that men do not hunger for truth but for belief.

Is that right. And what do women hunger for?

Men.

She smiled.

In any case, he said. Truth holds little sway in the hearts of the devout. The geologist had *wanted* this assignment. He'd been angered by what the creationist had done, he was eager to teach the truth. But he found that nobody believed what he said. His students were suspicious of his science and countered his facts with the creationist's theories.

How? What did they say?

The old man shrugged. What are facts when stripped of their authority? Just testimony. The students demanded the geologist account for various mysteries in the world and when he'd fumble for an answer they'd laugh. *What is air for?* they'd ask. *What's the point of water?*

The geologist was troubled by this. But when he spoke to his colleagues he found many of them had been persuaded by the creationist's claims as well and he too began to doubt. Not the facts, of course, the old man said quickly. But the purpose behind the facts, whether it mattered what men believed. He would lie awake in his small rented bed at night with his heels hanging over the edge of the mattress and he'd watch the headlights slide across the far wall. The school library had many books which supported creationism and when the geologist brought in books and films with photographic images of erosion, fossils, sedimentary deposits, all were dismissed as fakes. Evidence from assorted journals was shrugged off. The students believed it was all a scientific hoax of the greatest magnitude, a conspiracy. The creationist's firing had only fuelled their conviction. What source could be believed? What evidence upheld? In their minds, if all the world was deceived, who could be trusted?

He regarded her, wetting his lips as if unsure how to proceed. He said, At last it occurred to the geologist to take his students on a field trip. He'd show them the badlands. He'd explain to them the sandstone hoodoos eroding there beyond the old museum. He rented an old bus. Its folded doors leaked and whistled with wind while he drove and its tires roared up through the steel wells so that he had to shout to be heard but still it took his students there in one piece. And so they went.

The old man described the features of that country with great precision and care. The low grey sky and its flat light and the alluvial shifts and patterns of wind. A moonscape of sheer rock wall and hawks in slow spirals overhead like curls of blown dust. The museum itself an inelegant wood structure flexing and contracting in the dry air through whose dark windows their watery reflections strode warping and strange. In the grainy light sat cabinets of tagged bones and water-stained skulls many millennia lost. Garish paintings. Herds of monster lizards. A gruesome wire-strung devil like a thing of nightmare suspended in the air overhead. A local guide led them along a walk discussing the rock formations and her voice shivered and distorted in the smooth rocks and came back and faded. Lichens and weeds and fierce yellow grasses among the stones. The geologist had phoned in reporters from the city who also spoke with the students. Free books were distributed. A film shown. In the museum courtyard boys clambered up the spine of the Albertosaurus and girls grinned shyly under its painted fangs and the geologist snapped their photos.

Surely it failed, the woman said. Surely they weren't convinced.

On the contrary. They returned to their town convinced by evolution and of the gradual nature of geologic change. And that evening they all watched the national news. It was a program on the students and they were interviewed and discussed.

The woman frowned. What about the parents?

The old man nodded. The parents. The parents had been convinced by the creationist's claims too. The school board's forcefulness on this issue appalled them. They kept their children home from school in protest. A public meeting was called one Tuesday night in the high school gymnasium. A chance for all sides to speak out. And so once again the reporters came back.

The old man watched his cigarette stub burn steadily down and with great delicacy he transferred it to his other hand. Thin webs of stars were shining in the blackness.

Chairs were set up in rows and the big steel doors wedged open onto the night air as the hall filled. The parents were seated in the folding chairs, and in the back other townsfolk stood in a blue haze of smoke under the basketball netting where the backboards had been dragged aside and tied off. A microphone stood at one end of the aisle.

Anyone who wished to speak was allowed. One man said that if the earth were even half its age the land would have eroded as flat as a table millennia ago. A woman announced that studies had proven the ocean's accumulated sediments not older than four thousand years. The local pastor plucked the microphone from its stand and spoke about grace and God's presence among them and of the uprightness of their town. Shaking and with the microphone unclipped and pacing the aisle with the strut of his god in him like a revivalist preacher.

The coffee was still hot and the old man removed its lid and sipped grimacing.

You're not exaggerating? the woman asked. Just a little?

The old man held out a hand. In the end the creationist's sister got up and made her way to the microphone. The hall went quiet.

Her left arm was withered and she held it to her side by its wrist
but despite this she was very beautiful. It seems this girl had
slipped from a wagon as a child on a patch of sandy earth and
landed under the rear axle and been crushed but in a sort of miracle hadn't died. As if she were touched by that very grace their
pastor swore to. The old man coughed and held up the glowing
stub of his cigarette as if to consider its worth. He blew on it, its
ember flared briefly. Then he continued. She spoke not of what
was true but of what was right. She said there were many truths
all of them credible but of varying worth and she said it seemed to
her the immorality of evolution should not be ignored.

The woman shifted her feet. How is it immoral? It is what
it is.

But what is that? the old man asked her. After a moment he
shrugged. The creationist's sister said that such thinking led to
the evils of racism for if all men were born of monkeys then those
who lived closest to them must yet be near relations. She said such
thinking led to the strongest laying claim upon the weakest and
the weakest being unworthy of survival. She feared to so contra-
dict the teachings of the bible and warned that without a moral
compass no sense was to be made of the world. And as she spoke
she gazed sadly at the geologist in the audience and her eyes were
very clear. She said to live by such a theory was to remake God in
man's image or to deny Him altogether and no good could come
of either. She shook her head and warned, *If we teach our children
they are beasts, we must not be surprised when they behave like beasts.*

The old man fell silent. He wet his thumb and forefinger and
crushed out the embers of his cigarette and pocketed the butt in
his shirtfront. His wristwatch glinting in the floodlights.

What did they come to at that meeting? the woman asked.
Did it amount to anything?

Does it ever? What is ever possible between men of opposing
faiths?

Evolution isn't a matter of faith.

What would you call it?

Science.

Science is a secular faith.

The woman smiled. Not in the way that you mean it. Why would the geologist agree to the debate?

It wasn't a case of agreeing.

Those people weren't going to be convinced by anything he had to say. Why would he go through with it?

The old man inclined his head, breathing softly. Who knows why any of us do anything? he said. Even in stories something acts upon all of us and we don't know what that is.

You don't mean God.

The old man waved his hand irritably. The trouble with that sort of talk is that God means many things to many men.

He watched the woman sitting in that blackness with her hand knotted in her lap and her eyes shut tight as if some more consoling darkness lay within. The far lights below darkened her eye sockets, carved more deeply her tired face. She opened her eyes.

You were the geologist, she said abruptly.

What makes you say that?

Tell me I'm wrong.

You're wrong.

I don't believe you.

The old man opened and closed his hands in his lap. Out in the ruins a small bulldozer was scraping into its maw a crumbled retaining wall and a crash of rubble carried up to them where they sat. It sounded muffled and very far off. A cloud of white dust drifted past the floodlights and out to the night.

He said he had lived his entire life looking for answers to just a few questions. And when he found one, he lived badly with it. He slid a handkerchief from his hip pocket and coughed and wiped at his chin. He said a spirit of inquiry deserved respect but that it had to be tempered with modesty. He did not mean humility. He had little time for those who would suggest men should not seek answers. But an answer is only ever the edge of an outer question. And all of us keep moving outward. His eyes were stinging with the late hour and he rubbed at them and blinked. I wasn't the geologist, he said. I've been a painter my entire life and I wouldn't know where to begin. You don't have to believe me.

She watched him quietly.

I'll be sixty-nine years old this year, he said. And I don't know what to believe. He gestured grimly out at the darkness. When my wife died I turned from all of that. She died in 1964. She wasn't even thirty-five. A child to me now. Almost a grandchild. I've smoked all my life and here I am healthy as an ox. God? Grief? He shrugged. You live long enough and you come to see your own smallness in it.

So what do you think? There's no sense in any of it?

No, he said. I don't think that.

Why are you looking at me like that?

You're wondering how the creationist's tale ends.

Is there an ending?

Of course. There are three of them.

Three.

The old man nodded.

You said this was a true story.

Again the old man nodded. He said it was this very concern for the truth that made the ending so complicated. That in a certain light this problem of truth grew insurmountable for it was in fact the riddle of the world itself.

She frowned. That's ridiculous, she said.

Why? he asked. You believe a great earthquake struck the city. But in reality many thousands of quakes struck. All of us lived through a different disaster. How does it go? *No two can meet one on one road for though there be just one his shape is manifold.* You doubt this but it doesn't matter. Whether the world is one or many matters to few. It is what it is.

I don't know. I don't.

The old man shrugged. Men find a way regardless. It's not what happens but what's said to have happened that matters. We tell stories to make sense of the world. And any struggle for meaning is hopeful. And there are as many stories as there are men and stories do not die.

The old man stared at his knees. He rested his palms upon them. Well, he said. So the years passed. The geologist went on teaching evolution in that town and the newspapers turned to fresh controversies and the creationist in his anger moved away. He packed up his truck early one morning and was gone. Without even a goodbye to his sister or his father. And he didn't write them in the years that followed. But what man, he asked, ever knows what his future holds? Or which fate plucks at his string?

The geologist, you see, had been devastated by the withered sister's beauty on that evening. And he courted her with great gentleness. He drove out to her farm in the evenings and played bridge with her widowed father at their kitchen table and he spoke to her of the cities he had lived in and of the West Coast where he was born and she listened boldly with her cobalt eyes upon him. She told him of the gulls confounded by the prairie sky, which had trailed the dying salmon into the mountains many years before, and confessed she'd never seen the ocean. He said he'd never known God. She assured him he would someday although he didn't believe her. They didn't speak of her absent brother, the creationist.

The old man shifted slightly. He said, They were in time married. And very few objected though he was from the city and she touched in her strange way and he agnostic and she devout and when she became pregnant the geologist felt himself truly blessed, and when she lost the child he grew fearful, and when her rupture wouldn't stop bleeding and she too died his life also ended for a time.

The old man fell silent. He breathed, troubled. A dog slouched up the hill towards them but stiffened some yards off its ears cocked and fiery eyes shining and then it slunk west across the grassy slope.

After a time he continued. He said the creationist in his disgrace could find no employment as a teacher and in the months which followed he drifted northward finding work in the oil fields for he was a large man and strong. He carried little with him but his anger which burned dark within him and in his new brutal life he soon turned again to drink. There were women who lived with him for a time but none who stayed for he argued with his fists and drank heavily and he was fired occasionally and drifted on. Yet in that line of work he came to believe the geologist correct and one night in a trailer broken and drunk he began to scream at his God for the madness he had suffered in His name and though he cried out no whirlwind appeared to him, no voice admonished him, his dreams did not urge him to repent. When he awoke in the morning his eyeglasses were broken and his shirt pocket where he kept his old bible was empty. Thus did he lose his faith.

The geologist meanwhile was drowning in his own grief. And each day his dead wife's father came to him and cleaned and cooked for him and the geologist did not rise from his bed but lay frozen and mute and each day the old widower spoke to the young widower of mourning and of faith and of the many shapes loss can take. And time passed.

You must understand, the old man said. Eventually it was summer. The world beyond the geologist's windows turned sun-drenched and very fine and one day the old widower arrived to find the shades lifted and the bedroom dazzling in its brightness. And the geologist frying eggs in the kitchen. There seemed to be no reason for it, or the reasons were too many, too complicated. Thus did the geologist turn to an immense and consoling God and thus was he able to walk again in the light among men.

The old man studied the ruins of that hospital. The creationist never did regain his faith, he said. He lived bereft and aimless in the long decades he had left.

And the geologist? the woman asked. Did he ever remarry?

No. And he didn't ever meet another woman he could have loved. But what woman could compare to a memory? It's always this way. No, the geologist moved to Edmonton to teach in the schools there in the hope of getting away from his grief. Of course it didn't work. We carry some burdens all our lives and never set them down.

The old man cleared his throat. So which man was the happier? The one who believed himself free at last from illusion, or the one with a new-found sense of purpose? The old man drank from his coffee and he cleared his throat again. He said, The creationist's eyesight had always been poor. And in his old age it failed him entirely and he moved into a home for the infirm where he could wait out his days. A stooped figure with shaking hands. His eyes weeping a little always under the lashes. He'd smooth out his sheets each morning through the grey fog of his vision and shuffle with great care to his bench by the hall windows and he'd sit listening in the sunshine.

And the other?

The geologist too got old. And because he was alone he too had to move into a home and, yes, it was this very home, and sure enough he shared a room with the creationist.

I see.

The old man shrugged as if to apologize for the twist in his tale. He said a true story and a truthful story are not the same thing. That the ways of the world are strange and many and that what happens often is not to be believed.

It's unlikely, the woman agreed.

Yes, he said and nodded. Nevertheless, The two men in the course of their confinement became friends though both were long accustomed to solitude. After a while the blind creationist asked his roommate for a favour. He said that although immersed in darkness he lived in a kind of light and that he knew his life was nearly done. When the geologist protested he wouldn't hear of it and asked only that his friend might write out a letter to his sister whom he hadn't seen in many years. Of course he could not have known of his sister's death, of this man his friend's great grief. He said he'd at one time been a religious man but had strayed, for his life with God and his life without God were no different. And now when he looked at the world he saw nothing but darkness and if there were a God He must be a god of darkness. But this he could not accept. The old man looked up. Neither man knew the other, you understand.

The woman nodded.

Well. The geologist listened to his friend and at last he said that he too had lost a great deal in his life but for a brief time he'd known happiness. He said he wouldn't give up those days now even for all that followed. He said real goodness was possible and if so then why not God?

Why not. The old man smiled bitterly and peered up at the woman. I've always thought that the most elegant defense of faith. Why not. At any rate, in the days to come the two men sat together listening. And in the evenings the geologist transcribed in a trembling hand the words of his blind friend. He'd hold each sheaf close to his eyes and carefully read back what he'd written. Lines were struck out, lines added in, until at last the letter seemed complete. But the creationist wouldn't sign his name and the geologist lowered his pen and regarded his friend. *I'm sure you're forgiven*, he said. *Absolutely sure. Given time enough nothing matters but to see again those we once loved.* The blind creationist's eyelashes were wet and his face was turned towards the fading sunlight and the geologist asked one last time for the address and name of his friend's sister.

Not just yet, said the creationist. *Tomorrow.*

At least you must sign it, said the geologist. *Please.* It was a Friday evening and many of the staff at that facility were leaving for the weekend. The geologist was holding out the pen in the late sunlight to his friend. They were sitting on the porch. It was a moment of great clarity. And the geologist understood, I think, that he was offering his friend a kind of absolution.

Go on, he was saying in his quiet way, holding out the pen. *Go on. Take it.*

The old man waited. The woman sat with her face hidden and her ear tilted down towards him and she sat silent. After a time he said, This is the first ending.

The woman shook her head. That's the first ending?

Yes.

Did he sign the letter?

The old man opened and closed his hands in the darkness.

So they both end up blind, she said.

Well. Blind to certain truths. But absolved.

Absolved.

The old man nodded. It is a hopeful ending. The two men who lived so differently come together and find a common ground. The creationist's reunion with his sister lies still in the future. Everything is possible.

After a time she said, They didn't deserve such unhappiness.

No. They didn't.

Whoever does, though. What's the second ending?

The old man cleared his throat. He shifted his hips. The creationist's father, he said, the father-in-law of the geologist, the man who was supposed to receive that letter, he lived a long time after the geologist departed. He was a good man and gentle but solitary and marked it seemed by his long tragedies. He was treated with a kind of deference but it was the deference of the old and the mad. Which he in time came to be.

The old man pursed his lips slightly as if mocking his own words. Well, he said. He fell ill and grew suspicious of the world. Wrapped himself up in his faith with a kind of hopelessness. He came to believe the world capable of little but betrayal. That the economy was ruled by a cabal of bankers. That men had never walked on the moon. That a global pandemic threatened to engulf the earth at any moment. He would walk the roadside ditches in the evenings muttering to himself in his loneliness, ragged and unkempt.

No man at the end of a long life should find himself so alone. His wife and daughter were dead, his son was vanished in the northern oil fields, his son-in-law was silent and grieving in the city. He lived out the years left him praying for darkness. Who could blame him? The old man shrugged and picked a bit of tobacco from his lips. I guess he'd walked in the light too long and he'd been burned. But the world had one last mystery in store for him. As it often does.

It seems he was wading the long grass in the ditches one after-noon when he looked up at the sky and saw something extraordi-nary. The world went still, and the sun went black, and the sky burned itself out. And darkness covered the earth.

It was of course an eclipse, the old man said. And after a moment it passed, the shadows eased, the sunlight returned, as is the nature of things. But the old widower who'd been standing with his arms slack and his mouth agape when it came over him had collapsed.

The old man studied the woman. There are midnights in all of us, he said. The heart lives in a glove of darkness and its dark-ness is entire and without end. I believe the widower came to understand this. I believe he saw something in that eclipse that was in him already. The world's heart isn't so different from the hearts of men and men's hearts too are a kind of fire.

What do you mean, collapsed.

The old widower died three days after the eclipse. He was buried without ceremony beside his daughter. He died in silence and alone.

Jesus, she said. How is that an ending? That's awful.

I guess it is.

That's the second ending? Really?

Yes.

He doesn't get the letter from his son.

The one addressed to his daughter? No.

But she was shaking her head and holding her bad arm. No, she said quietly. No. I see just the one ending. Just the one sequence of events. Once the second ending happens, the first isn't an ending anymore.

The first ending remains true, the old man said.

But it's not an ending. The second ending wrecks it. It eliminates the hope.

Does it? That is not how the two friends would see it.

It doesn't matter how you see it. It only matters what happens.

How we see what happens becomes what happens.

That's not my experience.

Is it not?

The woman gestured at the destruction below. A dark figure was walking slowly between the medical tarps and the low yellow bulbs strung up at intervals there blackened one by one as he passed. Look at that, she said quietly. What do you see out there? You see exactly what I see.

Some would see the hand of God.

The hand of God. There.

His mercy, yes. If God's ways are not our ways then we cannot hope to make sense of them.

The woman leaned forward and regarded him in the darkness. You don't believe that, she said.

He shrugged.

This is a world of horror and sickness, she said fiercely. Whatever else God may be He is not only goodness and mercy and love. There's brutality in him too. If anything comes from him then this does too.

He said nothing for a long time. When at last he spoke his voice was low. I'd guess that if grace exists then it's probably a simpler thing than we imagine, he said. Not a case of means and ends, of God willing this for this purpose, that for that. Not a method but a mystery.

He thought the woman was staring at her bandaged arm but then he saw her eyes were closed.

You won't make sense of it, he went on. There isn't sense in it.

She waved a tired hand at him. You said there were three endings, she said.

Yes.

What was the third?

He shifted his hips on the bench, his bones creaking. It doesn't matter, he said. You should get to sleep.

Tell me.

He looked along the hill into the blackness. The third ending is no different from the first two, he said, but it elects cessation over conclusion. All things end. Nothing is ever finished.

I'm sure you're forgiven, the geologist told his friend, begging him to let him know where to mail the letter. *Not just yet*, the creationist replied. And he took his friend's arm and told his friend to wait just one more day. There was one more thing he needed to add. They would finish it in the morning, he promised, and then they would send it. Of course, as is the way of things, the letter was already finished. For the creationist died that very night.

No, said the woman.

Yes. Is there some meaning in all of this? Some common thread to bind these three? The old man blew out his cheeks, growing tired. I think not. There's one irrefutable truth in our lives and everything else is doubtful. Everything. He removed the lid from his coffee and hurled the dregs into the grass with a kind of disgust. You just get old, he said. You don't think you are and then you are.

She said nothing and they were silent a long while.

At last she stirred. I'm sorry about your friend, she said softly.

Well.

If there's anything I can do.

There isn't anything.

I know it.

I keep looking for some good in it but there isn't any.

No.

He ran a begrimed thumb along the skin under his eyes.

Where will you sleep, Arthur? Out here?

I don't know that I will.

You should try.

I know.

Try to sleep.

Okay. I will.

The woman slid down to the grass and crunched around the truck and the old man heard the door open and close with a soft click. Then he leaned back. The blue stars in their great wheeling tracks brutal and perfect as clockwork. Glinting in their gauzy webs of light. Closing his own eyes to imagine some fixed eye on some icy otherworld. He stretched out, his hands interlocked at his stomach like an indigent and he felt the cold metal through his jacket and after a time he slept.

When he awoke the moon had risen and the world lay waxen and strange in its stark light. He could smell the wild grass among the trees and also the dust in the air and there was a darker smell also like pitch or tar rising from the pits below. He lay very still with an arm across his eyes. Finally he sat up and rubbed his unshaven face with his hands.

The wind had died. Out in the pit the low-slung tarps shivered in the light like the rippled surface of a sea and the weird crumpled heaps of the buildings loomed up behind. All of it below in a kind of crater as if the earth itself had opened. He thought of the woman's shattered arm. Along the far slope in the hooded moonlight passed what seemed a long line of refugees ascending out of that place and they shuffled with their heads low and shoulders dipping and though they trudged without break their

numbers did not diminish. In the broken dark they seemed penitent and scourged and in the pooled light their strange figures
twisted trembling and sad. He watched for a time but could make
no sense of this vision and he sat with his big hands deep in his
pockets and stamped his feet for the cold.

In the morning the low sky was dark with cloud blown in during the night. The old man ran his hands through his hair, grimacing. His cold jeans slucked to his legs heavy with dew. Above
the trees a rent in the clouds pulsed smouldering and red as if
some more fiery world lay just beyond this one and he sat looking
at it and then he looked away.

I suppose it was already over before we left for Greece. It must have been.

I guess she would have gone regardless. I guess so. It was the only overseas journey we ever took. The sunlight in the Mediterranean was what struck me first. It was a different kind of seeing, it was beaten flat and very white and it seemed to seek out the edges in things. It was a distinguishing kind of light. I expected Callie to be drawn to the statues. The ancient frieze in its eaten relief around the Parthenon, the votives with their flat lifeless eyes. But it was the general decay that seemed to hold her. I wonder now what she was seeing. The famous pieces she completed after we returned, in that year before her death, were filled with a kind of ruin. A decay. I heard a feminist critic wrote once that this reflected her despair at our marriage. Maybe that was a part of it. But her name was Callie Andersson before we married and I always thought of her like that. Never as a Mrs Lear. I don't know. I still do things I don't understand the reasons for. Art is truthful when it does that to you. I don't know if I thought some of this would have settled down by now. That I'd have known myself a little better. I can say that after sixty-eight years the heart is still a mystery and when I say that I don't just mean my own.

I remember wandering through the overturned stones, the rubble, on the island of Delos. The pale light felt so clear it blinded us. The heat was terrible, there wasn't any shade. I wondered at the time at the silences. There was nobody around. This was before the days of the big tourist buses, the big ferries. I think now of the ruined houses and their atriums opening up onto the blue sky, the terrible pink and white dust in our clothes, the hopeless silence, and wonder if the Greek idea of the afterlife was anything like that. Sun-drenched and quiet and empty. There were dozens of cats like living shadows weaving in and around the stones. All of that turned something in her, I think. Callie used to say about her work that there was always a point where the gesture exhausted itself. But that you couldn't see it until you were on the other side of it.

The other side of it. I can't say that now without feeling an obscure anger. Our last morning in Greece we spent walking through the narrow quarters under the Acropolis. The light was dazzling. The air was muggy and warm and old and I remember it felt strange breathing air that had been breathed for three thousand years. There was an age to everything man had made there. So old it might have been inhuman. I guess that's truer than I mean it. You live long enough, you stop resembling the living.

In the shuttered doorway of a small café Callie put a hand to the lines at my eyes and told me I was getting old. I was just thirty. It's a kind of sadness, remembering. Some things you want to forget. The sun was blurred and painful in the sky behind her. When I closed my eyes I could see the perfect negative of her form burned into my eyelids. I can still see it.

QUESTIONING THE DEAD

Astonishment. That was what she felt. Seeing the old man tilt his face down towards her son, murmur some kindness, seeing her son grin back. Astonishment and a kind of gratitude drenched golden in that wash of golden light. She watched his yellow eyelids, his sunken cheeks, the play of early shadow in his stubble like steel wool as he tied off some bundle in the bed of the truck, banged the tailgate shut. He clapped his hands across his dusty trousers. Mason went around to the cab, swung himself up and in. The old man kneeled to inspect the rear tire.

Why are you doing this? she asked after a moment.

He peered up at her in surprise. Doing what?

Watching out for us.

He coughed a wet thorny smoker's cough into his fist.

Isn't there anyone looking for you? she said. Anyone you need to find?

I suppose there must be, he said. There's always someone.

When she climbed up into the truck she could see leaves still on the chestnut trees along the street and leaves scurling in the ditches also. The old man got in after her. The windshield was rimed with dust and he flicked on the wipers over the dry glass but they dragged raggedly to no effect. Then the motor wheezed, cuttered in, roared to life.

At the hospital overpass he let the engine idle and leaned low over the wheel and told her he thought her daughter had probably gone home. If you want to know what I think, he said. His eyes scanned the bad road ahead.

Kat won't be there, she said firmly.

But we should check there first.

No.

The old man peered across at her.

We'll start at her school, she said. If she's not there, then we'll see.

Your house is closer.

Arthur.

It just makes sense.

Arthur.

What.

Take us to her school.

His elbow bumped the keys where they swung from the ignition and the sharp metallic crunch was startling. You're as stubborn as Mason, he muttered.

I'm not stubborn.

The old man frowned. Not compared to your mother you aren't.

He punched the truck into gear.

They turned south, then south again, over asphalt burning off white in the rising sun. Past storefronts shuttered dark. The old man gripped the steering wheel in two hands sitting very erect in his seat. Despite the hour there were many on that road and the driving was slow in the cleared lanes. Over a traffic divider she saw the roadbed crested in a frozen comber of pitch and tar. She lifted her eyes to the side mirror. Crows were circling some kill on the highway behind them and she looked to see if her son had seen them but he had not.

She thought Kat might be anywhere. She did not believe she would find her at her school but did not know where else to begin. She stared at her son's sticky unwashed hair and wondered where her daughter must have slept last night. If she was cold. If she had gone back to the house. Mason was slouched in the seat between her and the old man with his safety belt loose around his waist and his eyes fixed on the lanes ahead.

Within the hour they had left the highway. A few survivors swaggered weirdly off before them into the ruins. After a time they reached a shopping mall and then turning west they saw the mall storefronts on that side shattered and a slab of the roof fallen in. Its parking lot filled with chunks of concrete, shards of glass long as a man's legs. Some cars were crushed. Fire crews stood in the rubble smeared black with ash. The old man drove on. Down roads labyrinthine and thin and some of them impassable with bricks, fallen telephone poles, abandoned cars. The dormer windows of many old houses had crumpled or sheared off and swaths of cloudy plastic sheeting had been nailed across the holes and as they passed Anna Mercia thought she could see figures moving greyly within like blurred phantoms.

On the radio a seismologist and a professor from the university were being interviewed.

Our instruments indicate a series of shallow crustal quakes, the seismologist was saying.

Crustal quakes?

Yes. Ruptures in the earth's crust that occur very near the surface. Usually on minor fault lines. Because of their epicentres—

Epicentres?

The seismologist cleared his throat. The precise places in the earth's crust at which earthquakes occur.

Sort of the cradle of the quake, the professor interjected. Where it's born.

I see, said the interviewer.

Our instruments have indicated a kind of zipper effect, in which a small crustal quake originating outside Nanaimo appears to have triggered a secondary quake, and this a third, and so on,

rippling the earth throughout the region. So what should have
been damaging over a small area was actually devastating over a
much broader region.

And where were these epicentres located?

Well, yes, that's the question. Many struck directly underneath
the major metropolitan areas. Vancouver, Victoria, Seattle—

And that accounts for the destruction?

Excuse me—

.Yes, we think so. We've never seen anything like it. Our instruments are very precise.

Professor Michaels, you were going to say something?

Thank you, yes. Our instruments are also very clear but they
suggest nothing of the sort.

What do you mean?

What we've experienced is what we call a megathrust subduc-
tion quake—

The Big One—

Mm. And all of our data is in perfect agreement on this point.

The seismologist again cleared his throat. We think otherwise.

Gentlemen—

This is absurd, the professor said angrily. Nobody has ever
heard of such a thing as a zipper effect.

You just mean *you* haven't heard of it. Despite all of Professor
Michaels's confidence, the truth is we don't really understand
how the earth's crust works. I mean in any detail. Or even how
earthquakes happen. Let alone why.

Are you suggesting there might be even more explanations?
the interviewer asked.

Yes.

No. We know what we know.

Which doesn't sound like much at all, the old man muttered.
He leaned forward and switched the station. Is there nothing
else, for god's sake?

There, she said. Wait. Go back.

A recording of emergency shelters and routes of travel was being repeated and then the announcer came on the air. He said many roads were open and that although rescue operations continued the destruction was now well under control. He said the earthquake was estimated to have registered at 8.1 but the damage was far less than previously feared. Nor would the death toll be so high as dreaded. He urged citizens not to panic and he explained that the army had been called in to keep the peace and that public safety would be ensured.

The old man frowned. 8.1, he said. I heard 8.6 earlier.

It's like a beauty pageant. Yesterday they were saying 9.0.

It all means nothing. Unless they indicate which scale they're using. He reached for his hip pocket squinting across at her and then he fumbled at his shirt flaps. You wouldn't happen to have a cigarette?

I never took it up.

Good for you. Mason? You got any cigarettes?

Mason grinned.

Now on the radio a cheerful woman was informing listeners that the water in their toilet receptacles was still safe to drink.

Didn't a tsunami strike on Tuesday? the old man said.

She shook her head. I think everyone was afraid it was going to happen. But I don't think it did.

Are you sure?

Pretty sure. It was all over the radio earlier. Why? Where did you hear of it?

The old man grimaced. The radio.

Jesus.

No one knows anything.

I guess not. I did hear the downtown core was burning.

The old man nodded. You can see it from here.

A cloud of smoke like a deep twilight was thickening out across the sky and a grey finger encircled the low sun and then the daylight fell down around them and faded out and a grey pall passed

over the truck. The worn treads of the tires crunched sadly over
the debris in the road.

She heard the old man sigh heavily. A yellow bruise at the
corner of his mouth made his profile sullen and ugly. Mason did
not lift his eyes and she glanced down at his hands knotted before
him and then up and out at the streets. His knee was jumping
under his interlocked fingers but his gaze seemed fixed on the
dashboard as though he studied some darker gauge.

The quietness from the morning had passed and now there
was something clammy and grim among them and Anna Mercia
did not speak of it.

The road was narrow and they were driving now through low
shuttered warehouses with ramps leading down to loading bays.
She saw no people. They came to a four-way stop and the old man
glowered out at the streets. Two of the streets were filled with
rubble and the crushed hulks of cars blocking the way. It did not
look accidental.

Well, he said. He folded his long grey arms over the steering
wheel. What do you think?

She frowned. What do I think is down there? Past those cars?

He rubbed his shirt cuff over the glass. Can you see anything?

No.

It doesn't feel right.

No. Somebody's blocked off those streets. To keep traffic out,
I guess?

Or direct it elsewhere.

It could just be to keep us to safer roads.

But there aren't any signs, the old man said. They'd use signs
for that.

People ignore signs.

Well.

So what do you want to do?

The smoke over the city twisted ochre and brown in the daylight as if some refinery burned in the ruins. A wind was roiling

out of the south scuttling papers and leaves and debris into the
roads and the pillars of smoke bent sluggishly northward.

She shrugged. I guess we keep going.

The old man nodded.

The road turned sharply not fifty yards farther on and as they
came around the narrow corner they rolled crunching to a stop.
They'd reached some kind of barricade. A police car with its doors
open blocked the way. Two men with rifles stood some yards off.

I guess we keep going? the old man muttered sarcastically.
Jesus.

Turn around, she said.

They've got rifles.

Turn the truck around.

Jesus. Are you serious? He gave her a hard look.

She said nothing.

The squad car sat empty, its slow blue lights swivelling. The
windows of the tall buildings around them glinted dark, inscrutable.
Something was wrong. One of the men waved angrily. He was
wearing white gloves.

What's he saying?

I don't see any police, she said.

The engine ticked quietly and they sat in the truck unmoving.
The old man set his hands on the wheel and shifted his weight
and the leather creaked under him and he regarded her in silence.

Then the men were knocking at the old man's window. Twin
blurred figures dark and faceless through the dirty glass.

He rolled the window creakily down.

The men looked dirty, unshaven, as if they had not slept in
days. Something in their faces frightened her. Both wore red strips
of cloth tied off on their sleeves. A rifle was slung over the shoulder of the shorter man. The taller held a pistol loose at his thigh.

What's going on? the old man said. Is the road closed?

We've had some trouble with looters, the taller man said.
Where are you headed to?

We're trying to find a missing girl.

Sure you are. This was the second man, the shorter one. His face was oily with sweat.

We're going to have to ask you to step out of the vehicle.

Why?

The shorter man opened the door roughly. Get out, he said. His eyes were dark.

And what do we have here? the first man asked. A thick pale hand vanishing low into the footwell. He withdrew the old man's rifle from beneath the seat, checked the chamber expertly. You got a licence for this?

It was destroyed in the quake, the old man said.

Sure it was, the shorter man said.

Shouldn't be carrying this inside the vehicle. You know that.

Of course.

She leaned across, arms folded around her son. Who are you? she asked. Are you police?

That's right. Police.

I want to see your identification, she said.

We're not police, the first man said. He gave his companion a grim look. We got special dispensation. We're stopping all the vehicles and checking for looters.

What special dispensation? she demanded.

The second man muttered something then.

What happened to your hand? the taller man asked.

She hurt it in the quake.

Sure she did, the shorter man said.

In the quake? Or breaking into a store?

Jesus Christ, she snapped. We don't have time for this. I mean it.

But the shorter man swore then and he leaned in and hissed, Get out of the fucken truck.

Don't get out of the truck, Anna Mercia said.

The old man unbuckled his seat belt. It's alright, he said. I'll just be a minute.

Arthur, she hissed.

But he climbed out and left the door standing open and a bell in the dashboard chiming. The first man came back to the truck and withdrew the keys from the ignition and took them with him. She said nothing. She could see through the windshield where the old man was being questioned at the front fender. In the waxen daylight his skin looked plastic. His shock of white hair plastered wetly at his neck.

Mason twisted in his seat, peered back over the ribbed leather. She heard the canopy open with a clatter and then the first man called across to his companion. Got a lot of food back here, he called. All sorts of things. Flashlights. Water.

When she turned back she saw a movement across the street. A third man lurked just beyond an open window. He had a gun trained on their truck. She swallowed nervously.

They're not police, Mom, Mason whispered.

Hush, honey, she said. I know. Just stay quiet, okay?

He frowned. Arthur needs to know.

He knows, honey.

The old man came back to the cab and ducked his head in and gave her son an uneasy smile. It's okay, he said. They want us to wait in the building over there. They just need to check some things.

No, she said firmly. Absolutely not. We're not going anywhere.

His eyes were pained. Anna Mercia, he said.

I said no.

Think of Mason.

There was something in his voice. Then her door opened out and the shorter man stood there, studying her. Get out, he said flatly.

What are you going to do to us?

Get out, he said.

They got out.

The two men led them across the street towards a mound of rubble and then cut past two cars standing with their doors wide and their trunks popped and pieces of clothing strewn in the dirt. Just behind these stood a blue truck with a tarp crumpled on the ground and Anna Mercia stopped when she saw its cargo. She felt suddenly terrified.

What the hell is that? she said.

In the bed of the truck lay the sprawled corpses of a half-dozen people. Looking boneless and swollen. The old man coming up beside her swore softly and held his nose and shielded her son with his body. Some of the corpses were in a bad way, the flesh furred where it had started to come apart and laid out between the bodies were a number of mismatched human legs some still dressed in trouser leg and sock and shoe. A soft black wax of thickened blood had collected in the grooves of the floor and they could see where boots had smeared and tacked through it, where heads had dragged lolling. Anna Mercia stepped back holding her mouth. Her eyes watering.

Oh my god, she said. What are you going to do to us? She was shaking.

What is this? the old man demanded. What's going on here?

The two men grinned at each other.

Relax, said the taller. Hey, take it easy. That's on its way to Henderson Field.

The old man had pulled her son away.

Henderson Field, she said softly.

Come on, the shorter man said. It's disgusting. Let's go.

He led them into the apartment complex across the street and up a narrow flight of stairs to the third floor. Unlocked a battered green door and held it wide.

She followed the old man through. It was a small apartment.
In the entrance lay piles of winter coats, empty wire hangers. The
kitchen was small and dishevelled, a table and chairs toppled
against one wall. The windows at the back had been boarded over.
Toaster and microwave on the narrow counter, cupboards at all
angles and tins cluttered and dishes smashed on the floor. In the
sink were stacked old breakfast plates and she saw brown dregs of
coffee crusted in the bottom and it seemed none had eaten there
in days.

What is this place? she asked.

The shorter man grunted from the doorway. Wait here, he
said. We'll get you when we're ready.

Ready?

But he had already closed the door. The scrape of a key in the
lock, then the heavy tread of boots on stairs.

She tried the tap. It gasped dryly but no water came. Flies
dead on the sills, dust on the shelves. She went to the closet door
where it stood closed and she opened it and then stood listening.
She could hear the old man moving in the next room and she went
out to the living room and saw her son standing in the corridor.
She was frightened.

How much trouble do you think we're in? she asked.

It's not good.

She laughed bitterly. For god's sake. Do I look shaken?

It's okay Mom.

This was stupid. Stupid.

But it's done, the old man said.

He sat in the gloom at the edge of a hardwood chair beside the
television with his hands between bony thighs and his head lowered. She watched her son go to him and murmur some word and
he put a tired hand on the boy's shoulder. To her eye there seemed
a thing conversant and alien between them which she could not
comprehend. When at last he looked at her there seemed a fierce

reproach in his eyes. His lined face drained and grey, his eyes sunken with the strain.

Don't look at me like that, she said.

Like what.

Like this is my fault.

The ceiling creaked as if some footfall faltered there. The building felt huge and dark and silent.

This isn't your fault, Anna Mercia.

That's right, she said angrily, it isn't. She crossed to the front window and tried to lift the pane but it had been painted shut. Through the greasy glass she could make out three men hauling the old man's provisions from their truck. A fourth leaned into the cab, rooted under the seats.

They're taking your stuff, she said.

Yes.

Then her eye was drawn to a low doorway across the street. The shorter man with the gun was speaking to another figure and then that figure turned and peered up towards her where she stood. Even at that distance she could make out the bandaged head, the gauze over the punctured eye, the black beard. His uneasy limp as he moved to one side.

Oh my god, she whispered.

It was the barber.

What is it? the old man asked in alarm. What's going on?

But when she looked again she was not so sure. The man had turned and limped back into the building and he had seemed somehow too large, too bulky. The shorter man with the gun was crossing the street towards their building and she turned now to the battered apartment door.

We have to go, she said. We can't wait here.

The old man wrinkled his brow.

What do they want? Mason asked.

Lower your voice, son.

What do they want.

Whatever we have, I suppose.

She could see her blue hands trembling. Arthur, she said. We have to go. I mean it.

How?

She crossed back into the kitchen, began to rummage through the drawers. Help me, she muttered angrily. Then she was prying at the hammered boards over the back window with a butter knife. Goddamnit, she hissed.

The old man wrapped his big hands around a loose board, pulled, straining.

Goddamnit, she hissed again.

And then the boards were breaking off and swinging on their crooked nails and she was smashing out the broken glass with a pastry roller.

Mason, she called. Get over here. Get through here. Go on.

And then they were slipping down the metal fire escape, the rusted bolts groaning softly, their shoes clanking on the rungs. Jumping the last few feet to the sidewalk. Running.

Mason gets it from me, I'd say. He always was watchful, had such a sense of trespass, a compass for betrayal. Not Kat. When she was little she loved animals, cats, birds, fish, dogs in the street. She gets that from her father. Mason would scream blue murder if a dog came near him. I don't know how Kat got so quiet, she wasn't like that as a baby. It's hard. They're both stubborn, they get that from me. Mason's the sensitive one. Kat can be emotional but I think it's because she doesn't feel things as deeply. She's the optimist. She's always been popular. It'll be hard for her as she gets older, she's so beautiful. I think of those sullen girls who haunt shopping malls, defiantly smoking, flashing their pierced bellies. There's this way of undoing you that can feel almost physical, this attempt to hollow you out. I'm not talking about sex, never mind about sex. It can be done so delicately you don't even realize something's been taken from you. I want to keep that away from her but I know it's not up to me. That frightens me something awful.

A girl was found murdered out in the woods last June. Two boys from her school did it. They burned her body, I don't know why. I guess to make it harder to catch them. Who does a thing like that? I unfolded the Times-Colonist *one morning to see the face of the murdered girl, heavily made up, hair in an elegant bun. It was obviously a graduation photo, something taken on a day of great importance. I hated that they'd used that picture. That they'd taken such a precious moment and linked it forever to her death. I guess they wanted her at her best, I can understand that. Jesus. Sometimes it gets so exhausting, reading the news in the mornings. I laid the paper on the table, set my coffee aside, brought my brow down to rest against its cool print. The pages smelled faintly of dust and ink. I was thinking of that girl. I don't know. I don't know.*

Mason came in and I raised my face, smiled. He stood on his toes to reach the cupboard with the cereal, his face straining with the effort. I watched him get out his blue bowl and his dented spoon, pull a brown place mat from the drawer. He's a good kid. You forget it sometimes. He was humming to himself, some tuneless little song, drawing out the last notes.

And then he sat down beside me, like he belonged nowhere else, and I wanted to cry.

They ran. In a whorl of streets, alleys, doorways, they ran, and then she saw nothing not her feet not her own hand wiping the dirt from her face. Not the ugly swaddled skull of the barber in that open door. Not the glister of sweat on his arms. She gasped, the sharp edges of masonry scraping her ribboned shirt. The shush of the old man's pale cloth, the cool of Mason's hand in her own. Not her little girl. Oh her little girl. When Mason stumbled she drew him up and his shoes clattered echoing off the pavement. The old man had come to a stop.

What is it? she hissed. The galloping of her own heart. Her son's shallow breaths.

There, Lear whispered. Across the street.

Is it them? Mason asked.

Lear shook his head. I don't think so.

A figure in a long dark coat was picking his way along the sidewalk. He peered down the street both directions then disappeared into a tall apartment complex.

They'll know we're gone by now.

Do you think they'll follow us?

He frowned. I don't know. I doubt it. I guess it depends on what they were going to do.

You mean to us.

I mean to us.

Mason, she grimaced. Get up.

I'm up.

We need to keep going.

I know. She closed her eyes. She closed her eyes and thought of her daughter, buried. Thought of her plunging downward. How she must have awakened choking in blackness. A panic in her. The sharp rubble gouging her cheek and how she must have cried.

Anna Mercia?

She opened her eyes. I'm ready.

Sometimes she imagined her daughter buried alone and sometimes she imagined her with a friend. But always she saw her little girl's knees folded back, the soles of her soft feet atlasing hard a chunk of wall. Her small heart battering in its cavity of blood amid the creaking of her own flesh. The hot webbing of her fingers in the dirt.

And too sometimes she would imagine the strong hands lifting her out, into the blaring light. Away from where she had been. Where she still might be.

They saw no one else for many hours. The doors of the grocers and corner stores they passed had been broken or pried back and the windows smashed in. The old man went from shop to shop peering in and at last he stopped, gave her an anxious glance, slipped inside. He came out looking grim.

Nothing?

It's what I thought. The shelves are empty, everything's already been taken.

I'm starving, Mason said.

She put her hand on the back of his neck. But you found something.

Lear's lips whitened. No.

It is something. What is it.

Her son was rolling an iron cross-hatched bar with the toe of his shoe. Was it dead people?

Lear glanced at the boy and then at her. His grey eyes were dark.

Oh god, she murmured. That's awful. It's been four days.

He nodded and glanced at the sky as if only just noticing it. It's so quiet, he muttered.

It is.

I'm sure there are people around. We just don't see them.

They were walking again. Mason slipping easily ahead, peering into the locked cars as they passed. We shouldn't have let them take our truck, he called back to them.

No.

Or our food.

Mason. Be careful.

Her son gave her a look.

Just then Lear hissed at her and she glanced across at him. What?

His brows drew down into a dark knot and he gestured ahead, past Mason.

A large black dog stood with its long tongue loose in its jaws, watching her son. It lifted its snout, turned, studied her and Lear.

Mason, she called sharply.

Her son stopped, peered back.

It's not alone, Lear said quietly.

She felt the skin on the back of her neck prickle. What do you mean?

I saw a different dog following us before. A yellow one.

What do they want?

He gave her a look.

She shook her head. It's only been four days, Arthur. They can't be wild already.

And what do you think they've been eating for four days?

Mason, she called again. Mason. Come here.

Her son wandered back towards her swinging the iron bar. They moved on through the empty streets and after a while she saw a second black dog join the first. The two dogs did not approach, simply moved along loose-limbed and silent in their wake.

Why don't they bark? she asked uneasily. They're so quiet.

Just leave it alone, Lear said. Just walk. As if you know where you're going.

What is it? Mason asked. Is it the dogs?

Yes, honey.

Stop looking back so much, Lear said. Mason. I said stop looking.

Mason swung back around.

They crossed a small parking lot and kicked through the weeds of a closed electronics outlet and turned into the nearest street. It was narrow and cluttered with rubble and the old man swore softly when he saw it and then just stood with one hand on his forehead and stared up the road in each direction. The sun had slid behind a screen of smoke and in its red light his face looked drained and grim.

Where exactly are you leading us? she asked.

Are they still behind us?

Yes, Mason said.

There was rubble in the street where the wall of a warehouse had slewed out over the shells of parked cars and they clambered over chunks of masonry and crushed windshields aching with the exertion. When Anna Mercia paused she could hear the click of claws on stone.

I hear it too, Lear murmured. Just keep going.

The going was slow. Low buildings in disrepair stood close to the road and cast them in darkness, in sudden light, as they passed the gaps where walls once stood. Her boots slid in the loose mortar and gravel and then she was down the hill of rubble and climbing up over a car and ascending another pile.

Mason, she murmured. Mason, honey. Come on.

Then some dark thing slid past at the edge of her vision and she turned.

Arthur, she called out uneasily. Did you see that?

But Lear had passed from sight and she took her son by the wrist and scrambled after him. She could feel eyes boring into her back and when she reached the rise and looked down she saw Lear staring back at her from below. His back pressed up against the fender of a half-buried car.

Then she looked back and saw it. A large yellow dog was watching her. It bared its teeth and loped loosely towards her.

Don't run, Lear called up. Just come very slowly down.

She could feel her son trembling beside her.

A smaller brown dog had materialized to their right. It barked once then studied them with yellow eyes. Two more dogs appeared at their left. She kept her head high and turned her face very slightly to keep the dogs in her line of sight. The yellow dog stopped short and swung its wet snout from side to side as if catching some scent. Then it came again forward along the ridge of the rubble.

Don't do anything, Lear said to them in a calm slow voice. Just come here as if it's nothing. Easy. That's right.

They reached him and he was walking again. She felt a rush of air pass her by and she glanced over and saw the dogs were now level with them and moving alongside them though they did not attack. There were more dogs now and she could not count them all.

Arthur? her son said in a frightened voice. Arthur? There were tears on his cheeks.

Just take it easy, son.

They moved with careful slowness along that street and the dogs moved with them. They did not raise their heads nor did they slacken off and they poured alongside them like a strange dark river. Lear said very softly, There. We'll go in there.

She followed his gaze.

It was an old cinema house and she could see as they approached that the double glass doors had shattered around their metal frames.

How do we keep them out? she said.

He said nothing.

She could feel the hot sides of the dogs now where they bumped against her legs. Her son was crying. The dogs bumped and muscled past, their unwashed fur bristling.

Here, she said. Here we are, honey. Here.

As they slipped under the marquee the dogs stopped as one in the street, stood watching. Their jaws agrin, fangs yellow and mossy. Her son stared back at them from the lobby and he did not move.

Mason, Lear said in a low hard voice. Mason. What are you doing.

Maybe they won't come in, he said. He looked very frightened.

They will. They will if we don't get these doors blocked.

How do you know?

Get over here Mason, she said angrily. Help us with this.

And then they were dragging a big steel garbage can over to the doors and tilting it over with a crash. Lear hauled across a big chair. A glass popcorn machine screeched over the concrete floor, fell shattering. The dogs did not flinch.

The cinema itself seemed safe enough. The door to the projection booth stood open and Lear made his way up to look around. Anna Mercia followed her son into the dark theatre.

Twin grey shafts of daylight fell through the collapsed ceiling over the screen, low now and deepening yet as the day faded out. She stood at the top of the aisle peering down at the dim rows of seats, the big white screen. There was dust on the shabby seatbacks, rubble in the carpeted aisle. Mason wandered up onto the stage, ducked his head behind the screen. She turned away. A sleeve of newsprint had blown in with the leaves and caught in the armrest of a chair and she plucked it free and smoothed it out.

There's no one here, Lear called down from the booth.

Mason, she said. Stay close to me.

He nodded from the screen.

She swallowed painfully. Thinking of the barber at the road-block and how unlikely it seemed. She thought she must have been mistaken. When she glanced down at her hands she saw they were trembling. Arthur? she called.

Yes?

Hold on. I'm coming up. Mason, she called.

They made their way back to the lobby and through the broken door and up the narrow stairs to the small projection room. In the corner a slab of the roof had lifted and driven down like a ramp and Lear was sitting on the roof peering down at the street. She left her son in the projection booth and came through and joined him and sat on the tarred roof with her knees drawn up to her chest.

Everything alright? she asked.

That one hasn't moved, he said. He nodded to the lee of the building across the way. A yellow dog crouched with its head turned up the street. Something passed through her, something illicit and wild and furious.

Is it the same one?

He shrugged. I don't see any others. I think we'll be alright in the morning.

The air was colder here. A blue shadow seemed to pass over them where they sat and then it passed on down the street and she glanced quickly at the sky.

Look at this, Lear said. This will cost a fortune to rebuild. We'll be at it for years.

She nodded.

He looked at her, his face drawn tight with regret. I'm sorry this is taking so long, he said.

It's not your fault.

We'll find your daughter tomorrow. It's not too far from here.

She leaned her temple against the low wall. Curled the fingers of her good hand and studied the broken skin. You know what I keep thinking? she said and she was surprised by the anguish in her voice.

He raised his eyes.

Did I or didn't I appreciate it.

He frowned. Well. You're not through it yet.

At the hospital Mason asked me if I thought Kat was alive.

What did you tell him?

I started to say yes and then I couldn't say it.

Well, Lear said. He shuffled his feet.

I can't stop thinking about it. I keep wondering where she is. What she ate last night for dinner. If she's cold. She didn't take a jacket with her to school. I didn't remind her to.

He said nothing.

I should've made her take a jacket.

Lear looked away.

She picked up a loose stone and threw it at the broken wall of a hotel across the street. Shabby curtains billowing in the seedy rooms. It clattered hollow and sad off a sunken drainpipe and the yellow dog lifted its head, peered suspiciously up. She said, I lost her once. Kat. She wasn't even two.

You lost her?

I lost her. I was with my mother in a department store shopping for a snowsuit for her and when I turned around she was gone. She smiled faintly remembering her little daughter quick in her cruel birdlike investigations. In love with a world of her own devising. Leaves and bits of twig in her hair, her dark hands on her darker knees as she squatted in the department store aisle to see beneath their silver cart. Her husky brown corduroy trousers, yellow knit sweater. And her tiny perfect milk teeth. The scent of her skin was like sap and twilight in a dusky hall. Oh lord. How she had run in a frenzy towards the escalator leaving her old mother with their cart, frail and clutching her purse to her breast and peering sadly about. The sightless white mannequins. The branched candelabra of the clothes racks. A harsh fluorescent

light shining off the faces of all she passed. I thought somebody
had taken her, she said. I nearly died.

They watched the dog slip long and thin around the building
and into darkness.

Where do you think he's off to? Lear muttered.

He must have heard something.

They always look like they know exactly where they're going.

Jesus, she said suddenly, angrily. This time last week it was a
different world altogether.

It wasn't.

She swallowed.

I didn't mean it like that, he said. I'm sorry.

I know.

Tell me what happened.

With what?

Your daughter. In the department store.

Oh. She had been thinking of the barber's wife and she glanced
at him guiltily and gave a short laugh. I was desperate. They were
stealing children back then, it was just starting up again. It was on
the radio all the time. She of course never even knew she was lost.
She'd crawled under one of the clothes racks and was sitting there
behind the clothes watching us the whole time. I don't know what
she was thinking. I could've killed her.

A helicopter whupped high overhead and she stared at the
dark underbelly, the dome of glass glinting and vanishing in the
late sky. She watched the bank of cloud into which it vanished for
many minutes. The chop of its blades fading.

I used to think I was a poor mother, she said.

I'd guess if you worry about it, that probably means you're
not.

You never had any children?

No.

You didn't want any?

I never thought I did, he said quietly. Callie died so young. I don't know what would have happened if she'd lived.

She was silent for a time and then she glanced down at the projection room. Her son was poking about on the shelves, clattering his iron bar along the metal grates. Mason, she called in. What are you doing?

Her son looked up at her.

I have something to ask you, she said to the old man.

What is it.

I want to know what it was like in there. What you found.

I found you. And Mason.

But what was it like?

He rubbed his eyes. I was so tired. I can't remember.

Mason remembers, she said.

I know he does.

I wish he could forget it.

I wish all of us could.

They were both peering down into the projection room where Mason crouched reading an old film magazine, turning the thin pages.

She said after a moment, His father and I never married.

Mason never talked about him.

We were just kids when I got pregnant with Kat. We met at the university. We were both students in our first year. He had this big, broken shovel of a nose. I thought it was terribly romantic. We went backpacking through Thailand and Cambodia and that's when it happened. Of course we didn't know it until later. I think it does funny things to a man. Getting his girlfriend pregnant. At least it did to him. I don't know. He was a good man. We had our differences but he was a good man.

Lear shifted and studied the boy. Is he in Mason's life at all?

Not really.

You don't miss him?

It's just how it is, she said with a shrug. He was gone and back for six years until I got pregnant with Mason. Then I decided it was time. But things were never smooth with us. I guess we were young, I don't know. Maybe that trip to Asia did something to us. You imagine you're seeing the real country. But you're not. That's a myth we make up, there is no real country, not like that. That's why you never do make any sense out of those countries. Places like that. They live closer to death than we do.

Lear shifted his back and groaned. He had large irregular ears and they were very pale in the twilight and when he turned his head slightly the shadows fell across obscuring his face like a dark storm descending.

She closed her eyes. The hot mingled stink of cooking and laundry and trash in the streets and the rough fingers picking at their sleeves and the crowds of the friendly poor. The ancient cities in the jungle carved with the terrible visages of vanquished gods. Mud streets. The staggered signs along the roadbeds indicating land mines. Beggars in swaddled robes with feet and hands missing and bowls cradled between their raw ankles. The chickens in hostel yards and the squeal and spray of slaughter. And the tower of human skulls and the elementary school with its tiny caged rooms and the black stains on its floors and the images of the bloodied incarcerated men and women and children and her standing beside a tree and digging with her shoe a small pale root which was no root but a fragment of bone from the thousands buried in the killing fields as if the earth itself were the author of such brutality.

She scratched at her shattered hand. But out of it all, I got her, she murmured.

They were silent for a time. The streets darkened. She could no longer make out the old man's face when he shifted on his haunches.

Anna Mercia? he said.

Mm?

Do you want to tell me who you saw at the roadblock?

She gave him a sudden hard look. No, she said.

She could see him nodding in the darkness.

It wasn't Mason's father though.

Jesus. No.

Well. I just thought.

Why would you think that?

I don't know. I just thought it might have been.

It wasn't.

He nodded again in the darkness. I haven't been sleeping, he said. I keep seeing her when I close my eyes.

Who?

Callie.

Something in his voice arrested her and she leaned across and took his big cold hand in hers. Somewhere far off the faint clashing of cathedral bells could be heard. He rubbed at his face as if only just waking. A wind blew scurls of dust through the deepening intersection and a dark cat passed without sound in the street. The old man sat and she sat with him and they waited like that as if guests in a house not of their choosing. Which in a way they were. As are all the living in this world.

Escape isn't about ropes and cages, dark closets, prisons, bad marriages. True escape is absence. It eludes you, it's what you can't have.

My father's an ongoing escape. He's a door I can't quite close. I wonder if I will see it closing in Mason or Kat, if that's how it will end. I don't know. He wanted back in our lives though I couldn't see why he should be given that privilege. He wanted to know his grandchildren. He came back to Victoria after my mother died. I don't know why he waited, he shouldn't have waited. But he did. He bought a café in Fernwood. I didn't know what to think. He didn't call us. I only heard about his return through friends months later. Imagine that. I didn't believe it, walked down to that corner in Fernwood and stood in the doorway of a barbershop across the street watching the little brick café. It was like seeing a ghost. He looked so old, and tired, and unhappy. I didn't go over. He's been buried three years now and I'm still angry.

He wasn't a bad man. He was never a father, but he wasn't a bad man. I tell myself this over and over, thinking maybe it will stick. In the late sixties Trinidad like everywhere else had been corrupted and was in strife and my mother could see it burning in him, that desire to go. She called it that. A desire. It was already a kind of infidelity. It was more his blood than we were.

Jesus.

What you can't have. Mason was a miracle baby, he shouldn't have happened. I'd been sick with uterine lesions and the doctor, under the weight of his pouchy face, lifted his heavy eyes and told me I wouldn't have any more children. David was crushed. He'd always wanted a son.

I don't know. I guess we kept trying, though there was something bitter and desperate between us after that. Things got worse between us. David already had one foot over the threshold when we learned I was pregnant again.

That was Mason. It was enough to bring David back in for a time.

I'd hear him creeping about the house at night, going in to check on Mason, on Kat. The floorboards in the hall shivering like a haunting. After he was gone, sometimes even then I'd feel him there, padding softly down the hallway.

In the afternoon of that fifth day they reached the black gate. Its iron spikes and ornate crossed bars wheeled back, standing wide.

Anna Mercia held her son's hand. He led her past the head-master's house with its weathered yellow paint and she slowed and they looked down over the school grounds. It was a boarding school and a day school and she knew there would be many teachers and students down there yet. Sloping off and stretched flat across to the far staked fenceline lay two playing fields, their lime markings looking sutured in the weird light. A tendril of smoke vanished in the charcoal sky. Beyond the fields stood a cluster of hollowed-out buildings like a reef which the destruction had broken upon and fallen back from. The washed light on the wimpled brickface of the ruins.

The old man came slowly up. I know this place, he murmured. I know this school.

Kat should be down there, she said. But in her voice she heard something lift, strange and frightened, and she knew her son could hear it also.

Yes, Lear said.

Mason said nothing.

They went down. The grass they trod was grey and the brick walkways grey and mortar dust lay in a fine grey ash over all. Their heels crunching glass, stones, splintered chips of desks. Windows gaped darkly down. The school was built around an open quadrangle of grass and benches and she made her way among the ruins. Her neck was stiff and her fingers in her good arm ached and she felt nothing else that she would admit to. She did not want to think about her daughter until she had found her. The facing doors standing open on hallways buried in darkness. Men shouting in the ruins somewhere. Where the gymnasium roof had fallen a crane was dragging roped and tackled slabs of concrete to one side and the rubble scraped and boomed.

And then she could not go on. She stopped in the grass beside a jumble of metal chairs and stood amid the whorled dust with her one fist gripped tight and her face dark. When her son called to her she did not turn.

Mom, he called. Mom.

The old man approached her slowly and she raised her eyes and he said, It's alright, Anna. You don't know what's happened here. You just don't know.

She realized she was crying and she rubbed the heel of her hand in her eyes. A gash in the shingles of the main schoolhouse where the bell tower once had stood. She looked away.

A fireman with a broken arm saw them then and he lifted his own sling at her in greeting. His eyes troubled. You and me both, he said to the woman. You looking for someone?

My daughter, she said quickly. Katherine Clarke. She's in grade eleven—

But the fireman shook his head. His skin was leeched grey and streaked with grime and his eyes were very black. I'm not the guy to talk to, he said in his gravelly voice. Try the office. He wiped grimly at his nose with two fingers and then stood looking down. His fingers were black. My nose keeps bleeding, he said. What do you think that is?

Where's the office? the old man asked.

The woman nodded at the ruined schoolhouse. In there, she said.

No, the fireman said. They moved it to one of the boarding houses. You know the music teacher? Singh?

Ray Singh?

He's been in charge of the salvage these last two days. He might be able to help you.

Thanks.

He looked at the woman dully and then he nodded. Sorry I can't help you more.

It's alright. Thanks.

Sure.

The music teacher was a big dark bearded man. They found him standing in the lee of a shadowed wall in his shirtsleeves and with a tie tucked inside his shirtfront and he lifted his eyes at their approach. He seemed to stand shimmering in the shadows and he did not step out into the light. In his fist he held some manila document.

Mrs Clarke, he said gravely to the woman. He lifted his face, peered past the old man, the boy, to the ruined quadrangle. Where's Kat?

Anna Mercia shook her head. She's not here?

Isn't she with you? Then all at once the man understood. Jesus. You haven't found each other yet? He looked at her and stepped forward. You know she's alive, right?

Anna Mercia folded her arms and glanced at the goalposts standing against the skyline lean and polished like strange bones and breathed. She was afraid to speak. The music teacher gripped her shoulder and his meaty hand was hot on her skin.

He said, I saw her myself right after the quake. Right here. She's alive.

You saw her.

Yes. I saw her.

She felt herself starting to cry. She hardened her face, looked away.

Kat was right here, on the field, when we took roll. Jesus, and his voice drifted off. I would've told you at once. I'm sorry.

I knew it, Mason said. I told you.

The music teacher looked down at him quickly, then back at the woman. In the strange light a crescent of darkness scythed along his jaw and his eyes were luminous in the shine. Kat said she was going home. I think that's what she said. She was going to look for you.

We haven't been home yet, the boy said.

Anna Mercia has, the old man interrupted. No one was there.

Her head was still reeling. You're sure it was her? she said softly. You're absolutely sure.

Ray, a man was calling from the rubble. Hey, Ray.

The music teacher glanced back over his shoulder.

She blew out her cheeks and she saw that her legs were trembling and all at once she sat down and started to shake. Her son put his arms around her.

Mom, he said.

She wasn't hurt, the music teacher went on. I can tell you that much. Maybe she went to a friend's house? Most of the students got bussed home late Wednesday afternoon. Listen, I got to get back to this. He peered across at the salvagers then crouched down next to the woman where she sat. Go on up to the office, Mrs Clarke, he said. They have records up there. They'll tell you where Kat was heading off to.

I thought she was dead, she said.

Just go on, he said.

She picked her slow way across the quadrangle, her shoes crunching, following the old man and her son. She did not recognize the feeling in her and then she did and it was not relief but a dark joy. Two boys were lashing a tarp over a stack of desks and a man stood and was shouting but she could not make him out and she did not stop. She started to laugh and then she started to gasp. A red dust had risen from the brickwork and the air smelled of dirt and broken timber and it felt cooler on her hands and face. As if autumn had come.

She saw her son reach up and take Lear's hand as they walked. There was that thrumming in her spine as if a small engine were pistoning away and she could not help the happiness building there.

Lear stopped, waited for her.

You knew this place? she said.

He nodded. When I was a boy my best friend lived near here. Tommy Gates. His father built motorcycles. He coughed into his fist, withdrew a rumpled cigarette from his shirtfront with two fingers.

Kat wants a motorcycle, Mason said.

They're very dangerous, Lear said.

That's what Mom says.

Lear looked at her and she felt herself staring with great intensity. *Do not lose sight of this Anna Mercia*, she thought. *Keep it clear until you have found her.*

This school was built the year I was born, Lear said. He turned his shoulder to the wind and lit the smoke and drew deeply on it then shoved his lighter into his hip pocket with a thumb. You wouldn't know it, he said. The school seemed old even then. Tommy and I used to come throw stones at the lit-up windows on Sunday nights. He smiled at the crumpled schoolhouse, the dark slash in the roof.

What happened to him?

Tommy? He died in 1987. We weren't close at the end.

I'm sorry.

Her son's skin like smoke in an autumn sky. What must her daughter have lived through. She swallowed painfully.

Lear said, I remember a Chinese cook hanged himself in the bell tower one night during the war. They had a hell of a time getting ahold of his legs. And the bell clanged at each pass of the body. Imagine. It woke Tommy's whole neighbourhood. Lear looked all at once embarrassed and he glanced away and then after a moment he said, Everything crumbles I guess, given time. He took a long drag on his cigarette then crushed it under his heel and said softly, There are things in this world that I will miss.

You have some time left yet, I'd guess.

The steel weights of the flag ropes were clanking against the poles in the quadrangle and it sounded hollow and thin and sad. She shivered.

Here it is, Lear said. Lock him up. Gone sentimental and old.

I don't think so.

Arthur? her son said.

Mm?

I think you are wise.

She saw the old man flush with pleasure and drop his chin and turn aside and she thought in an upwelling rush, *So you too then. So it is the same for you as well.*

In the small office a tall grey secretary with a faint moustache shading her upper lip received them. Clenched her jaw and studied them.

Yes?

Anna Mercia said, I'm looking for my daughter. Katherine Clarke, she was here—

Clarke?

That's right.

The secretary held a thick plastic binder of papers and she flipped the pages crisply and she ran her finger along the lists. Her nails were blunt and very clean. She flipped to the back of the binder. Scanned some page further.

Is there a problem?

Hm? No. The secretary took up a red binder from below the counter filled with loose sheets and turned the sheaves carefully.

She was beginning to feel distinctly uneasy. She peered about at the shabby office, the mismatched furniture, the damp thick silence in the walls. Something was not right.

What's wrong? she asked. It's Clarke. With an e.

The secretary frowned. Yes, yes, she said. I know Kat, she's a lovely girl. I just can't find anything in here. Nothing's where it's supposed to be. Could you just wait a moment? I'll only be a moment.

She can't find Kat? Mason asked.

Anna Mercia put her good hand on his shoulder to stay him. Why don't you go sit down, she said.

The secretary had turned to speak to a tall man in a brown sweater who looked at Anna Mercia and then shrugged and then she went on through a glass door into some adjoining office. After a moment she returned. Anna Mercia could feel some part of herself shutting down. She studied the secretary only half-hearing what she said. A light dusting of dandruff at her collar. A throat wattled with age. She was staring at it and could not stop. When it swallowed a deep cleft of skin sank and rose and settled at her collarbone.

Mrs Clarke?

We were told you'd know where to find her.

Yes. If you'd please come with me, the secretary said. Dr Philips maybe can help you.

The headmaster?

She nodded. Just this way, Mrs Clarke. He'll be with you shortly. Then she glanced across at Mason and back at Anna Mercia and said, softly: Maybe your son should wait out here.

She told herself to be calm. *It is only that they do not have a record of her. It is just that he wants to tell you himself. It is nothing bad. There is no need to be nervous.*

Still she hesitated. Arthur? she said.

I'll stay with Mason, Lear said. We'll be outside. Take as long as you need.

The secretary led her through a thick oak door, into a library. Nodded and withdrew, shutting the door with a click behind her. The lighting was dim with the overcast sky slanting in through the drawn blinds but even so Anna Mercia could see the room was not large and the furniture was dark, and moth-eaten, and old. Bookshelves lined the facing walls and two dormer windows were inset along the outer wall and photographs in rosewood frames hung crookedly over the papered walls. Here and there she saw pale squares where some had fallen or been removed. Nailed above the windows were lacquered wooden plaques emblazoned with the names of students many decades gone. She did not know what to do and after a while she sat.

The desk stood cleared of all papers and books, its polished mahogany gleaming in the faint light. In the middle of its wide expanse stood a solitary white box of tissues. It seemed to glow in the darkness. Anna Mercia tried not to look at it.

A short man in a dusty suit entered after a moment through the same door she had come in by and he crossed the room and held her hand a long moment. His wrists were hairless and very white.

John, she said hollowly. Where is she?

Mrs Clarke, the headmaster said.

But when she looked at him something very cold and very heavy turned over inside her.

I'm sorry to keep you waiting, he said. We're entirely overwhelmed by what's happened. As you can imagine.

She nodded slowly. She felt nervous, frightened, her limbs liquid and sluggish as if moving through dark syrup.

Where is my daughter? she said again.

The headmaster released her hand and then rolled a chair on its castors from the desk and drew it in close and he sat and set the box of tissues on the floor at his feet. Anna Mercia stared at the box.

Well, he said. What have you been told so far?

Nothing. No one will tell me anything.

Okay, he said.

Her throat felt suddenly sharp. I talked to Ray Singh outside, she said. He saw Kat after the quake. Out on the field. He said I should come here.

I'm afraid Ray is mistaken, the headmaster said in a soft firm voice.

What do you mean?

He breathed heavily.

Where is Kat, John?

He's made a mistake, he said again. He steepled his fingers before him and he leaned forward and his eyes were fixed on hers. Kat, he began. She wasn't at the roll call we held on the field after it hit. I'm sorry. We don't have any record of her after.

I don't understand.

Her car's still out in the lot.

I don't understand.

The headmaster took her good hand again in his own and she shuddered but could not pull away. His soft hands were warm and moist. She watched the white cuffs of his shirt creep from his blazer sleeves. A silver ring on his hand shone like dark pewter.

It was a very confusing time, he said. We organized the kids as best we could but we know some of them went off on their own without telling us. So the records we've got aren't at all thorough. I want you to know that. I know of at least two kids who came back yesterday and we thought we'd lost them. They went home right after it hit. He wet his lips and then he went on. On that first day some of the students we recovered were taken to the morgues before anyone thought to write down the names. I don't want to scare you, he said. Kat was in one of the buildings that was worst hit. We haven't found her.

You haven't found her.

We haven't found her. No.

He released her hand and she slumped forward and her hair obscured her eyes, her mouth. She could feel her shoulders lifting at each breath. The throb of pain in her bandages.

How do you know Ray didn't see her?

He frowned. Kat's not in the register. If she was on the field—

Maybe she was missed.

Maybe.

Maybe she went off looking for me or Mason.

It's very possible. It was a confusing day.

But already something in her was burning down and when she looked at the headmaster she saw him very coldly. But you think she's dead, she said.

I don't know where she is. That's all I can say.

But she's probably dead.

No.

And if she's—

But her voice caught on the word that third time and she did not finish the sentence. She sat in that chair shaking and shaking and the headmaster did not touch her. *Do not cry*, she told herself fiercely, *do not let this man see you cry. Do not.*

Mrs Clarke, he said at last. Anna. Have you checked the emergency shelters? Her friends' houses?

She said nothing.

Kat could be anywhere, he said. When were you last at home? She might be waiting for you at home.

She said nothing.

I wish I had something more to tell you.

She looked up and when he saw her face he fell silent.

I lost her John, she whispered. I can't find her. I can't. She wiped the wet grime from her cheeks with the flats of her hands. Something terrible was rising in her.

Anna Mercia, he said.

She stood. She stood and she passed from that library without sound and her legs were thin and insubstantial as smoke. She felt herself loosening at the joints, her limbs lean and prickling, and all of what had been in her was suddenly gone as if it had not been there ever.

Mrs Clarke? the secretary said as she came out.

She said nothing. But went past and descended the stairwell in the slanting grainy light. On the lower landing she stood a long while breathing and then she smeared a hand across a pane of glass but the dirt did not come off. Slats of daylight, slats of shadow. Her son would be down there eager for news. She did not know how long she could wait and at last she continued down. Her hands rattling the wood banister.

How did it go? the old man asked as she came out.

She felt scorched and thin and when she saw her son she kneeled and pulled him to her with great fierceness and the old man did not ask anything more.

Where's Kat? her son said.

Oh, honey, she said. She squinted up at the old man. I need to be alone with Mason for a minute, she said. Can you give us just a minute?

He nodded sadly down at her and he gestured out at the weather-stripped rugby posts. I'll be just over there, he said. Come to me if you need me.

She met his eye and nodded. Then she was watching his hunched shoulders as he picked his way across the quadrangle and as soon as he was out of sight she took her son by the hand. She did not look at him.

Kat's not here, honey. They think she might've been hurt.

Is she at the hospital?

Maybe. I don't think so.

Maybe she went home. Should we go home?

There was a charred taste in her mouth.

She crouched down and touched his face. Not yet, honey. Not just yet.

Talking about my father. Jesus.

At the end of our weeks in India, I left David for an afternoon and borrowed a bicycle and went into the hills. It was only April but already there was a smell in the air of burnt flowers, an earthy sweetness so rich it made you hungry. We would be going back to our lives in Canada and I didn't think I'd found what I'd been seeking. I pedalled up a hill, panted through a lane of sweltering shaggy trees, and then the whole sky broke open.

On one side lay a field of yellow grasses, breathing in the wind. On the other side rows of tilled fields, green and upright. I pedalled slowly. Over everything loomed the strange shapes of windmills. I don't know if they're still there. I guess it must have been some kind of foreign development back then. I don't know. They were behemoths, huge industrial flowers. I felt alone up there, the hot wind spitting at my clothes, loud in my clotted ears. That was freedom, and wildness. Like I'd ventured into a treacherous place in order to save myself.

A building emerged from the grass. A tiny stone temple. I could just make out candles burning. A little open temple in the middle of all that nothing. I slowed, and stopped, and dropped the bicycle in the grass. In the soft sun the candles were a vague illumination, like a torn piece of sky. I went in. The room was narrow, the stone walls cold and black from centuries of candle smoke. The floor smelled of wet ash. It was no bigger than a great hearth, and yet the silence—my god—was immense. I sat on the lone stone bench. The silence had a depth beyond itself, like an echo in a concert hall, and I sat and I raised my eyes.

Carved into the stone walls was a kind of relief sculpture. I don't know if that's the right word. It was blackened from smoke or age, I don't know. It looked very old and I couldn't quite make out the scenes carved there. It seemed to tell some kind of story. I remember turning around, and studying the figures over the stone lintel. A man in a robe was kneeling before a horse, or a donkey. A halo surrounded his head. He had four arms and was holding what looked like a pair of black-smith's tongs. But there was a cart attached to his shoulders, and in the cart what must have been the sun. He was in a harness, and a man with an elephant's head was striking his shoulders with a whip. I don't know if it was the dark stain in the stone, or the years rubbing down the edges, but the blurred figure's face looked almost exactly like my father.

I felt, very distinctly, something like fear on the back of my neck. It's one of the sharpest memories I have of him. It wasn't even of him.

INTO THAT DARKNESS

He stood a long time at the edge of that field with one hand on the rusted lid of an old rain barrel and his face turned back to the ruined schoolyard. He did not see the woman or her son and after a while he understood they were not coming. He felt suddenly foolish, and old, and sad.

He turned away, crossed under the posts of the rugby pitch. Here the ground sloped up into scrub and trees and flowers grown wild. A strange silent corner of the campus. He scrambled over a knot of roots and turning shaded his eyes to study the salvagers below. The dappled leaves, the cantilevered branches gone grey with old weathers. He thought of the woman wandering out there in her grief and of the boy trailing behind her through the ashen daylight.

His wife did not die in autumn. Still something in the late golden grass, in the shimmer of leaves dying slowly red, in the strange lingering light that pressed itself into the back of his neck like a warm hand and held itself there, something in all of that led him back to her. He saw in a flat bench of earth the cracked and weather-sprung marker of some forgotten fence and he stood a moment in that place staring. Then kicked through a shunt of leaves run up against an oak trunk in the nettles and went on. Thinking of those weeks after his wife's funeral. How he would go to the cinema and sit alone in the dark, his big hands pressed to his face. He would get to his feet and the seat would creak shut behind him and he would make his way back up the aisle and out into the hot evening air half-blinded by it all. *Oh, Callie,* he thought, *it does not ever cease and we do not imagine at the beginning how long we will have to carry it with us.*

As he came out on the road above the school property he saw in the tangled silence two children like apparitions wending down the hill. Wearing collarless shirts and cricket caps from some decade long past. One paused in his descent and raised a pale and watery face towards the old man and held him in his eyes and then both were gone and the old man could hear only the chop and hack of their shoes in the leaves and then nothing. The trees darkening.

He stood a long while in that road staring after them. Then he heard the boy calling to him, and he turned, and he saw the woman watching him from the road.

I thought you'd left, he said.

The woman's eyes were dark.

We didn't, the boy said. Are you coming with us?

He looked at the woman. He understood that she was going to search among the dead at Henderson Field. He thought of this and then he thought of the boy going into that place.

I guess so, he said quietly.

They walked in silence. The air felt cool on the back of his shirt. The streets were empty.

He felt very clearly his heart settling in him. A weight that had lifted for a time was now creaking heavily back down onto its joists and he walked the more slowly for it. He understood something was ending.

A flock of starlings gusted up out of the oaks and funnelled past and the flock shifted shadowy and mutable and crackling against the sky like some sentient weather come upon them. There was no sun, only a luminous haze in the west.

Gulls were ghosting far up in the wimpled sky and the houses they walked past sat dark and forlorn and cold in the cold light.

The grey sidewalk was badly cracked. They passed a smouldering storefront, white vapours billowing out of the gaps in its boards. The old man felt weary and unwashed and sad. He thought of her socks laid out to dry in the broken cinema that morning, hanging like the turned-out skins of dead things. The shine of the boy's bent spectacles.

Henderson Field was not far. They turned down a street the old man recognized and passed a clapboard church. A rubbled churchyard where he had stood every Sunday of his childhood. The grass and flowering shrubs were coated grey with mortar dust. He could hear the faint clang of a hammer from within the church.

He could see at the end of the street a crowd gathering and beyond that the tall weathered boards of the fence surrounding Henderson Field. There were crows circling in great numbers under the grey sky. He slowed, and the woman stopped, and looked at him.

What is it? she said.

He ran a hand across his eyes. Peered back at the church they had just passed.

You don't want all of us in there with you, I guess.

She nodded.

We can wait for you here. At the church.

She glanced past him at the ruined churchyard. Here?

I grew up here. I went to this church as a boy. It'll be safe until you're back.

Mason, honey, she said. She crouched down.

I want to come with you.

She shook her head.

Mom, he said.

No, she said. I need you to wait here with Arthur. Make sure that he's okay.

What about you?

I'll be as fast as I can. I promise.

It seemed to the old man that something was in her, something very white and pure and hot. She was staring at her son a long moment as if in farewell. It was not farewell.

I love you, she said to him. I won't let anything happen to you. Okay?

Okay.

She held him. And then she straightened and turned and went on down the street without looking back. The old man came forward and put a hand on the boy's shoulder.

Come on son. Let's find us a seat.

The boy nodded, his eyes fixed on the diminishing figure of his mother.

The old man sighed. His knees were very sore and he reached slowly down and rubbed them one at a time and then he straightened and led the boy up the walk to the church doors. *I think you are wise*, he had said. That sudden flush of pleasure he had felt.

The heavy carved doors were propped open on wedges of wood. The old man entered the vestibule and stood amid the old smells of varnish and cotton and smoke like the child he once had been. The soft pews gleamed dully in the oiled darkness. He could just make out the big cross where it had fallen and been propped up at a sharp angle over the altar. Through a hole in the stained glass a grey light filtered in. But in that cold church the smokey dark reminded him of a darkness the more absolute and he shivered and turned and glanced at the boy.

What do you think? he said.

There was a cough from within and the old man turned sharply.

Hello? he called.

Something moved in the darkness.

Arthur, the boy whispered.

Hello? he called again. Who's there?

It came towards them slowly looking larval and strange in the smokey blue nave and it moved with a kind of measured tread as in a dream. Short and thick and strong-looking despite its age. It was a man about his own age and came forward wrapped in a moth-eaten brown blanket and he eyed the old man and the boy from over the rims of his wire spectacles. His left hand clutched a hammer and a paper bag of what the old man imagined must be nails.

I guess that was you we heard from the street, the old man said.

The old custodian ran his tongue along the inside of his mouth, his cheek belling out. His knotted fingers clutched the blanket close.

We heard you hammering, the old man said more loudly. We didn't mean to intrude.

Never mind it, the custodian grunted. What do you need?

I beg your pardon?

He regarded the boy. What do you need?

Nothing. We just came in for a moment. Don't let us bother you.

The custodian rubbed a knuckle under a greasy lens. You can sit if you like, he said.

Thanks.

What's wrong with your legs?

The old man smiled angrily down at them. The knees are a little sore, he said. But they're alright. I'm just not what I once was, I guess.

You look alright, he said to the boy.

None of us are alright, the old man murmured. You've had some trouble?

The old custodian peered about as if to assess the damage for the first time and then he nodded. Some, he said. It could have been worse.

Yes.

It is worse elsewhere.

That's true.

We didn't have any dead here at least. The old custodian frowned as if arguing some point within himself and then he let the blanket fall from his shoulders and he swaddled it in a ball and set it aside on a pew. It folded stiffly, reeking of boiled cabbage.

I don't guess you're hungry, he said. I don't guess you'll be wanting something.

He led them down past the chancel to a thin door of painted wood standing open and he passed into the dim corridor beyond and turned left and descended the stairs to the basement. His wispy head vanishing round a corner into darkness, his shoes scraping the boards. There were no windows in that stairwell and the shadows fell long and deep and the smell of dust and varnish was in the air. The custodian called to them to mind their step and the old man followed the creak of his voice, ducking his head low and trailing a hand against the water-stained wall.

This is Mrs Tanner and her granddaughter, the custodian said from below. They're resting here a bit.

It's just Becky, a reedy voice said from out of the darkness. This is Kayla.

Arthur? the boy whispered.

I'm here. The old man stepped through. Where are you?

The custodian was standing hazy and indistinct in that dim underground chamber and then he crossed to the far wall and tugged at the dusty curtains. They squealed on their threads exposing a row of high barred windows. A weak grey light sifted in. He could just make out two figures seated at a low folding table near the far wall.

Come in, the custodian muttered gruffly. Come in, sit down. Becky used to be our organist.

I still am, she smiled from the gloom. Don't mind Sal. You go away for a bit and it's like you were never here. I didn't catch your name.

Arthur Lear. This is Mason.

They came forward. And then something in the old man lurched, leaned to one side, righted itself. The organist was looking up at him, her cropped white hair in frame at her face, her puckered lips drawn and sad. There was nothing in her to resemble her. She was not her. And yet when he looked at her he saw his wife.

What is it? the custodian asked. You're alright? He was at creaking open and brushing off a metal folding chair for the boy.

He cleared his throat, blushed. It's nothing, he said. He glanced again at the organist, glanced away. His heart gone liquid inside him.

A fire was burning in a black cast-iron heatstove. In the shadows of that long room leaned stacks of blue gymnastics mats and a pew cluttered with cardboard boxes of many sizes and the tiled linoleum had been left unlaid along the walls. The old custodian dragged the metal card table out. A pale yellow tablecloth hung crookedly off it looking ghostly in the weak light and the old man sat uneasily down beside the boy.

We only just stopped in for a rest, he said. Mason's mother is down at Henderson Field.

She's at Henderson Field?

Not like that, the old man said. She's looking for his sister.

Oh, sweetie, the organist frowned. She looked at the boy. She had sad grey eyes. Sal why don't you get them something to drink. Are you hungry Mason?

The boy looked at him and then at the organist and he shook his head no.

We're alright, the old man said. Just a little sore. Are you tired? he said quietly to the boy.

No.

Are you sure?

Yes.

Why don't you lie down on the mats over there? the organist said. She pointed to a shadowed corner, a stack of gym mats. We were resting on them earlier. Come on.

The boy looked at the old man.

Do what you want, he said.

The boy stood and went over to the mats and lay down.

Mr Lear's knees are bothering him, the custodian said.

The organist frowned. Her wrists were ropy and liverspotted and frail. Would an aspirin help? I've an aspirin out in the car.

But he shook his head. That peculiar blue tone that entered his wife's voice when she asked a question and knew the answer. The grey coveralls she would work in, one long white hand resting on the stool as she chipped away. The soft clink of tools in the low light of the shed. He was suddenly very tired.

The custodian opened a cabinet and took down a set of teacups and saucers and he set these clinking upon the table and he returned and took down a bowl of sugar and a creamer and a single dented spoon. He chunked the kettle on the stove lid and went to the cabinet and lifted down a glass jar filled with tea bags. Then he upended the teapot and shook the bags into his palm and held the pot up to the light with his thumb gripping the inner wall and he peered into it and blew some dust free and replaced the bags. An orange cat poured between his ankles purring as he worked and he pushed it off with the wall of his shoe.

It's strange being in this church again, the old man said softly. I haven't been in years.

The organist studied him. No?

I came here as a boy, he said. Maybe that's why.

Did you hear that, Sal? she said. Another prodigal.

The custodian waved her off gruffly. The cat was wending between his feet and he took it in both hands and walked to one side and pitched it unceremoniously into shadow. But you're back here now, he said. Perhaps it's not a coincidence.

The old man smiled. He felt the big sadness welling up in him again.

You think I'm joking, the custodian said.

I don't think you're joking.

Sal doesn't believe in coincidence, the organist said.

The custodian came over and sat across from the old man. Coincidence is just another word for providence, he said. Except it is not so frightening.

The tobacconist shuddering in her stained bedsheets. The weird bandaged stumps of her arms twitching. I feel like I haven't slept in days, he said. Do you have some water?

Of course.

The organist leaned forward conspiratorially. His wife's cool wrist on his shoulder, the steady rise of her breathing. The bite of her rings in his neck. *What is the matter with you? Hold it together*, he thought.

Sal's a great one for his faith, she was saying. My father was very religious too. I've had a harder time of it.

That seems to be how it works, the custodian said. Faith breeds uncertainty.

She nodded. I remember when I turned eighteen my father gave me a bible for my birthday. Not much of a present for a young woman. I found it a few years ago in a box in the attic and when I opened it up what do you think fell out? A hundred-dollar bill. It must have been in there all those years and I never knew about it and he never mentioned it. It would've been a lot of money back then.

Yes.

Imagine. I'd had it all those years and never even opened it once. He must have known.

A hundred dollars. That's quite a reward for opening a bible.

She laughed. Well it seemed pretty miraculous at the time.

The little girl looked up at her grandmother. I saw a miracle once, she said.

I know you did.

I saw Jesus in a piece of toast. Remember?

I remember. What did you do with the toast?

The girl smiled shyly.

You don't want to tell them?

I ate it.

The organist nodded and smiled. That's right. You ate it.

She shifted her granddaughter in her lap and the old man peered at the two, at the shadow of the one in the skin of the other. What he did not ever have. As he did not ever think the hour. The kettle was warbling a low pained warble from the stove and he looked away.

The custodian leaned back in his chair. God's hand is in more than we know, he said.

Well. For those who believe it.

Which is not you?

I can't accept any god who would allow this to happen.

The custodian studied him from behind his wire spectacles. You mean the earthquake?

Yes.

Well. There is agency even in that.

Sal, the organist interjected. Leave it alone. No one did this to us.

The custodian lifted his dry bony shoulders. His dusty green sweater, his leathery skin. Of course not, he said. But how much good has come out of this, how much charity? God is more visible in what's taken from us than in what is given.

The old man was thinking of his wife in the small kitchen of their house those long years ago. The *chunt-chunt-chunt* of her chopping vegetables, the throaty low hum as she sang along to the radio. A wash of traffic in the street outside. How long ago was that. For how many years had he tried not to remember. The kettle began to whistle and then to shriek.

The custodian got to his feet. Mr Lear doesn't agree, he said.

I don't. I'm sorry.

We call the evil within us sin and the evil outside us suffering. But it's all one.

Suffering is evil?

The organist was murmuring to her granddaughter and then looked up as the custodian picked up the kettle. The shrieking fell away into silence. All at once the church felt immense and quiet above them.

I can't accept that, the old man said softly. The boy's eyes were closed in the half-light and the old man saw him again as he was on that first night, climbing out of the ruins. Thinking of that and then not thinking of it. I don't think evil has anything to do with it, he said. Sometimes we just confuse the thing. Sometimes there's just no sense to be made of it.

It is what it is?

I suppose so.

The custodian drew his thorny brows in tight as if weighing the old man's doubt. Evil is the suffering which afflicts us, he said. All of us. It is manifest in us, it is a part of what we are.

The old man shifted in his chair.

God frightens me, he went on. Without such fear I don't think faith is possible. Fear and love are very close. Many people claim to love their God but they don't fear Him and I don't see how this is possible. To know God is to see how unlike us true holiness is. It's overwhelming. It is what it is and we are what we are. There's no apology for it.

You have a hard view of it Sal.

Maybe. But there's adoration in the man who trembles before the Lord. He stood with his ropy hands on the metal seatback. I know what you'd ask, he said. How can anyone believe in a God who permits such suffering. What could be the purpose. He shook his wispy head with great seriousness. Fear is a lesson we don't learn easily. God's a stranger to all of us, believers and unbelievers alike. Which is as it ought to be. There's no answer to it beyond faith. You wonder how can God love us and still cause us pain? It's a meaningless question. God does not love us.

You don't think God loves us?

What is there to love?

The old man frowned. But a god like that? Capable of such brutality?

God is not an elected official. He does not act to please us.

You sound so sure.

I am sure. It is called faith.

That kind of faith is blind faith.

The organist turned her brown eyes upon the old man. Faith is seeing without sight, she said quietly. If you're looking too hard for it, Mr Lear, you won't find it.

I'm not looking for it.

Of course you are.

The old man was quiet for a long while. At last he said, I don't know. It seems to me faith is nothing or it's everything. There's no middle to it.

It's all middle, said the custodian. That's why it's so difficult.

It's as real to me as air or water, the organist said.

But not to me. Not without proof.

Faith is a kind of proof.

But only to those who have it. That's the problem with it.

Which is not you.

The old man sighed. Which is not me.

When did you lose it?

My faith?

Yes.

He lifted his big hands. The dry rasp of ropes as her coffin settled into the earth. The black overcoats under that whitening sky. The slow cold dap of the rain. I don't know, he said. I just one day looked inside myself and didn't see any resemblance. There was no echo.

The custodian studied him gravely. I will pray for you, Mr Lear.

He smiled a sad smile but he said nothing.

The custodian returned to the heatstove and wrapped his left hand in a towel and he took up the boiled kettle in his right and with his left hand supporting the base he bore it smoking to the counter. His spectral figure soundless in the grey light. He clapped the ornate lid onto the teapot and set this down onto the table and he sat. The string tags of the tea bags dangling out of the pot. The rising steam luminous in the fallen light.

The old man peered back at the boy curled up on a mat on the floor, his small ribs rising and falling in time. He leaned forward on the table.

I keep thinking about his mother, he said quietly.

The organist studied him. She's your daughter?

He looked up. No, he said. No, I didn't know them from before. She lost her daughter during the quake. We didn't find any sign of her at the hospital and she wasn't at her school and when she went home the girl hadn't been there either. A teacher at her school thought he saw her after it hit. But he didn't. The old man passed a hand across his eyes. He could see the woman's bruised yellow mouth and her sorrowful eyes and he thought of her weeping in the ruins of that school and he looked up. You tell me, he said. What did she do to deserve that?

The custodian held his spectacles loosely in his fingers and pinched the bridge of his nose and closed and opened his eyes. That's a terrible thing, he said.

Yes.

He slid back on his spectacles and weighed the old man. I don't know, he said.

But you think there's a reason for it.

The custodian went to the stove and unhooked the charcoal poker from a low nail behind the stovepipe. I think there's a shape to it, he murmured. It's not the same thing. You said a teacher saw the girl?

The old man nodded.

Then I trust she will be found. You should have faith.

She'll find her daughter, the organist said. I know she will.

When she said this he looked across at her and he was struck again by the overwhelming presence of his wife. He could not explain it. There was no way to explain it. He sat in silence feeling an enormous gentleness come up in him. The boards above creaked and went still as if someone walked over their heads. The old man looked up and the little girl took his hand gently and touched his wrist and he thought of his wife. No one spoke and he thought of his wife. Her soft fingers cool on his skin and him light-headed and warm in that warm dark.

He glanced across. The boy slept on.

The tablecloth glowed with a soft lustre as if some lamp burned below it and the dark tea smoking in their china cups burned also with a strange light and the old man poured a dollop of milk and watched it bell murkily up out of the depths pale and cloudlike. The organist across the table was stirring her own tea and she tapped her spoon in a flare of steeled light against her saucer and the ringing was dazzling and clear and pure. She held out the spoon to the old man and bent her head down to her granddaughter's cheek as the heatstove smouldered on. The old man waited. The spoon was shining in that light. He reached out his hand.

Go on, she said. Take it.

I told her I didn't know if anything of us goes on afterward. I said I wished I believed differently. I guess death never seemed to me half the mystery that life is. She said when you look back on your life what do you see and I said I know that what I lived is not what I recall having lived. Is that any kind of answer? I don't know. I guess you build something out of it that seems true whether it happened that way or not.

I didn't tell her about that day. She asked but I wasn't going to tell her. I remember it was a Sunday. This was April 1964. I was in my studio at the back of the house and didn't hear the knocking for some minutes. When I opened the front door it was Aza. She was standing with her bony arms folded and then she held them down at her sides and then she folded them again. She was looking at me. She told me Callie had been killed in a car accident the day before. Her taxi had hit a streetcar. I stood there looking at her for a long moment. I didn't understand. Callie? I said. She nodded. A bus went slowly past in the street behind her. Yesterday? I said. I still had one hand on the door handle and then I let it go. I sort of shook my head. Callie's boxes were still stacked in the hall and I wondered if Aza had known Callie had left me. I suppose now she probably did. I screwed my face up and it seemed I could feel every muscle in my cheeks, in my expression. I didn't cry. For many years I was ashamed of that. But I guess there's no sense in it. We are what we are.

Then Aza stepped forward and reached up and put her narrow arms around me and she started to cry. And what seemed strangest to me right then was the reality of this second person, this second flesh, touching me.

The feel of her knit sweater under my fingertips. That we could be there at all.

Some things you just can't talk about. Faith is like that. The words just aren't there. My grandfather didn't go to church though he believed in God. He didn't talk about it. When I asked him he said heaven seemed unlikely but hell was a very real possibility. A few years back, out at Esquimalt lagoon, city crews had to halt some excavations on the headland when they found the burial site of a native woman. It was a thousand years old at least. I didn't know they buried their dead in places like that. Maybe they didn't usually. Her bones were being exhumed and moved to reserve land. I don't know what I believe but I guess if there's any kind of an afterlife, it's like that. What you were goes on in the world. You just don't go with it.

She drifted along the high-planked fence of Henderson Field in that slow crowd and she did not speak and the daylight was very pale. The air bloomed with a terrible sweetness. She could see the corners of a scoreboard standing forlornly beyond the tall fence and there were wreaths and photographs tacked to the boards and she observed the lonely and bereaved and otherdead through the afternoon light. The sky ahead was a storm of screeching crows and when she looked back the telephone wires swayed heavy with them.

The crowd poured and poured itself forward. Towards the iron gates.

She passed her hand across her eyes. She was watching a group of children at the fence with their eyes pressed to the knotholes. She listened to the valves of her heart shunting, the moist cumulous sacs of the lungs. As if an act of salvage were at work within her. She did not feel what she thought she would feel and she wondered when it would hit her.

The fug of unwashed flesh, of rags and filth and sour blood, hung over the crowd in a low mist and she pushed on through it. She could hear a bulldozer somewhere near, its heavy treads scraping and hauling down wreckage. She breathed and it hurt. She breathed and it hurt, sorrow stitching itself in her side like a cracked rib. Her son's face. When he was small the ropy dark arms thrown about her neck in the morning kitchen, the warm pall of breath on her throat whispering *I love you a hundred and a hundred and a hundred and a penny and a penny and a penny.* The shriek of high laughter, that flour-dusted roller in her fist, then her daughter hiding in the kitchen curtain. Wrapped and mummified and giggling in silhouette. Oh she did not love them enough.

She rubbed her face with her shoulder and she pressed on. When she turned to look back she could not see the old man nor her son. Then someone was calling her name. She saw a man with burnt-looking eyes pushing towards her, his skin yellow. She knew his slouched shoulders, his big soft empty hands. Her daughter's swimming instructor. He was dressed in a dusty black shirt and he had dark eyes as if he had not slept and when he touched her she shuddered as though she had not been touched in a very long time.

Anna Mercia? he said. Jesus. He looked at her arm.

Hey, a man behind him hissed. Hey. He fastened a claw on the instructor's wrist. You got to get in line like everyone else. You can't just budge in. Hey.

He glanced back for only a moment. But when he turned again towards her his face looked strangled and all at once something heavy turned over inside of her.

Anna, he started to say.

You found her, she said abruptly. Her voice sounded thick.

He nodded.

She's inside.

He nodded again but he did not seem able to say anything more.

She understood and yet she did not understand. Then she felt stunned and light-headed and she looked at her trembling legs as if they were not her legs. The instructor gripped her good arm. Deep in the black slough of his eyes some grey weeds adrift like leeched hair.

I'm sorry, he said. I'm so sorry.

She tried to say, *You cannot be sorry, you cannot know what it is to be sorry, you cannot,* but her voice gave out and she could not get her breath. Then something like a half-strangled sob came out and he drew her to him and her soft face was mashed up against his chest and the thumb of her good hand was at her own throat as if to stopper the words back up. He held her wrist and then her legs gave out and he stumbled to hold her up. She could feel the blood in her skull.

You don't want to go in there, he was saying. Anna Mercia? Look at me. I can ID her for you.

How did she look? she whispered.

Jesus.

Joshua.

Yes?

How did she look?

The instructor swallowed and blinked and looked away.

She was still shaking her head foolishly and then she started to cry. My little girl, she said. O my little girl.

He pulled himself free after a time and lifted her to her feet and she just stood breathing, very quietly breathing, just very quietly gulping air. A lady in the crowd turned and looked at her and then glanced away in embarrassment. Across the street she saw an old woman in a lawn chair get to her feet and fold shut her chair and go into her house. The crows on the telephone lines plunged off flapping then lifted and circled and cried.

A white van passed and the crowd parted slowly. The mesh gates at the far end were unchained and rolled wide and the van went in. She wiped her eyes angrily. The grey light felt scrubbed and raw.

She could hear the steady clack of typewriters behind the iron gates. There were folding tables set up in rows just beyond the entrance and the crowd swelled up against the gate chain and then fell back. A man in a red shirt unpinned the chain and counted through twenty visitants and refastened the chain and his eyes roved the crowd as he spoke into a radio. She watched this, feeling gutted. What had been her heart now just darkness and heat.

Then the man waved them past and they were in.

It was a small ballpark in a small suburb. She had been here before. A softball game in the late summer dusk, hot dogs and mustard and beer in big plastic cups. Her daughter asleep in her lap. The air was afire with the stink of disinfectant now and under this a steady sickening sweetness. She knew that smell.

They were led past a sign reading Sanitary Carpet and they stood in a row upon a swath of tarps spread out on the asphalt behind the locked and shuttered concession booth. A small wooden sign for the ladies' toilets creaked in the wind.

The instructor pointed to a line of tables along the fence with computers set up to a generator. Over there they should have a record of her on file, he said. Go to the Identified Table. He furrowed his brow slightly. If you need anything.

Yes. Thanks.

I mean it.

Yes.

If I don't see you again.

It's okay.

He looked like he might hug her and she turned aside and then he did not. He returned to his place in the line as volunteers in white coveralls and white haircaps and bearing whirring disinfectant units strapped to their shoulders made their way among them. They handed out face masks and thin plastic gloves. The tanks tilted and slouched as they moved and were slung crosswise from hip to shoulder, the steel cylinders vibrating fiercely.

A man gestured for her to raise her good arm. He wrapped her sling in a clear plastic bag and tied it off under her armpit. She slid the cloth mask over her mouth and stood with her legs wide as a volunteer with brown eyes approached. His voice was muffled through his mask.

It's the Formol, he said. Shut your eyes.

She shut her eyes.

As he sprayed, her skin felt chilled and though she held her breath the sharp peppery stink of the chemicals made her choke. When he tapped her shoulder she nodded blindly and he waved her through and as she left she could see him rubbing the toe of his boot across the place where she'd stood as if to erase her passing.

Her bloodied hand had clouded up the inside of its glove and she stood a moment regarding it and then looked up. Her skin was grey in the slats of shadow where she stood below the bleachers. She walked to the ramp. Past the folding tables where typists filled in the brown cards of the dead she pushed into the crowds that lined the edge of the field then stood and shielded her eyes.

The first thing she saw were the gulls. Circling and alighting and slapping back into the air. The smell was brutal even where she stood. She saw rows of low mounded tarps amid bags of ice and these she knew were the dead. There were figures walking the rows slowly, stopping and staring and then going on. At the far fence under a tarpaulin tied to the batters' cages she could see an area marked Remains and she thought of the bodies there poured out, dumped in, zippered up in the black bags and then she remembered suddenly waking in that field of the dead after the quake and she turned and made her way under the bleachers.

She went to the tables the instructor had indicated and stood in line. When she reached the front a man with a thin white moustache and spectacles gestured her near. A stack of papers in a manila folder at his elbow, a pencil behind one ear. Sad brown eyes. He was wearing a shirt with silver tassels in a fringe across the pockets and she looked at them uncomprehending.

He glanced at his computer screen then back at her and he nodded. His voice was high, thin, scratchy. Yes? he said.

I'm looking for my daughter. I was told if I came here.

Yes. She's been identified?

She nodded.

Last name?

Clarke.

I'm sorry?

Clarke. With an e.

He typed with the first two fingers of either hand and studied the screen and after a minute he dropped his chin and looked at her over his spectacles. It's not here. Would she be under another name?

She shook her head. Kat? Katherine? With a k.

I'm sorry. Do you have her identification number?

Her what?

ID number.

She stared at him foolishly. I was just told she was here, she said. A friend, he knows Kat, he saw her in here. I don't know. She's sixteen. She's an inch shorter than me. Her hair is—

But the man had shut his eyes and he was shaking his head. He removed his eyeglasses, held them in one hand, rubbed the bridge of his nose.

Mrs Clarke, he said unhappily. Please understand. There's hundreds of bodies here. When we ID them we give them a number and then we file them according to that number.

I know.

Without that number there's only one way to find her.

You can't look it up?

It's not here. I don't see her name here.

She nodded but did not understand.

Listen, he said. I need a name or a number. Something that'll come up here. You start one of two places. If she's here, that is. It seems everyone's getting told conflicting accounts and I imagine you're no different. But if your daughter is here she'll be in either Identified or Unidentified. Did your friend identify her?

Yes. He was sure.

But did he report it. I mean, to someone here.

She was afraid she might start to cry again.

The man leaned forward. Mrs Clarke? Mrs Clarke. Listen to me. Without that number there's just no way of knowing.

She swallowed.

Mrs Clarke?

Just give me a minute. Please.

Okay.

After a moment she murmured, Can't you check again? Maybe it's spelled differently.

He folded his hands in front of him. We could be here all day, he said. If you really want to find your daughter you need to go out there yourself. It's the only way to be sure. I am—

I know. You're sorry. Everyone's sorry.

He watched her with his sad eyes.

Then she was on the field. She was walking out onto the turf feeling hushed and strange with her mask itching at the corners of her mouth. There were papers blowing across the field and trash in the wires of the fence and everywhere she looked she saw the lonely seekers of the dead. She could hear hammers at work behind the dugouts where stacks of unpainted coffins leaned, pale and hastily cut, and under that the cries of the grieving calling across the field. All of this she heard muted and dim as if through water.

Where she walked the grass lay trampled in little yellow clumps and as she passed a cordon a volunteer in tennis shoes who had been studying a clipboard looked up and nodded to her. Twin steel chairs marked the Unidentified section, a rope tied to one and looped in the grass. On the pitcher's mound a wooden sign had been nailed to a post and two soldiers stood beside it in the dirt, their rifles lowered. They wore very white cloth masks over their mouths.

She went past them. Past them and into the bodies.

All at once she could hear no sound except her breathing. Her ankles were cold where she walked. Many of the coverings had been kicked aside and left in crumpled heaps and she walked with her eyes to the ground and she did not look at the dead. She did not see a naked woman with blonde hair, heavy breasts flattened, her pubis shaved. There was no long red incision seared across her abdomen. Nor did she see a little boy with his bruised eyes open, his blue lips upturned in an eerie grin. Nor an old lady whose seamed face looked peaceful, unblemished, without a mark on her, as if she were only dreaming. Her body below the sternum was not mangled, was not horribly pulped. Nor a boy with his legs crushed holding a baseball glove to his chest. Nor a man with a swollen belly, the flesh gone soft as molasses. Nor another with his throat torn out and a newspaper stuffed in the wound. Nor a plump girl in pink pajamas, her cheeks pocked with acne. Nor two brothers in yellow sweaters, their faces dirtied, blood in their ears and hair. Nor a baby gone grey in the face with its black tongue poking between its lips nor a man with no hands nor a naked boy in sunglasses nor did all of their faces in the late clarity of that day seem to her peculiarly beautiful. She did not see these dead nor did she see across the rows a crow hop off a boy's chest with something in its beak and she did not see one of the soldiers walk towards it and it did not flap lazily away. She swallowed in the cold light.

She went on. The blue canvas sheets rustled where she stepped in close to see the faces. The creased tarps in the dirt underfoot reflected a weird blue light back up over all. She began to notice very small details. The prickled dandelion weeds in the grass. A bottle cap. The ants forming their tiny black script over the dead, cold in the grey light. When she looked up she saw in the outfield an elderly couple, the man in his good grey vest, the wife leaning into his arm. She stood watching as they murmured and paused and their voices carried across to her indistinct. He stooped to read some face and nodded to his wife and then they strolled on.

What was this world. What was this true world. She started to cough and turned aside and saw a man in a threadbare undershirt

stained yellow with sweat or grime and he was kneeling next to a
body. A boy in thick boots and a heavy fireman's jacket was fumi-
gating the bodies and she watched the spray lift and blow awry
the coverings. The boy stooped and adjusted the settings on the
cylinder strapped to his back and kicked back up the tarps and
moved on.

The small man in the stained shirt was calling out across the
corpses. No one paid him any mind. His skin was so white, his
unshaven face hard with long grievances. There seemed no fair-
ness in it. He called out again and she heard no word in his cry.
The clouds were mottled and suffused with a fierce light as if some
luminous world hung obscured above. She crouched on an open
tarp and tucked her chin against her collarbone and her legs felt
thick with sorrow.

He was still calling and at last the two soldiers on the pitcher's
mound looked at each other then wandered slowly over. The small
man gestured loosely.

How much for a coffin?

What?

How much for a coffin.

Did you find someone?

How much do the coffins cost?

I think the caskets are free, aren't they? The first soldier looked
at his companion and his companion shrugged. They give you one
right away. Just go over there. Right over there. He pointed to the
stacked coffins behind the dugout.

The small man stood with his head lowered.

What is it?

I can't lift her all that way.

The soldiers looked at each other and then one of them set
his rifle butt into the grass and leaned on the barrel. He looked
down. They got volunteers to help with that, he said.

We're just supposed to guard the bodies. Make sure no one
steals anything.

The second soldier folded his arms. Anyways it doesn't matter. You got to get a death certificate first before you can remove anyone. You got a D.C.?

The small man stared at them. The soldier with his arms crossed looked off.

She came over to them and the men stepped back as she leaned over the body. A girl in a floral dress, in white socks crushed at her ankles. Her skin was greenish and oddly lumped. The small man had laid his thin sweater across her face for modesty. The grass under her was stiff and burnt and she stared at it a moment and said without raising her eyes: Who was she?

My niece.

She looked at the small man and then at the soldiers.

I'll help you, she said. I'll take the legs. Her voice was hoarse. He doesn't want to leave her like this, she said to the soldiers. She was surprised to find she did not feel angry. Why don't you bring a coffin over here for us.

The two soldiers looked at each other.

Our orders are to stay here, ma'am, the one said. I'm sorry. They got volunteers.

She said nothing.

After a few moments the first soldier looped his rifle over his shoulder and shook his head and went off towards the coffins. A tall stooped man in a grey sweatshirt passed them and he checked his wallet then tucked it back into his pocket with two fingers. A flock lifted from the telephone lines and wheeled overhead. When the soldier returned he bore the footed end of a coffin and an old volunteer was with him. Its unfinished planks were rough and splintered and the small man stepped into it and bent down the heads of the nails with his boot.

The volunteer slid a fold of tarp under the girl's body and straightened and the small man gripped the tarp in his fists and she stood opposite the volunteer and all three lifted and conducted the girl's decomposing flesh to its casket. The body's hips sagging

low over the grass. The head thunked the lip of the coffin bonelessly but the small man's concentrated expression did not alter.
She looked down. The girl pale and lovely in her resting. Thinking of her daughter asleep with her hair dark and liquid at her face,
her savage brown eyelids. She was not well. There was the smell
of fresh lumber and of cooled iron. She rose. Bent by grief perhaps. Her lips moved wordlessly as if arguing with some unseen
judge. Against some law greater than the flesh. Be merciful.

The two soldiers slipped away as the volunteer and the small
man bore the coffin slouching towards the stadium wall and then
the man set off for the tables of typists.

You okay? the volunteer asked.

She did not reply for a long while.

At last she said, I don't think I am.

She stood to one side. He collected the sheets of lumber and
stacked them against the iron rails along the wall and he watched
her as he worked.

All at once she knew she could not bear another cadaver and
she took the mask from her face. She unzipped her jacket and went
up the steps and sat high in the bleachers. Grooved steel seats.
Chewed gum flattened underfoot. Far below the dark figures
stood among the corpses. She peeled off her glove with difficulty
and dropped it under the slats and she sat for a long time staring
at her hand. It looked very wrong.

She looked off.

Finally she rose.

At the end of the third row she found her. Her clear face was dark
and softly furrowed as if she dreamed. She did not dream. Anna
Mercia breathed. Child of darkness, child of glass. Laid out on
her back, her dark hair in storm upon the grass. Her white shirt
was rumpled and streaked with dirt and her school tie hung aslant
her flattened breasts. Anna Mercia lowered her head and stood a
moment but it did not help. She made her way crinkling between

the tarpaulin mounds and sat in the grass beside her daughter and after she had watched her for a few minutes she began to cry. She was still so much a child. Anna Mercia cried harder and harder but made no sound, her dark mouth hanging open. She turned her head and looked out past the fence at the low clouds. The sky a dense black shroud of vapour and ice, water and swirled dust. It did not fall. A shadow slipped across the earth and she groomed her daughter in her waxen sleep her fingers tracing the eyelids and then her hand hung and lifted over her unmoving as if to ensure her safe passage. She sat like that and looked about at the figures wending slowly along the aisles of the dead and the soft crinkling of the corpses and her eyes grew very clear. It did not end. Her wrist was limp in the cold grass, her palm was empty and very dark. It did not end.

In the dream I'm a young man again and walking out to my car at the airport. I don't have any luggage. It's a vast parkade in the dream. I don't know that it ever seemed that big in life. I go up and down the rows in the cold working my way up through the levels until I reach the roof. A grey rain clatters off the parked fenders there, punches off the dahlias and rhododendrons planted around the lampposts. I blink the water from my eyes. There's no one around. When I turn back, my wet shoes have left prints across the darkening asphalt.

Then I see the car. It's always like that. I turn slightly, see my shoe prints, see the silver Volvo parked under the open sky. There's a silhouette in the passenger's seat. It's Callie. I knock on her window but she doesn't hear me and I can see water beading coldly on the glass and coursing in slow rivulets over the door. I climb into the back seat, shut the door with a bang. I wipe my face with my open hands. I stare at the back of her head.

I know that it's her though I can't see her clearly. I understand she shouldn't be here and I'm afraid to disturb her, afraid she'll realize her mistake. The rain daps loudly on the roof, it flecks the windshield. Then the world outside in its darkness darkens yet further and I peer sadly through the dappled glass. Shadows of raindrops mottling Callie's hands. Her skin looking spotted and old. Below us I see the black airport out-buildings warp and bend through the rivering pane and the black trees and parked cars beyond also go strange and the world seems to stretch and distend. I lay my head back upon the cold seat and then the keys in my hand darken and Callie's skin in the front seat seems to darken and then the very air itself. Beyond the airport over the fields the sky is white and blinding and I cradle my eyes thinking the leeched sun must set but it doesn't set. The darkness comes on.

Callie? I say quietly.

But she is gone in the darkness. I think at that moment I will wake up but I don't wake up. The darkness comes on. It comes on overtaking car and parkade and airport and I shift in my seat, stare back through the rear window at the blackening world. Until it too has passed, as all things pass, into that darkness.

The old man's tea had gone cold. He held the gold-rimmed cup in both hands and stared hard into it as if to divine some meaning there. Turning the cup slow on its china base in his thick fingers, the tea whorling the more slow within. The little girl coughed. A spoon clinked. He looked up. The heatstove ticked softly and the custodian rose and took up the poker and hefted back the hinged lid to stir the smouldering logs. A wall of heat rising through the basement. His wrinkled face cast in a red glow of corded wood and ash like some inchoate demon at its forge and his features cast in stark lines of shadow, lines of light. He shut the lid with a clang. Stood wiping his hands on his shirtfront.

If that teacher saw her then I expect she'll turn up, he said.

The organist was staring into the stove. She'll find her, she said. Maybe his mother's found her already.

Of course she'll find her. I can feel it. He bent then to hang the iron poker over the bricks and it swung creaking on its nail.

The old man weighed them both in his dark eyes. The cloistered air smelled faintly of things burning and he pushed his teacup away in its saucer and stood.

I think I will take those aspirin, he said. They're in your car?

The organist lifted her head slowly. Sal?

The custodian rose from his chair but the old man waved him down.

No. No, he said. I'll go.

They're in the glovebox, she said and held out the keys. It's a blue Prius.

He studied the boy sleeping in the corner, his hollowed eyes.

He came up the water-stained stairs and crossed the chancel in the grey light, his heels echoing up the empty aisles. The church felt sad and hugely vacant. The thick doors stood open to the street and the old man grimaced there at the threshold to see the blue world beyond. He began combing his hair with his fingers and clapping the dust from his sleeves. Sat on the nearest pew and bent over and retied his laces then straightened and studied the overcast sky. His face was tanned with grime and his hair still bent up in white tufts from the crown of his head and he looked like a man confounded by grief.

A car drove slowly past. The old man walked out into the dusk and down the peeling wood steps. The handrail rattled and jounced under his weight like a gangplank. A wind was up from the east and the side of his face went cold with it. He thought of the woman bowed with grief on the dark sofa, her stillness. He went slow and his heart felt sore and he was crossing the lawn towards the drainage ditch when his feet went out from under him and he fell. He fell hard onto his side and the breath went out of him. The street was dead and the shuttered houses dark and where the old man lay it seemed suddenly that the light had dimmed and the noise of the world been shut off and he lay listening for the sound of his blood but he heard nothing. A slight wind still coming down cold upon him, ripping at the grasses without sound. He shut his eyes.

After a time he got to his feet. It was starting to rain. His trouser leg was grimed with clay and there was grass in his fingers and he could see his skin through the thin shirt. He wiped his hands in the grass. He could just see in the rising dusk the boarded-up fence of Henderson Field, the grey figures ghosting past. A shadow came to the open doors of the church and stood staring out at him but he could not make out the face. Thin and enshrouded and cadaverous. After a time the figure went back in and the old man shivered and turned away.

Across the road an old chestnut tree stood impassively on a rise of grass and all through his childhood he knew that tree must have stood as it stood now. All of the dark yards surrounding had been forest then and he remembered prowling the trees with sticks and pine cones after church, his good grey slacks greased with mud. He ran a wet hand across his eyes. He heard the faint laughter of fathers drifting out of the sunlight, the cries of children in the trees. He turned his face to the darkening sky. At the edge of the cold light he could almost see them, blurred and fading. Shadows of mothers, shielding their eyes. Calling their loved ones in.